'Simon Van Boo͟,   ͟s a grea͟   complex longings of the
human heart, and he articulates those truths in his stories with pitch-perfect
elegance. *Love Begins in Winter* is a splendid collection, and Van Booy is now
a writer on my must-always-read list.'

Robert Olen Butler, author of
Severance and *A Good Scent from a Strange Mountain*

'Simon Van Booy seems to start with a story in mind and then to turn it
into a poem without losing its narrative power. *Love Begins in Winter* is an
exquisite show of force.'

Roger Rosenblatt, author of *Lapham Rising* and *Beet*

'*Love Begins in Winter* brings to life the wistfulness of youth and the possibili-
ties of young love with clear and graceful prose.'

Jamie M. Saul, author of *Light of Day*

'The stories of *Love Begins in Winter* are stylistically brilliant and emotionally
beautiful. I found myself gasping, literally gasping, at surprises so perfectly
attuned as to be inevitable. Simon Van Booy is an extraordinary writer, and
this is a book to be read and reread again and again.'

Binnie Kirshenbaum, author of *The Scenic Route*

'Beautiful … each of these stories has moments of sheer loveliness.'

Publishers Weekly

'Pitch-perfect … Convincingly shows how love rights the world.'

Kirkus Reviews

THE SECRET LIVES OF PEOPLE IN LOVE

'These tales have at once the solemnity of myth and the offhandedness of
happenstance.'

Publishers Weekly

'Van Booy shows an uncanny ability to create intense moods and emotions
within the ͟͟͟͟͟ ͟ ͟ ͟͟͟ ͟ ͟ ͟ ͟'

Booklist

'Lovely and genuinely touching. This talented author bears watching.'

Kirkus Reviews

'Breathtaking … chillingly beautiful, like postcards from Eden.'

Los Angeles Times

THE ILLUSION OF SEPARATENESS

'A delicate, complex, moving novel, one to withstand – demand even – an instant second reading.'

Telegraph

'There's a crispness to his writing … It is the beginnings of poetry.'

Independent on Sunday

'The elegance of Van Booy's evocative prose has led to comparisons with F. Scott Fitzgerald; it's some claim but one this little gem of a book completely justifies.'

Daily Mail

'Van Booy writes with muted, unsentimental elegance about the impulses that bind us together.'

The Times

'There is a sustaining pleasure in wondering how the strands of the story will tie together.'

Guardian

'The reader finds herself entranced by the strange turns that occur in these invisibly connected lives, and which then alter them forever.'

Siri Hustvedt, author of
What I Loved and *The Summer Without Men*

'The writing is what makes this remarkable book soar.'

Publishers Weekly

'His writing is consciously poetic and at times aphoristic, and he deftly portrays his characters' raw emotions.'

Wall Street Journal

'If F. Scott Fitzgerald and Marguerite Duras had had a son, he would be Simon Van Booy; this is a truly special writer who does things with abstract language that is so evocative and original your breath literally catches in your chest. This is a novel you simply must read!'

Andre Dubus III, author of *House of Sand and Fog*

'There is ... an integrity to [Van Booy's] vision and a haunting element in his portrait of friendship and, ultimately, resolution.'

Daily Mail

'Vivid and meticulous ... the floweriness of his prose is skilfully balanced by his short, precise sentences.'

Metro

'A book that is timeless but not rootless ... highly sophisticated and absolutely sincere.'

Irish Times

'A tender, earnest first novel ... Van Booy wisely resists romanticizing torment, instead suggesting that grief – tied as it is to fate and faith – can give way to promise.'

Publishers Weekly

'A swift and engaging story.'

Wall Street Journal

'His prose is music, and his characters are warm-hearted, gentle, bemused, philosophical beings ... It's as if Shakespeare's Sonnet No. 30 has unfolded into a full-blown novel.'

East Hampton Star

Also by Simon Van Booy

SIMON VAN BOOY

The
Secret Lives
of People
in Love

Includes the award-winning collection
Love Begins in Winter

ONEWORLD

A Oneworld Book

This edition first published in Great Britain by Oneworld Publications, 2014

The Secret Lives of People in Love © Simon Van Booy 2007

Love Begins in Winter © Simon Van Booy 2009

The moral right of Simon Van Booy to be identified as the Author of this work has been asserted by him in accordance with the Copyright, Designs, and Patents Act 1988

ISBN 978-1-78074-559-6
ISBN 978-1-78074-594-7 (eBook)

Stay up to date with the latest books,
special offers, and exclusive content from
Oneworld with our monthly newsletter

Sign up on our website
www.oneworld-publications.com

The author wishes to acknowledge his generous publisher, Juliet Mabey at Oneworld Publications, and her team: Lamorna Elmer, James Magniac, Paul Nash, and Lucie Uwarow, for their brilliance, hard work, and great friendship, all of which made this volume possible.

CONTENTS

PART ONE

Love Begins in Winter

Part One

Love Begins in Winter

to

If you are not here, then why are you everywhere?

Love Begins in Winter

I

I WAIT IN THE SHADOWS.
   My cello is already on stage. It was carved in 1723 on a Sicilian hillside where the sea is very quiet. The strings vibrate when the bow is near, as though anticipating their lover.

My name is Bruno Bonnet. The curtain I stand behind is the color of a plum. The velvet is heavy. My life is on the other side. Sometimes I wish it would continue on without me.

The stage lights here in Quebec City are too bright. Stars of dust circle the scroll and the pegs as I am introduced in French-Canadian. The cello belonged to my grandfather who was accidentally killed in World War II.

My grandfather's kitchen chair is also on stage. I can only put weight on three legs. The wicker at the center of the seat is ripped. One day it's going to collapse. When the chair arrives at the concert hall a day or so before a performance, a frantic music director will call with bad news: "Your chair has been utterly ruined in transit."

An eruption of applause and I take the stage.

Who are all these people?

One day I will play without my instrument. I will sit up straight and not move. I will close my eyes and imagine life taking place in the houses outside the concert hall: steaming pots stirred by women

7

in slippers; teenagers in their rooms wearing headphones; somebody's son looking for his keys; a divorcée brushing her teeth as her cat stares; a family watching television – the youngest is asleep but will not remember his dream.

When I clasp my bow, the audience is suddenly very quiet.

I look out at their faces a moment before I begin.

So many people and yet not one single person who knows anything about me.

If only one of them recognized me, I could slip from the branches of my life, brush time from my clothes, and begin the long journey across the fields to the place where I first disappeared. A boy leaning crookedly on a gate, waiting for his best friend to get up. The back wheel of Anna's bicycle still spinning.

For ten years as a professional cellist I have been raising the dead in concert halls across the world. The moment my bow makes contact with the strings, Anna's form appears. She is wearing the clothes from that day. I am twenty years older. But she is still a child. She flickers because she is made of light. She watches a few feet from my cello. She looks at me but doesn't recognize who I am.

Tonight the concert hall is packed. By the end of the final movement I can sense her fading. Perhaps a single hand remains; a scoop of shoulder; a shimmering mane of hair.

But she is turning inward quickly now – quickly drifting from the living world.

Some concert performers turn their backs to the figures that float upon the stage: figures that move with the confusion of sleep, with the grace of unfurling smoke, figures conjured by guilt, love, regret, luck, and happenstance. Some performers I've read about can't take their eyes off them. Some crack and fling themselves off bridges; others drink themselves into oblivion or stand in freezing rivers at midnight.

I think music is what language once aspired to be. Music allows us to face God on our own terms because it reaches beyond life.

I feel moments from the end.

The muscles in my bowing arm tighten. The final notes are sonorous; I steady my bow like an oar held in a river, steering us all toward the bank of now and tomorrow and the day after that. Days ahead like open fields.

And night pools outside the concert hall. The city is still wet. The concert hall is glassed in and overlooks a garden. Eyes of rain dot the windows and shiver with each breath of wind. Stars fill the sky, then drop to flood the streets and the squares. When it rains, even the most insignificant puddle is a map of the universe.

When the performance ends, I stand and raise my bow to the audience. I can hear things landing on the stage – flowers and small letters taped to the plastic.

The applause is deafening. I feel for Anna's mitten in my pocket.

I drip with sweat under the lights. Each drop holds its own tiny clapping audience. As always I want something sweet to drink. I hurry off the stage, still holding my bow. When I reach the steps, I feel again for Anna's mitten and suddenly see her face with terrifying clarity. Such straight hair and so many freckles. The only authentic memories find us – like letters addressed to someone we used to be.

I hurry to my dressing room. I find a towel, drink orange juice from a bottle, and fall into a chair.

Then I sit very still and close my eyes.

Another concert over.

I wonder how many more I can do. How many Annas are left. She was twelve when she died. Her father was a baker – and since that morning, every twelfth baguette he bakes bears the letter A.

He lets children eat cakes in his shop for free. They talk loudly and make a mess.

A porter knocks, then enters my dressing room with a cell phone. He gestures for me to take it. He has the sort of square shoulders women like. There are deep lines around his eyes, but he doesn't look over forty. I give him my bottle of juice. He holds it at a distance from his body. I cup the phone to my ear. It's Sandy. She wants to know how it has gone. She couldn't hear because of the static on the porter's phone. Someone had given her the number so she could listen from backstage. Sandy is my agent. She is originally from Iowa. A good businesswoman; understands how creative minds work – in other words, she's pushy with everyone but her talent. I tell her it went well. Then I ask if I can tell her something.

"Like what?" she says.

I seldom volunteer anything. For most of my thirties, I have seen little point in telling people anything. But as a teenager, I loved passionately, spent whole nights crying (for what, I can no longer remember). I followed women home and then wrote sonatas that I left on doorsteps in the middle of the night. I dived into ponds fully clothed. I almost drank myself to death. In my youth, all conflict was resolution – just a busier form of emptiness.

Sandy knows only that I'm French and that I never forget to send her daughter a postcard from wherever I go.

I tell Sandy about a dream I had on the flight to Quebec City. Sandy says that dreams are either unresolved conflicts or wish fulfillments. According to Freud, she says. Then she doesn't say anything. I can hear a television in the background. Then she says her daughter needs to go to bed. I ask what she's done wrong. Sandy laughs. They are knitting and there's a film on. Sandy is a single mother. She went to a facility and had herself impregnated. I've always thought that if

Sandy died, I'd want her daughter to live with me. I could teach her the cello. Though she'd be alone a lot because I go away.

Still, I would leave her "notes" all over the house. We could name the two eighteenth-century portraits that hang in my apartment. They could watch over us. We could watch over each other.

I give the porter his telephone back and thank him. He asks if it is good news.

My plane is not leaving for New York until the next afternoon. I have an entire evening to wander around. I arrived in Quebec City just this morning. The taxi driver was from Bosnia. He wore a wool hat with the symbol of his favorite football team.

About half an hour after my performance at the Musée de la Civilisation ended, several couples flooded my dressing room and invited me to dinner. These couples are the same in every city. In the ancient Sicilian town of Noto (where my cello was made), their garments would have borne the most intricate patterns. I imagine faces, people sitting in courtyards: the luxury of shade; lips wet with wine; dusty feet resting atop sandals; the smell of horses from outside; children running through the house, curls bouncing off shoulders; laughter turns to crying – the scope of human feeling hasn't changed.

I'm always asked to dinner or to spend the weekend somewhere with the trustees – perhaps I might even bring my cello? they ask.

When I was young, I was too shy to refuse. For the past several years, I've politely declined. Sandy says I'm getting a reputation for being difficult.

I explained like always that I must recover; that I have been hampered by a rather serious cold. I took a few deep breaths for effect. A woman laughed. Her husband put his arm around her. He was wearing a canary-yellow bow tie. There were dark patches under his eyes.

Before the performance I looked at myself in the mirror. I wondered if I should shave. It was my birthday last Wednesday, and I have thirty-five years attached to me like a belt of weights. Actually, years mean nothing. It's what's inside them. To some I am a famous cellist. Bruno Bonnet. I don't know what I am to myself, probably still a scared little boy enchanted by the world, or, at best, the boy whose face has remained glued to the misty back window of the family sedan, a brown Renault 16. As a child, my family would take long drives, often not even stopping for the night. I think my father drove the way he thought. My mother would break bread and give my brother and me handfuls each. When the bread was gone, we would finally stop. Bread was the civilizing force of my childhood.

My father was one of the few men I knew growing up who didn't smoke. His father was killed in the war. As Paris filled up with Nazi soldiers shouting and pointing things out, the roads south were clogged with people – their possessions loaded onto cars, horse-drawn wagons, baby carriages loaded with radios, family pictures, and cutlery. Hitler wanted the roads destroyed.

It wasn't difficult for the pilots of the Luftwaffe to spot the roads from above because they were literally moving. My grandfather was plowing a field. His head was clipped by a piece of shell. My father was ten.

When I was ten, my father gave me a photograph of his father holding his ancient Italian cello. He told me to save it, that one day it would mean something. I remember telling him that it already meant something. Then I asked casually if I could learn the cello. I wasn't aware of what I'd said.

A few weeks later on Christmas Eve, there was a priceless eighteenth-century cello sitting under the tree. It was my grandfather's; the case bore his initials. My mother had tied a ribbon around the case. As I approached it, my father got up and left the room.

My father listened to me practice with tears in his eyes. That's the secret to my success as a cellist.

As my dressing room gradually emptied, the man with the canary-yellow bow tie asked if he and his wife could take my cello in their car to my hotel, the Chateau Frontenac, where they planned to dine at Jean Souchard's restaurant. His wife said they would be more careful than I could imagine. I thanked them and explained how the music director had already arranged for the cello to be escorted to the hotel "vault" by several members of the museum staff. The couple looked disappointed, and so I walked them to their car. They seemed to want something from me. I wanted to explain that trusting is harder than being trusted.

I love walking. Especially when I have nothing to carry (which is not often). On my way back to the hotel it starts to rain, lightly at first, and then hard, half-frozen drops. On the street that leads to the Chateau Frontenac, I stop walking. The road surface is slick. It reflects the world with a beautiful inaccuracy.

My old geography professor once told his class how the music, paintings, sculptures, and books of the world are mirrors in which people see versions of themselves.

There is something about the rain slipping down the hill that prevents me from moving. People hurry past, going somewhere but nowhere. Cars slow down. The people inside want to see what I am looking at. The sweeping whites of the headlights like strange animals.

When I get back to New York, I'm going to memorize the opening lines of Dante's most famous work. I think it begins, "Midway on our life's journey, I found myself in dark woods…"

I think of Horowitz's Träumerei. Twenty-five seconds longer than anyone else's. Or did I imagine that? If you haven't heard this piece…

It's about childhood.

My parents back in France spend their evenings watching television in the socks I sent them from London. I love my parents and forgive them. Above the couch is a framed watercolor of a mountain lion. If it fell, it would kill them. It's a limited-edition print. There are 199 others in the world.

They will only ever be my parents once. They are the only parents I will ever have in the history of the universe. I wonder if they feel me thinking about them here in Quebec City in the rain – I wonder if they feel me like a small animal gnawing them affectionately.

I continue up the hill. The Chateau Frontenac towers over the city like a benevolent dictator. From the eighteenth floor, you can see the Laurentian Mountains. Montreal is five hours southwest. The castle was built for well-to-do railroad passengers a few decades after the American Civil War. I suppose for some Quebecois, it's the biggest building they'll ever see. Lovers come here too and walk the city at dusk. You can see them on the promenade, sharing an umbrella, huddled together, stopping only to kiss and stare down at a cold black river dabbed with patches of streetlight.

When I play, I feel as though I am flying. I circle the auditorium. I am anywhere but inside my body. Without music, I would be a prisoner trapped in a sealed wall.

When I play, I sometimes picture my parents. And then the moment I finish playing, there is an eruption of applause. People cannot wait to give applause because they clap for themselves; they clap because they have been recognized by someone who died long ago in a room that flickered with candlelight.

I want to call my father, but my parents will both be in bed. They'll be annoyed if I call – but grateful tomorrow. My father thinks me eccentric anyway. He tells his friends at the café about me, about how eccentric I am. It's his way of talking about me.

In Noyant, the small French village where I grew up, it is too late to call anyone. I can feel the stillness of the town. The empty streets. My parents are asleep. The glowing numbers of the red alarm clock magnified by a glass set down in front of it. In the glass there are tiny bubbles that rise to the surface in the night. The remnants of supper will be in the refrigerator. There will be a cool skin of moisture on the car outside – a new Renault. My brother bought it for them as a Christmas present. I remember that my mother wanted to go for a drive in her nightgown; my brother was overjoyed with this. My father washed his hands and looked at it through the kitchen window before going outside. He stood next to it and put his hand on the roof. Then he went off to the vegetable patch beyond the far wall of the house and dug for a few forgotten potatoes. My mother took my brother inside and reassured him that we'd all go for a ride after breakfast. My brother has never understood our father. My brother is emotionally literal. Women have always loved him. I miss him. We grew up in a cottage that was part of a small bourgeois estate my father cared for.

The long eighteenth-century manor waits in darkness for its part-time occupants, who are spread across Paris for most of the year like different parts of a machine. They are a lovely family. Though one side is a little solemn, while the other is a little zealous. The house is long and white with many windows. In the attic there is a box of Napoleonic uniforms. In one of the bedrooms, three dozen Agatha Christie Penguin paperbacks. In another, engravings of birds.

Tomorrow I will return to New York, my home for almost a decade now. More concerts at the end of the week. One at the Lotos Club, another at a fund-raiser for Central Park, then Los Angeles – a concert at the Hollywood Bowl – then San Francisco, then Phoenix.

I love New York but miss the silence of rural Europe. Americans are literal. I think my brother would find a wife here in five minutes.

Bach's Suites for Solo Cello were written as pieces intended to teach but contain a mystery musicians unravel without knowing why; a map that shows the position of other maps. They are as popular as the stock pieces I play by Mozart and Haydn. Bach's Suites for Solo Cello are actually my biggest sellers. Bach and my brother helped buy my small apartment in Brooklyn. My brother doesn't know I know, but he bought thousands of copies of my CD and put them in his employees' Christmas bags. My brother's employees love him passionately. If there were a war on, they'd become his private army. It's amazing how he's done so well in business. He's crushed all competition. He's been on the cover of business magazines world-wide. For reasons known only to my brother and me, he has almost single-handedly made Renault the most popular brand of small car in Europe. I even have one here in New York. Everybody wants to know what it is. They always pronounce the "T". I have a mechanic in Queens. He's from Senegal and also grew up with Renault automobiles. In fact, I park it at his house and he uses it to drive his six kids around. I haven't seen it in almost two years. My brother doesn't know but would approve of the whole situation. My brother and I have the same brown Renault 16s, both from 1978. Perhaps we hold on to our childhoods because we can't hold on to each other. His girlfriends are always surprised when their millionaire boyfriend picks them up in a 1978 Renault 16.

An hour after my performance in Quebec City I walked right past my hotel into the maze of old streets. The rain was too beautiful to miss. Then I found Le Saint Amour, a little French restaurant. The food reminded me of home. I explained how I don't drink because I'm allergic, but the waiter brought little glasses of wine for me to sniff as I sank my fork into foie gras, filet mignon, truffled lentils. I'm not really allergic to alcohol; the opposite actually – my body loves the stuff.

The restaurant was packed with couples. A teenage girl sat quietly with her father. She was angry or disappointed with him. He knew it but pretended not to be bothered. I think all children are disappointed with their parents if they're lucky enough to get so close.

I left an enormous tip. I shall never forget my waiter. He kept trying to speak Italian, even though he knew I was French. He kept mentioning his daughters. He wore glasses that made him look too old. He loved being a waiter. He said that each meal was a memory. He said that he was a part of something good that had not started with him and would not end with him. As I left the restaurant, I felt a stabbing sadness. I would never see him again.

I passed several cold shops. Everything was closed. Puppets in a shop window stared out into the street, pretending not to see me. I walked carefully across the icy cobbles. It was snowing now, but only lightly. The buildings were silent, their occupants asleep inside. It was after one and so quiet I could hear the buzzing of streetlights as I walked under them.

The city looked different. I stood in the middle of the square before Notre-Dame-des-Victoires, a small gray, crooked church.

They once filmed a sad film there. It was about a boy whose father was a failure. Going back somewhere at night is almost like haunting the world after death.

I kept walking, making eyes at the statues, naming each one like a sentimental drunkard after lovers and friends.

And then I stopped walking. My eye was drawn by movement. I couldn't quite see what it was – most likely a human figure passing before a dark window like a fish barely visible beneath the surface of a pond.

Each window held its very own candle. But they weren't real candles, just electric lights shaped like candles. The long house was tucked into an alley that glowed with snow. The streetlights at the far end of the house cast a great shadow on the side of the crooked church. The house was almost a smaller version of the one in which I had grown up – the bourgeois manor my father had spent his life maintaining like a mute first-born child. There were other windows too, ones without candles, ones so dark it was almost as if there were no glass at all. An inscription above the door read, "Par le Coeur de Mon Fils," and then a stone relief of a hand entering what appeared to be a human heart. Also, a large crucifix carved into the heavy wooden door. The order and cleanliness of the corridor that was visible through the only brightly lit window, on the ground floor, made me think this was a convent.

Then I saw the figure pass by the window again. It stopped. Whoever it was had seen me standing outside in the freezing air. It was past three in the morning. We were the only two inhabitants of an entire city; footprints on each other's island.

The figure swiftly moved to another window, one with a candle, and I saw who it was.

I could distinguish her profile, but details remained a mystery. She stood with the poise of someone young. Her hand pressed up against the pane. Then, in the mist which had laid itself thinly upon the early morning glass — as if solely for the purpose of what was about to happen next — this woman whom I knew but would never know, this lost, sleepless figure who found herself wandering the corridors of an icy dawn, wrote something very slowly with her finger upon the pane. Then she lifted the candle against the letters she had drawn with her finger:

Allez

I took my hands out of my pockets. It began to rain and she disappeared. I turned and walked slowly away.

I said the word over and over again as I paced the city. And I felt suddenly warm, full of strength, full of life, and ready to give life. I suppose I need people to tell me what I already know.

My father and mother would be awake by now.

The kitchen sink full of vegetables freshly pulled from the earth.

My brother in Paris reading beside the window — his new girl-friend still asleep.

And Sandy, my agent — with her daughter in their hot bed, nestled in one another's arms. Their breathing is soft and private; mouths open against hillsides of pillow.

I must have returned to my hotel room around breakfast time the next day. I was out all night in the cold and soaked through. I left a small pool in the elevator. The couple staying on my floor with the miniature poodle will probably be blamed. The staff here is very gracious, and the grand Chateau Frontenac hotel is like something from the mind of Chekhov.

I am now soaking in a hot bath.

My chest protrudes from the bubbles like an island upon which the carved head of some great deity has come to life. I must remember to write in my diary that I spent the early hours of the morning making eyes at all the statues in the city and then soaked in a tub.

My shoes were so wet they had ceased to make a sound on the cobbles. I have put them in the sink. The leather is impossibly tender now; I don't think it will ever go back to normal. I think of the word. I can feel her finger moving across my back in the shape of letters.

Allez

When I get back to New York, I'm going to start getting up early. I'm going to invite my brother to come and see me. We will sit together in the park in heavy coats. We will watch the clouds pass. Sometimes I imagine that each cloud holds the weight of what will happen.

The water in my bath is cooling. I can see a version of myself in it. My eyes ascend to the window, then through it. They find the river and follow it. Quebec City was taken from its ancient people by the French when William Shakespeare was about my age. My hotel room overlooks the St. Lawrence River. Chunks of ice slip by with the current. Quebec women once set out hard rods of corn on planks of wood on the river's bank. I can see their cotton-white breath and their gray teeth as glimmering fish are spread across barrels. Their aprons are wet. Frost has dusted white the rich brown earth. The ground is hard as stone. Cold has cracked their hands. They laugh and wave to children on small boats drifting. Clouds churn in the eyes of the fish.

I like my room here at the Chateau. It overlooks part of the river but is directly over a park. In the park there are trees stripped by winter and blackened by rain. I can't stop thinking of the early settlers of the 1600s. The smell of wet leather. Stupid horses not doing what they're told. Babies crying. Wet wood. Ice on everything, ice cutting through the body. The earth too frozen to bury the dead. And nothing will grow. A few frozen berries dot the woods like eyes. New foods are tried but result in sickness.

I must have fallen asleep in the tub. I awake to a light tapping on my door. I don't answer and hope the person will go away. Tapping again. Perhaps my cello is ready to come up from the hotel vault they assured me exists. I find a towel, open the door, and thank the bellboy with some money. He asks if I want breakfast, then says it was an honor to carry my instrument. He walks away whistling. I think the staff like me. Two chambermaids think they heard me practicing in my room before my concert yesterday, but it wasn't me. It was Pablo Casals. I was playing one of his old recordings, a Toccata in C Major by J. S. Bach. They were shuffling outside the door. I made it louder. When it finished, they clapped. I should write to Bose and tell them their speakers are a success.

Most people never get to hear this music. Music helps us understand where we have come from but, more importantly, what has happened to us. Bach wrote the Cello Suites for his young wife as an exercise to help her learn the cello. But inside each note is the love we are unable to express with words. I can feel her frustration and joy as my bow carves out the notes of the mild-mannered organist who saw composing as one of his daily chores. When Bach died, some of his children sold his scores to the butcher; they had decided the paper was more useful for wrapping meat. In a small village in Germany, a father brought home a limp goose wrapped in paper that was covered with strange and beautiful symbols.

I open my cello case and smell my grandfather. I pick up the instrument and run my fingers tenderly up and down the strings. In each note of music lives every tragedy of the world and every moment of its salvation. The cellist Pablo Casals knew this. Music is only a mystery to people who want it explained. Music and love are the same.

I am staring at the fireplace in my room, holding my cello. I think of my parents again. My father doesn't listen to the music I record, but he sometimes comes to my performances when I'm in Tours or Saumur.

In my cello case is a mitten that belonged to the baker's daughter. I keep it in my pocket when I play. We sat next to each other in class. Her name was Anna. She had freckles and held her pencil with three fingers and a thumb.

Winter strips the village of my youth, but in spring the parks fill up again with children learning how to ride bicycles and not doing what they're told.

To SEE HIM IS a miracle. He stands at the fountain and gently raises a hand. Then birds swoop down from trees and perch on his shoulders. Some hover, then drop into his hands like soft stones. Children cry with joy. Parents want to know who he is. They call him the birdman of Beverly Hills and talk about him over dinners with friends who wonder what his story is. Some say his wife and child were killed. Others say he was in a war. Many people believe he's an eccentric billionaire.

He wears a dusty dinner jacket, and his pants are short enough to clearly see white socks. His hair is overgrown, with streaks of silver. Worn chestnut loafers tell of a different life.

Sometimes the birdman will raise a hand to his mouth and whisper something to the plump bird cupped there. Moments later, the bird will fly out and land on someone in the crowd: a boy's shoulder or the outstretched hand of a girl.

One Friday morning, not one but three birds landed on an old man's knee. He was sad because no one had asked him out to lunch that day, nor had he received any letters. When the birds landed on him, his mouth trembled and the clouds in his eyes parted.

When the birds flew away, he said, "What a nice birthday present!" The birdman nodded. The old man immediately went home, put away the length of rope, and went downstairs to ask his young Mexican neighbor to be his guest for dinner. They talked about many things. And over dessert the old man made a promise that he would teach his neighbor to read. They were both drunk. Every idea felt original. The next day, the neighbor took the old man a present and a piñada purchased in an East L.A. bakery next to the old Cat & Dog Hospital.

By the time the Mexican boy could read, the two of them had found that they fit the way jigsaw pieces do. They celebrated holidays together. They created for each other a world within a world and cast each other as stars.

Hope is the greatest of all gifts.

Once, a black-haired woman and her child asked the birdman his name. He sighed slowly. He didn't like questions. But the birds around him fluttered their wings. The tired woman and her young child peered up at the birdman.

"Please," the child implored. "Won't you tell us your name?"

The woman and child were holding hands. The afternoon sunshine warmed the tops of their heads. The woman tilted her left foot to the side as though pouring something out.

"Jonathan," the birdman said. Then he turned and walked away.

The birds flew with Jonathan, as though pulling his slight frame to the edge of the park with thin ropes. The park returned to normal. A homeless woman fell asleep to the sound of passing cars. Squirrels chased each other around tree trunks with acorns in their mouths.

III

S IX MONTHS LATER, the black-haired woman told her sister about the birdman over lunch at the Beverly Hills Hotel.

"The birdman finally spoke and told us his name was Jonathan," she said, laughing.

A woman sipping tea at the next table dropped her cup. It split neatly in two parts on the saucer. Tea escaped into the linens. A knot of waiters rushed out from behind a door. The stains would be hard to remove.

The woman at the next table stood up and quickly stepped toward the restrooms. She was wearing an old-fashioned sequin skirt and forest-green shoes. She had grown up in Wales. Her brother's name was also Jonathan.

It was almost five o'clock. Outside, the afternoon – heavy with heat – listed like an old ship and people rolled from one side of the city to the other.

The Beverly Hills Hotel is opulent. It prides itself on many things. There is a salon and several places to eat. For anyone who likes pink, it's paradise. In the bathroom, the woman who lost her teacup sat in the stall and sobbed. She could picture the waiters cleaning up; there would soon be fresh linens and shining silverware. Within a few minutes, all traces of her outburst would be erased.

The woman felt acorns in her pocket. She squeezed each one of them. Her Jonathan collected nuts. He kept them in small bowls around his bedroom. He wanted to feed the birds. He was obsessed with birds. And they built nests outside his bedroom in small dark places in the roof. He said he could see their eyes peering into his bedroom at night. Perhaps they knew all along what would happen to him. That was long ago in Wales, in a one-eyed village of sheep, mud, and stars.

Grief is a country where it rains and rains but nothing grows. The dead live somewhere else – wearing the clothes we remember them in.

IV

WHEN BABY JONATHAN CAME home from the hospital wrapped in white, I couldn't stop looking at him. I would sit by him at night. His breaths were fast and small. When his arms were strong enough, he reached for me, his sister.

Our house was a cottage warmed by hot coals that burned slowly and deeply in the kitchen stove. In summer the fireplaces in the main rooms were dark and full of winter's ashes. My mother would make salad sandwiches with lettuce from the garden. When Jonathan could walk, I took him into the fields behind our cottage and sat him down on a towel somewhere shady. I would build tiny huts from mud and straw as he held in his chubby fingers the brown plastic mice we both knew were our friends.

On Saturdays we would all go into the village. Outside the butcher's shop whole animals hung from hooks of brushed steel. Jonathan would point but had yet to find words.

When it was hot, I would take off his clothes and bounce him on the bed. I like to think this was his first memory.

My dolls sat in the toy box until Jonathan was two and he found them. Then began the great age of dressing them up. The two dolls became our younger siblings. Once we wrapped them in aluminum foil and pretended they were robots. Our quiet father would send the dolls postcards from wherever he traveled on business. I would read them to the dolls, and Jonathan would nod and then put them to bed, saying, "Wasn't that nice? A postcard from somewhere you'll never go."

When he began wearing underpants, he got in the habit of tying his unused diapers on the dolls. His underpants were small. When I came home from school, if I found them on the living room floor, soiled, I knew he would be crying on the bed waiting for me. I would take off my underwear and run it under the faucet and then show it to him. He would stop crying. All siblings have a secret life from their parents. Parents love their children, but children need each other to negotiate the strange forest they find themselves in.

It wasn't long before I was caught in the act. Jonathan stood naked at the bathroom door as I doused my underwear with cold water. He approached and wrapped his little body around my legs. The bathroom window held the final square of daylight. It was very bright and also very still. Downstairs, we could hear the sounds of cartoons pouring from the television. Jonathan never cried again when he had an accident. I firmly believe that while lies and deception destroy love, they can also build and defend it. Love requires imagination more than experience.

Nobody knows when Jonathan died. My father saw something in the snow from the bathroom window one morning. I wasn't allowed to go outside, so I sat in the bathroom and ripped out my hair. When my mother saw clumps of it on my bare legs, she decided to let me see Jonathan's body. I screamed and screamed and never stopped screaming until I met a man named Bruno Bonnet.

V

A RRIVING IN THE DARK for my concert the next day, I find Los Angeles pulsating with traffic; pairs of red lights thread the valleys with their flat houses and clear pools. The oldest houses have round edges and crumble a little more whenever the ground shakes. In the suburbs, imagine all-night Laundromats heavy with the freshness of clean clothes; young mothers with plastic flowers in their hair. Babies peer up through black eyes from hot towels. Gangs of men turn their heads to eat tacos at a roadside cantina. Trash blows from one side of the highway to the other, then back again.

Farther north, approaching Hollywood – hot-dog stands with neon arrows and faded paint; tattooed women with chopped black hair buying lip gloss at Hollywood pharmacies; a homeless man pushes a shopping cart full of shoes but he is barefoot. He keeps looking behind. His stomach hangs out. Sometime in the 1960s he was delivered into the trembling hands of his mother. If only it could happen again. Los Angeles is a place where dreams balance forever on the edge of coming true. A city on a cliff held fast by its own weight.

I like performing here, especially at the Hollywood Bowl. There's something about the movement of air. My music fills the thermals, and I imagine the notes flooding the city like birds. It's hot here too; a real contrast to Quebec City two weeks ago, where my feet froze after walking the city at night and conversing with the statuary. When my shoes dried, they were very stiff. I put them in a clear plastic bag and labeled it "Le Flâneur de Quebec." I think it's important to keep items of clothing that have emotional significance.

I've been thinking about that woman I saw behind the window in the middle of the night. Since that evening I've felt differently about a lot of things. I spoke to my brother about it. He thinks I'm finally coming around. He thinks I suffer from depression. But I'm just quiet. Solitude and depression are like swimming and drowning. In school many years ago, I learned that flowers sometimes unfold inside themselves.

After a good night's sleep, it's lunchtime and I'm eating meat loaf in the Beverly Hills Hotel. It's actually late morning. Outside on the patio is a Brazilian spearmint tree that died years ago. The waiter said it's now over a hundred years old – but does a thing continue to accrue years once it's dead? If so, if so… I stop myself. There are stumps of baguette on the table. The baker enters my mind. He is drying his hands on an apron. I stop myself.

Later, I will sink again.

Later, I will row myself out to sea with my bow to Anna's floating body. I can see her face so clearly. She died when she was twelve. I was thirteen. She hasn't aged with me, but sometimes I imagine her as a woman.

"A girl comes every week." The waiter was back, still thinking about the tree outside. "She plays with the plastic ferns in the branches."

I look into the branches and smile.

"Landscapers look at it and laugh," he said. "To them it must look stupid."

I like waiters – but you have to win them over quickly before you become just another client, just another table 23. The meat loaf is mediocre here, but the service is fabulous. I seldom eat at home; I'm on the road so much. This hotel is like having an adoring mother who can't cook.

The most delicious bread in the world is made in my village. It's something to do with salt in the water. The baker's daughter and I used to ride our bicycles to the edge of town. Remember that Noyant is a small village. We would leave our bikes leaning against each other as we climbed the swaying gate into the soft fields of Farmer Ricard.

He was a large man with eyes that seemed ready to fall out. His lips were very large too, and he wore green army sweaters. He once carried a baby cow on his back through waist-deep snow across several kilometers of fields. The vet in the next village was drinking chamomile tea and looking out the window. A broken leg was set and healed in a barn warmed by gaslight. Everyone in the village remembers what happened. The cow was allowed to die of old age.

Farmer Ricard has a photograph of his father in the kitchen. He was in the Resistance and was tortured to death. Madame Ricard is in the habit of talking to the photograph while Farmer Ricard is away in the fields. Sometimes she can hear him hammering in the barn. He likes to drink his coffee with both hands. They haven't made love for years but sleep holding hands.

A pianist here at the hotel is playing "The Girl from Ipanema." Lights behind the bar make the liquor glow. My napkin is pebbled at the edges. The hotel crest is faintly impressed in the center. The dining room is mostly empty. The dining room is split into many areas. Three tables over, an old man is doing magic tricks for his teenage granddaughter. It looks like she is wearing her prom dress. Her hair is pulled back. Her earrings are new. Every time the knife disappears into the napkin, she smiles.

At another table are a young Mexican and a very old man with white hair. They are reading from the same book and eating from the same bowl of ice cream.

This is the sort of place where pictures were snapped before the war. Glossy black-and-white prints now hanging in Beverly Hills above quiet beds in bedrooms that smell of mothballs. Women in black gloves. Smoking men with shiny hair. Palm trees in the background. Glasses, empty of gin, replenished by melting ice.

Once we were in Farmer Ricard's misty field, the baker's daughter and I would fill our pockets with stones. If one of us remembered to bring a plastic bag, that was even better. When laden with more stones than we could possibly carry, we dragged our heavy bodies to the edge of the field and made a pile. Then we'd split up and the search would continue.

We collected stones to save the plows.

Monsieur Ricard gave us a franc for every ten stones. If we managed to find one too big for one of us to carry alone (that was the test), that particular stone was worth a franc all by itself. When we got tired, we'd sit on the dirt and watch birds. Sometimes a farm cat would find us and its tail would go up. The cat would often turn around to look at something that wasn't there. For the past twenty-two years, I've been doing the same thing.

When I finish my lunch, I'm going downstairs to the Beverly Hills Hotel gift shop. It's opposite the hair salon. Rows of women sit with twists of silver foil in their hair. The stylists talk about celebrities, and soon the women start to feel like celebrities.

In the hotel gift shop I'm going to buy a hatbox.

Then I'm going to fill it with stones.

VI

FOR JONATHAN'S FOURTH BIRTHDAY, he was given a white hardcover book called *The British Book of Birds*. This was by far his favorite possession. When he was upset, he would clumsily sketch birds from the book, gripping his colored pencil in a fist.

About this time we had some lovely family vacations together.

Watching my father lift the caravan onto the hitch of our family sedan was like watching Atlas take up the world on his back. Then, on the motorway, my brother and I nesting in the back as my mother's hand appeared behind the seat with a smile of orange for each of us, my father quietly navigating our fortress to a field on a hillside at a distance from our Welsh village unfathomable to us.

By the evening, my mother, father, Jonathan, and I would be sitting in plastic chairs under a Cinzano umbrella somewhere on the Welsh coast. The smell of my father's cold lager beer, my mother's wine, cigarette smoke from another table. The sound of cars in the town, the smell of fish and chips, women in heels clopping along the narrow roads to the town nightclub. Then back at the caravan, Jonathan and I in bunk beds. We communicated by gently knocking on the thin wall against which our beds were built. The blankets were always musty, and the smell of dinner sometimes lingered until morning.

As an adult, I've realized where Jonathan found his gentleness.

Our father was a shy, good-natured boy – a handsome man from South Wales, strong enough to lift a caravan by the throat but wise enough to cup a moth as it slid its body against the flickering black-and-white TV. I remember the release from our caravan through a cracked door into the dark field, as though on its powdery back balanced the weight of his children's dreams.

The day was spent exploring the village and the countryside. My favorite memory is cooking sausages beside a river. We hiked through shallow woods and didn't see anyone. My mother grew up afraid because of what people did to her. And then afraid of what they might do to us. To her family she was shy, loving, secretive, and fiercely loyal, but in the world she stood poised, cunning, and glamorous. The perfect saleswoman.

I remember holding her slender hand as we crossed a river somewhere close to the sea, our caravan back through the forest on a concrete slab with other caravans. Little Jonathan held my hand. One of his shoes was wet. He had misjudged his steps. We all thought it was funny.

I wish I'd kept his shoes – that's one thing I regret getting rid of. I loved those shoes, and I loved the socks too.

And then my father with sausages wrapped in newspaper, who had not yet reached the bank. I remember our faces changing before us as we crossed the cold, blind, rushing river. I led Jonathan, carefully picking out stones whose heads poked out from the water, as though they wished to say something.

I remember looking back for my father, slowed by the weight of his joy from knowing that we were somewhere but he could not see us. I remember my mother's trembling voice as we neared the other bank and Jonathan's laughter like a tablecloth spread over his fear. Then my father tilted across on the stones, and we cooked sausages beside the water.

Jonathan disappeared that winter. It was a few days before Christmas. I remember asking my mother where he was. She told me to look under his bed. Potatoes boiled. The kitchen was full of steam. I wiped the window with my sleeve.

"He won't be outside, dear – look at the snow."

I will never forget that moment. Because he was outside.

My father had left a ladder propped against a conifer tree.

He was cutting branches with a chain saw before the snow came.

Jonathan had climbed the ladder. Nobody knew.

Once in the tree, he climbed and climbed. We don't know why. Perhaps he knew he had come to the end of his life and wanted to become a bird.

I hope he did become a bird.

I hear him call every morning from the tree outside my apartment.

By late afternoon we were all worried. My mother telephoned the police. My father searched the village, then young men showed up at our doorstep with flashlights and heavy walking sticks.

I fell asleep in the early hours of the morning without wanting to. I've felt guilty about that for most of my life. Perhaps if I'd stayed awake, I would have heard him call out.

The next morning several old Land Rovers with canvas backs were parked outside. The men at the kitchen table drank strong tea. Eggs spat in the frying pan. The farmers' waxed jackets dripped water on the stone floor.

They had found nothing and were half-frozen.

Dogs on the floor at their feet.

The dogs refused the bacon scraps offered them. The men said the dogs were sad because they couldn't find the boy. The scent of him lingered in their noses.

On Christmas Day, we sat and looked at the presents. My mother cried and threw her shoe through a window. I prayed by reading Jonathan's *British Book of Birds* aloud to the heavens. It responded in a scatter of soft white tongues that told us nothing.

In January, two weeks later, my father was shaving when he noticed a speck in the garden outside.

A smudge of color broke the white monotony.

Without wiping the shaving cream that smeared his cheeks, he rushed outside into the thick snow. Jonathan's body lay completely still. The branch onto which he had climbed and become trapped had broken that night in a storm. He lay in the snow faceup. His body was hard and his mouth was open. In one of his hands were three frozen acorns. In his mind, it was not yet Christmas Day.

It's still a mystery why he didn't call out. Perhaps he was afraid of being punished; children possess the most powerful fear of disappointing their parents.

After they took Jonathan's body away, my father went into the shed. He closed the door and then chopped off his right hand with an axe.

The police came and took him to hospital.

For almost three decades, I've kept acorns in my pockets. I check for them constantly.

Sometimes I roll them in my palms and hear laughter, then the sound of a breaking branch, something soft punching the snow from a great height.

Birdsong.

VII

T HE GIRLS IN THE gift shop at the Beverly Hills Hotel were kind enough to help me pack the stones into the hatbox with pink tissue paper. They asked if I was French. They said it wasn't so much my accent as the way I was dressed. They were excited to be involved in something eccentric.

The younger of the two wore blue eye shadow. She asked me what "*Voulez-vous coucher avec moi*" means. The older woman giggled and said she just wants me to say it. The girl with blue eye shadow slapped her friend's arm.

I asked for more tissue paper, and the younger girl asked why I wanted to wrap stones anyway. I told her it was just something I did.

Before I closed the hatbox, the young shop assistant reached in. I waited with the lid in my hands.

"Stones are really quite beautiful, aren't they?" she said. Her retainer glinted in the shop light.

I walked past the hair salon and then up the stairs. As I passed the Polo Lounge, a woman appeared from around a corner and walked straight into me. The force of her motion was enough to knock me down. I dropped the hatbox, and the stones rolled out with a loud clacking sound. The woman was carrying what I thought were small rocks, and they fell from her hands and scattered across the hard, glossy floor.

She glared at me. And then suddenly an arm of sunlight reached through a high window and opened its hand upon her face. I saw her eyes as clearly as if we had been pressed against one another in a very small space.

A bellboy rushed over and started to pick up her stones.

"Acorns!" he exclaimed.

The woman looked at him in horror.

"Please, I'll do it," she said. The bellboy was confused and continued to pick up the acorns, just more carefully.

"No, I'll do it, please," the woman said again. The bellboy looked at me for a few moments and then hurried off.

For some reason I didn't get up immediately. Instead, I watched her collect her acorns. She had beautiful shoes. And then the sunlight fell away and I noticed drops were falling from her eyes. I finally stood up and proceeded to collect the five stones I'd so carefully packed into the hatbox with the girls downstairs in the shop.

"Sorry," the woman said genuinely.

She had an accent I had never heard. Her hair was very soft, but I kept looking at her shoes.

For a few moments we stood opposite one another. It was awkward. Neither of us walked away. To anyone watching, it must have looked as though we were talking – but we weren't saying anything.

The most significant conversations of our lives occur in silence.

"I'm so sorry," she said again. I said I was sorry too. I wasn't sorry, but I felt like I should have been.

There were freckles on her cheeks and forehead. Her eyes were very green.

When she walked off, I sat on a bench by the counter and held on to my box. I sat there for some time and even considered leaving my box behind so that I might follow her, grab her arm, and force her to go somewhere with me and sit down. I wanted only to look at her green eyes and to hear the lilting song of her voice, as though her words were the notes I had been searching for, the vital sounds that I had never played.

The most important notes in music are the ones that wait until sound has entered the ear before revealing their true nature. They are the spaces between the sounds that blow through the heart, knocking things over.

I eventually went back to my room.

Later. My telephone flashing. A message from Sandy, my agent, some detail about my San Francisco concert and the music director's belief that my grandfather's chair is too damaged to sit on. I wanted to call her and tell her about this woman but felt for some reason it would upset her. Her daughter's birthday is coming up. Sandy asked if I would buy her a bicycle. Her daughter requested that I give her a bicycle and teach her how to ride it. I think when I am older I will be someone she turns to when her mother is depressed. I think Sandy is depressed a lot. More than once I've found her sitting at her desk in the dark.

I remember when my parents bought me a bike. In Europe of the 1970s, there was less production of things and so many of my toys and clothes were secondhand. In my village there was a weekend before Christmas when people sold bicycles. They leaned them against the wall of the church. From each handlebar hung a tag with the price in francs and the name of the person selling it. So if a child had outgrown a bicycle, on Christmas Eve it would begin a new life. Twenty or so bicycles circulated the village, changing owners every few years.

Sometimes, previous owners, unable to contain themselves, would call out to their old bicycles as they passed at the mercy of new owners.

"Isn't she a beauty – but watch for the front brake!" or "Be careful going over curbs like that – you'll buckle the wheels!"

It's amazing the details from childhood that can surface in a day. That's the best present I ever received. I remember watching parents walk the line of bicycles leaned up against the church, feeling for the money in their pockets, and the children who sat excitedly at home – forbidden to follow, even at a distance.

My bicycle was golden brown with a dynamo light – a small wheel spun by the back wheel that's connected to a small cylinder that uses the motion to power the front and rear lights.

I called Sandy and told her about my first bicycle.

"You get worse every day," she said. "But you're still my favorite client."

We straightened out the details for the afternoon concert in San Francisco. No chair, no concert, I told her. Then I tried to call my brother. His assistant picked up his cell phone and told me that he had gone shooting.

"Shooting?" I said.

"But he isn't shooting," the assistant said, "he's just in the forest with English."

I laughed. "English" was what my brother called his current girl-friend's father because he wore corduroy pants with small pheasants embroidered into the material.

"So English," my brother mocked.

"He's always glad when you call," his assistant said, and then she hung up without saying good-bye.

I never know when to hang up the phone, and try to say one final good-bye even though I can hear the other person has gone.

Then I ran a bath and let the heat settle. Before I slipped into the still water, I thought of the woman who walked into me downstairs. And suddenly I felt an extraordinary sense of hope for everything that was to come, a continuation of what I had begun feeling in Quebec City. It was something I had not experienced since I was a boy. Something I hadn't felt since the days of sitting in fields.

VIII

WHO IS THIS MAN, who like an apparition haunts my every thought? I thought about him last night in my small, steamy apartment. I took out my photographs of Jonathan and spread them on the kitchen table. Then I went to sleep and dreamed that the man from the hotel was sitting on the edge of my bed. Then I was watching the scene from above, and in the place of my body was stone. A person made of rock in the shape of me.

I thought about him this morning sipping coffee on the patio next to the pool no one ever swims in. There are leaves at the bottom. This man's face is like the end of a book, or the beginning of one.

If I thought I would see him in the park, I perhaps would not have gone. But the urge to see this birdman – another Jonathan... or my Jonathan. You never know.

You understand I had to make sure. Grief is sometimes a quiet but obsessive madness. Coincidences are something too great to ignore.

When I arrived at the park, I was of course too early. A few people slumbered under blankets beside their shopping carts. I stopped and looked at a homeless woman. The ridges on her cheeks were so deep her face could have been a map; the story of what happened. I wanted to touch it but didn't. She was somewhere far away in sleep, swimming back to the park through a dream.

All parks are beautiful when quiet and you see things like a book forgotten on a bench read by the wind. Other things too: Someone must have shed their shoes to walk in the grass and then forgotten about them. The shoes had remained neatly arranged for the duration of a night, jewels at their center. I wondered why nobody had taken them.

I chose a bench close to the fountain.

An hour later the birdman arrived. He was much too old to be my brother. And his skin was dark and cracked. His nose was wide and bulged awkwardly from a thin face. The whites of his eyes were impossibly white, but their centers were black. His clothes were beautiful but ruined. How strange that I was actually disappointed it was not my Jonathan. Another way to punish myself, to look behind for someone I feel but cannot see.

And then I noticed the man across the park. At first I wasn't sure if it was him, but then he looked at me and I was sure. He was more handsome than I remembered, and there was something serious in his movements – in the way he sat. A person with important messages but who has lost all memory of where he is going. And then I gasped because that was a description of me. Perhaps all my opinions of other people are opinions of another self.

I don't know why, but I wasn't surprised to see him. His legs were crossed neatly as though it were his favorite way of sitting. He didn't seem surprised to see me either.

Then children arrived and stood around the birdman. They shuffled their sandals in the dust.

He'd dropped his box of stones when I bumped into him. I can't understand how he fell over; I didn't think our impact was so hard. Perhaps he was off-balance. Perhaps he had been waiting all along for someone to knock him down and allow him to drop the weight he'd so faithfully carried.

For an hour or so, we both watched the birdman, laughing intermittently. I noticed he had a baguette next to him and wondered if he'd brought it to feed the birds. The birds flew around the children's heads, seemingly at the control of the birdman. They flew in arcs as though held with strings. The children laughed and jumped. They also looked at one another.

I glanced over at the man often and he looked at me too. It was inevitable that we meet. Like rivers, we had been flowing on a course for one another.

And so, at some point I stood up and walked over to his bench. My shoes crunching the small stones. I counted the steps. My heart bursting from my chest. I sat down and looked at his hands. He looked surprised and I wasn't sure what to do. My hand began to shake and he reached for it. I let him. With his other hand, he took from his pocket a handful of acorns and put them in my palm.

From my pocket I took a large stone and set it squarely in his open hand. If there is such a thing as marriage, it takes place long before the ceremony: in a car on the way to the airport; or as a gray bedroom fills with dawn, one lover watching the other; or as two strangers stand together in the rain with no bus in sight, arms weighed down with shopping bags. You don't know then. But later you realize – *that* was the moment.

And always without words.

Language is like looking at a map of somewhere. Love is living there and surviving on the land.

How could two people know each other so intimately without ever having told the old stories? You get to an age where the stories don't matter anymore, and the stories once told so passionately become a tide that never quite reaches the point of being said. And there is no such thing as fate, but there are no accidents either.

I didn't fall in love with Bruno then. I had always loved him and we were always together.

Love is like life but starts before and continues after – we arrive and depart in the middle.

IX

M Y FATHER ONCE TOLD me that coincidences mean you're on the right path. When the woman who bumped into me at the Beverly Hills Hotel approached my bench and sat down, I didn't know what was going to happen, and I didn't care. I only had the feeling that I always wanted to be with her. I had no urge to tell her anything – there was no need; she knew everything she needed to know without having to learn it.

As we sat side by side in the park, two birds dropped upon our knees. The birdman was looking at us. The children were looking at us too. The woman didn't move. She just stared at her bird, but her bird was staring at me. The small bird on my knee didn't seem to be thinking anything. Then he turned and looked at me. He rubbed his beak together and it made a sawing sound. I think he was asking for a seed.

When one of the youngest children in the group screamed, the birdman whistled and the birds flew from us back to his outstretched arms.

"Did you know this would happen?" I asked.

"It's why I came," she said. I drank down her voice.

"Are you French?"

"The baguette gave it away?"

She smiled.

"Would you like some?" I offered it.

46

She shook her head. "It looks too precious."

I ripped its hat off and she took it. She ripped it in half and gave me some. A scatter of pigeons suddenly swooped down.

"Where are you from?"

"The mountains of North Wales." She bit her lip. "Have you heard of Wales?"

"*Oui.*"

"Good," she said. "I can take you if you have warm clothes and like sausages."

For an hour we sat watching the many people who walked past.

Then she said:

"What are we going to do?"

I liked that she asked this. It meant we felt the same way about one another. I was still holding the stone she had given me. She had put the acorns I gave her into a pocket.

"I'm performing in San Francisco tomorrow night – will you come?"

"Who are you?" she said. "Tell me your name at least – I don't make a habit of following strange men around."

We both looked at the birdman.

"Really?" I said.

When she laughed, her eyes closed slightly.

"Bruno," I said. "This is my name, and I am just a small boy from a French village who can play the cello."

She seemed content with this answer. But then said hastily:

"Maybe it's the cello that plays you."

Then she added:

"I think you must be a very good cellist – a gifted one even."

"Why?" I asked.

"Because you're like a key that unlocks people."

"I doubt that."

"Not just people," she added.

She seemed suddenly confused, the way a woman does when she feels in danger of saying too much.

"What's your name?" I asked.

She smiled. "You could ask me that every day and get a different answer."

She bit her nail and looked away.

"That's not a very good response, is it?"

"It's perfect," I said, and meant it.

"Well, my name is Hannah."

The present grows within the boundaries of the past.

I asked if she had plans for the weekend. I couldn't believe I was inviting her to San Francisco – that I was allowing someone to trespass into my life, to climb over the gate and start across the farmland to the small cottage where I had been living for decades with just my music, my stones, my baguettes; a mitten.

I thought of the woman I had seen in Quebec City behind the icy window, the nun who wrote the word in the glass.

No beauty without decay. I read that somewhere else.

Every moment is the paradox of now or never.

If my brother back in France could have witnessed this event in the park with Hannah, he would have cried for joy. He cries a lot, and women love that about him, but then he can be stubborn and macho, and they love that too. I can imagine telling him about Hannah. He'll want to fly out and meet her. He'll want to send her flowers, chocolates, cheese – give her the latest Renault convertible. I can see them strolling the fields of Noyant, arm in arm, my brother picking up sticks to throw.

"Come to San Francisco," I say. "Fly up for my concert in the afternoon and we'll rent a car and drive back to Los Angeles together – this is where you live?"

"Yes," she said. "I have a shop in Silver Lake that sells prints, posters, and paintings."

"Of birds?"

"I wish it were just birds – but not everyone is like me."

"I think I like who you are."

"Well, it's not what I chose," she said.

I felt mild humiliation – as if *I* were somehow a part of what she hadn't wanted.

Then I said:

"Sometimes I think it's life that chooses us – and here we are thinking that we're steering the ship, when we're just vehicles for an elaborate division of life."

"Then why can it end so easily?" she said.

I wasn't sure what she meant. I risked an answer anyway.

"It ends quickly so that we value it," I said.

She turned her whole body to face me.

"No, Bruno, we value it because it's like that – but why is it like that? Why can life suddenly fly away when those left behind have so much to say? So much that silence is like a mouthful of cotton – but then when it's time to speak, one is capable only of silence. So much that's left undone. What happens to all the things a person would have done?"

I had considered all this.

"I'm not sure I want to know anything anymore," I said.

She bit her lip. I could tell she wanted to know everything.

★ ★ ★

49

We continued talking. Many of the things I said to Hannah in those first, long, heavy days just formed in my mouth without much thought. They formed silently like clouds and then rained down upon her. When we talked, I realized I knew things I hadn't thought I knew.

She agreed to come to San Francisco. And we would drive back to Los Angeles along the cliff – the very edge of a country we had lived in for so long.

Before I walked her to the parking lot, Hannah said she wanted to give the birdman something she'd brought.

We approached him, and the children stepped back to give us room. From her pocketbook Hannah produced a tattered volume. A book. She handed it to the birdman.

It was *The British Book of Birds*.

"Look inside," Hannah told him.

He did.

It read:

> *To our dearest child, Jonathan,*
> *May the birds you love always love you back*

"See – this book belongs to you," Hannah said sweetly.

"No, young lady," the birdman said. "It belongs to you – but you don't belong to it."

He leaned in very close to her.

"You belong to you," he said.

X

WE WERE TWO PEOPLE in a car not speaking. I think it was a
French writer who said that we perceive when love begins
and when it declines by our embarrassment while alone together.

Hannah flew up to San Francisco for the concert. It took place in
the afternoon. There were more children present than usual because
of the time. As I drew each note from the instrument, I could sense
her out there, watching, listening – biting her lip.

Anna's form appeared as always, but it felt far away. When I
turned to look, I could see only the outline of her body. She was
leaving me, and I wasn't surprised. I wondered where she would go.
I would miss her in a new way.

We left San Francisco that afternoon by driving in a straight line
over hills. The reflection off the water made the light seem golden;
many of the houses were red and wore small towers at their corners.
People sat in parks and drank water from plastic bottles. A man in a
black T-shirt walked his dog and chatted on a cell phone. A girl on a
bicycle ticked past. Her basket was full of lemons. Her hair was very
curly. The sidewalk cafés were packed. Faces hidden by newspapers.
Groups waiting for a table.

Our car moved forward slowly – it took hours to get out of San
Francisco, but we were together, the only two passengers on a journey

where the destination was unimportant. Hannah talked about my concert. She said she was the only person not clapping at the end. She said that for her the concert would never end.

When we turned true south onto the Pacific Coast Highway, Hannah said nothing for quite some time. I thought she was enjoying the scenery. A motorcycle passed us. Then we caught up to an RV and drove slowly behind it for several miles.

I began to ask Hannah questions, but she answered only with a word or two. I told her about the Metropolitan Museum of Art in New York – about the long fountain full of coins.

"I wonder how many of those wishes have come true," she said. More silence.

"Do you hear that?" I asked.

"What?" she said. "I don't hear anything."

"That's the sound of keys on my ring," I said. "Sooner or later I'll find the one that unlocks you."

She didn't say anything but placed her hand on top of mine.

I took several very sharp curves, and then the road straightened out.

I looked at the sea. I thought of fish bobbing along the bottom. The motion of weeds.

Then Hannah said, "I want to tell you about Jonathan."

And little by little, his life was placed before me like a map with a small and beautiful country at its center.

I saw him with his book in the garden, sketching.

Then a body stretched out in the snow.

The fist of acorns.

The severed hand of her father in the shed.

The dumb hanging ladder.

Years later:

The many meals that would sit in front of her mother and turn cold.

The guilt of her father as he'd laugh at something on the television, then suddenly stop laughing and leave the room.

One night, Hannah said, he went out in his socks, took the chain saw from the shed, and cut the tree down. Her mother didn't think it was possible. But he managed it somehow with his left hand and the stump of his right arm. It took six hours. When the tree fell, it crushed the neighbor's greenhouse. That afternoon they found a note in their letter box. It was from the neighbor. It read:

> *I never liked that greenhouse and was going to knock it down*
> *this week.*
> *I'm so very sorry for you.*
> *Bill*

Then I see my Anna.
The rainy day.
The accident.
A car speeding away.
The back wheel of her bicycle still spinning.

I stopped the car and we sat at a picnic table and held hands. After a couple of hours a park official with long gray hair came over and told us we had to pay five dollars to picnic, so we left. It wasn't the money, but the atmosphere had changed. I started the car with my foot on the brake.

When we were back on the road, Hannah said she was hungry. It had clouded over.

Fog wrapped the cliff in its thick coat.

Then it started to rain.

The swoosh of the windshield wipers was reassuring.

We turned inland at the first road.

The fog thinned out.

There were birds flying in the opposite direction — away from land. I couldn't think where they were going. Perhaps to a tall wet rock, far out at sea.

We stopped at a supermarket in Carmel for food. We held hands as the glass doors separated before us. I went for bread (the staple of my childhood). A few yards away Hannah held up an apple. I nodded. She selected another. I held up the baguette. She nodded. I decided right then that I would never tell her about Anna.

The man at the deli counter wanted us to try the different things spread before him in shiny bowls. He gave us pieces of cheese and meat on toothpicks. He asked how long we were together.

"Forever," Hannah said.

At the checkout, Hannah noticed a box of kites. They were on sale. She bought two.

The cashier scrutinized the kites for a bar code.

"You should get one," Hannah said to her.

"I'm not into kites," the cashier replied.

"Then what are you into?" Hannah asked.

The cashier looked up. "Music," she said.

Hannah and I spent the night at a Buddhist retreat center in the mountains perched above Santa Cruz. I had heard about it from Sandy, my agent. She thought it might be a nice place for me. It was supposed to be very quiet, with large prayer wheels painted in bright colors. I stopped in Santa Cruz for gas. A man opposite the gas station was throwing bottles at passing cars and screaming. I hoped he wouldn't come over. I thought about it as we drove away. Hannah asked if I was okay.

"I'm fine," I said.

The key to our room was waiting for us. It was not late when we arrived, but the surrounding forest threw dark nets over all the buildings.

Hannah stayed in the shower for a very long time. The drops sounded like a heavy rain, which made me fall asleep.

When I awoke, Hannah was sitting at the edge of the bed drying her hair in a towel. It was hot in the room because the window was open. I sat up and wrapped her in the sheet. She turned to me, so I kissed her shoulders, then her neck, then her cheek, finally her lips.

My mouth lingered on hers; I tasted her. I felt for her tongue with mine. I felt the blood surging through my body. We pressed against one another.

Impossibly close.

She gripped my arms. Her nails tore into me. Soon we both were burning. Sweat pooled in the ridge of my back as I moved like a tide determined to crash against those ancient rocks.

Then – a moment before – inside, I kept very still. Our bodies moved of their own accord. Hannah's body was swallowing, digesting all that was mine to give. For those final moments, we existed seamlessly – all memory negated by a desire that both belonged to us and controlled us.

After, we kept very still, like the only two roots of the forest.

The sweat on our bodies dried.

We lay on our backs with our eyes open. I would like to have seen her eyes then. Mine were clear.

Finally she turned to me with great tenderness. She asked if I was hungry. I said I was, and so in the darkness we dressed and slipped out to the car.

The first restaurant we found was mostly empty, but the hostess said they were expecting a large party any minute. She suggested another place. So we left our car where it was and walked.

The sidewalk was very narrow and crowded with plants. It was completely dark and there were no streetlights. Hannah held my hand and led me through. We passed a dozen Craftsman houses from the 1930s. People were inside. We could see them. A couple sat in separate armchairs watching television. They laughed at the same time but did not look at one another. In another house, a small boy sat before a kitchen table. He was peeling an orange. In another, a woman undressed and then turned off the light. I pictured Edward Hopper across the street in a fedora gazing up from the shadows.

When we reached the other restaurant, there was a wedding party at the bar. A band played mediocre but recognizable music, and the guests sang the chorus. The groom was surrounded by his friends. They had loosened their neckties. Each drink had an umbrella in it.

Hannah ordered a cold glass of wine. Our waitress was in high school. She wore makeup. There were several pens tucked into her apron, and her jeans were rolled at the bottom.

We ate the same salad but from different plates. When an entrée of pasta arrived, we ate from the same plate. Then we just sat and held hands under the table.

"Do you think there's an afterlife?" Hannah said as I signed the check.

"I think we're in it," I said, and we left without anyone noticing.

We walked back to our car through the dark suburb. Most of the lights were out by then. I looked for the small boy, but he must have gone to bed.

The next day we continued driving south. We had wrapped some of the food from breakfast in paper towels. The rental car smelled like a hotel. We were wearing the same clothes as yesterday, but our hair smelled of Hannah's shampoo. Hannah wore shoes she said she hadn't liked for a long time. They were maroon-and-beige heels. I told her I liked them. I also told her how I had noticed her shoes a few moments after we collided. She looked down at her feet and moved them around.

Hannah was in a better mood. She hadn't mentioned Jonathan, but whenever she thought about him, I could tell – she became quiet and still, like a statue. In Greek theater, the final breath of each tragic hero transforms the body to marble.

She told me about her life in Los Angeles, and then she wanted to know about New York. She was especially interested in Central Park. She'd heard there were parrots there. I told her the parrots were in Brooklyn.

I told her about my recent concert. The Central Park Conservancy had given me a "key" to the park. One of the benefits of possessing this key was a complimentary carriage ride. I recalled how I stood in line behind a man and his daughter. The little girl was about three years old. She had Cinderella clips in her hair. She was very excited that soon she would be riding in a carriage with her father. Her father bent down to her level to tell her things. Then he whispered something to her and she put her hands on his cheeks. Then I heard the girl remind her father that she was wearing underpants – that she wasn't young anymore.

The carriage attendant, who was watching a small television, hung up his cell phone, then stood up from his chair and informed everyone that the horse was very tired and would have to take a long break soon – so there would be only three more rides. The father and the girl were fourth in line. The girl tugged on her father's jacket and asked what the man had said. The father put his hand on her head but didn't say anything. The father looked around and sighed. His daughter asked him to tell her more about the horse.

"Has Cinderella ever ridden on a horse? Or does she just ride in the carriage?"

And then suddenly two women in sweat suits who were third in line walked away. The father grabbed his daughter's hand and they moved up one space. The daughter asked if the horse was married and if it liked apples.

One of the women who had walked away told her friend that she was tired and wanted to go back to the hotel. Her friend laughed and they held each other's arms.

Hannah thought it was a nice story. Then we passed what I thought were sea lions. They were sea elephants, and Hannah made me stop so she could take photographs.

Every forty miles we would stop, either to walk around or smoke cigarettes. We even kissed a few times.

I had a concert in Phoenix in two days. I wondered if the city was named after the mythic bird that rose from the ashes. Hannah said it had to be.

When it got dark, I thought we could take blankets from the trunk and build a fire on the beach. I pulled into the parking lot of a convenience store and suggested that we walk across to the beach so that no one would know we were there. Hannah thought it was a clever idea, and I went inside to give the cashier twenty dollars. He seemed pleased with the arrangement.

The beach was much cooler than we'd imagined, but it felt good because, after parking, we kissed in the car for twenty minutes with the air-conditioning off. Hannah moved her neck when I kissed it, guiding my mouth into all the spaces she wanted to feel me.

I wasn't able to build a fire because the air was too damp. It got quite cold too. So we just lay under the blankets and held one another. I could feel her hair pressed against my neck. Her body fit perfectly with mine. She pulled her legs up. We lay very still, making outlines in the sand. In the background, waves pounded a scatter of rocks not far out.

I woke at dawn. It was still cold, but the air felt soft and fresh in my throat. Hannah was nowhere to be seen. I sat up and looked around. The beach was deserted. I wondered if she had gone back to the car to get warm. I decided to look for her, and then saw her erect body a few hundred yards away on the bluff. She was flying a kite.

When I reached her, the wind had blown back her hair. The wind was blowing so hard her eyes watered.

At first I thought I'd just sit and watch.

At her feet lay another kite, already assembled.

"That's your kite, Monsieur Bonnet," she said without looking at me.

I unfurled the line quickly, and Hannah told me to start on the beach and then run up the bluff in order to launch it. I tumble-ran down the bluff.

I held out the kite and hit the bluff running. My kite took easily.

It was exhilarating. I had not flown a kite in thirty years. The force pulling on me was more powerful than I could have imagined. But I was the one who held on. I was not captive but captor.

We flew our kites for most of the morning, occasionally glancing at one another.

Then Hannah let her kite go.

It quickly rose, twisting brilliantly against the climbing sun.

Allez, I thought.

And my fingers released the strings of my own kite.

The force we had held fast against our bodies abruptly ceased.

The kites tore through the heavens. They were soon nothing more than two specks of color. And then both disappeared from our sight. Even though we knew they were out there, there was no way to ever bring them back.

Six months later I played for one night only in Paris. Instead of staying at the hotel, I rented a car and drove home to Noyant. I arrived about six o'clock in the morning. There were birds everywhere and the roads were empty. I sat with the baker in his small cake shop. I told him the whole story of how I collided with Hannah at a hotel in California. I wanted to explain why I hadn't been in touch for several months and also to confess how happiness still felt remote – as though I were watching it happen to someone else. It was a cool morning. Children trudged to school, not completely awake. The sky outside was rubbed gray. Clouds passed like open hands. The sky would soon be full of falling drops. The baker sat with me and dried his hands on his apron. His wife joined him from the back. I could smell fresh mushrooms. The radio was on.

The baker gathered my hands in his and told me how glad he was I hadn't been in touch – and that I must promise to stop sending stones. I suddenly felt very selfish and vain. I shrank from him. I pulled my hands away.

But then he said: "Bruno – we lost a daughter – we don't want to lose a son."

"That is what you would have been to us," his wife said.

"That is what you have become to us," the baker said and took his wife's hand.

"Send postcards from now on," he said. "No more stones, eh?"

Before I went to see my parents, the baker's wife suggested that when Hannah comes to France, perhaps I might introduce them to her. Perhaps they might make her a cake and serve it to her in the shop with a bowl of steaming coffee – that we might just be four people sitting down to a small meal in the evening.

XI

A LMOST A YEAR AFTER I met Hannah, the birdman died. His obituary was one of the longest ever printed in the *Los Angeles Times*. His life was unlike any of the rumors. There was a candlelight vigil in the park attended by thousands of people. Instead of birds, there were helicopters.

But I was far away in the middle of France, back in Noyant at the shop eating cakes with an old man and his wife. Children peered in at us through misty windows. They rubbed their mittens on the glass and talked loudly. They were excited because it was the first afternoon that bicycles would be sold against the church wall.

It was snowing hard. The baker was very round and his apron fit snugly about his middle. He went into the kitchen and then quickly reappeared with a tray of pastry scraps. The children saw him coming and stood by the door. Then we saw arms reaching for the tray and heard a chorus of "*Merci, Monsieur.*" When he came back in, there were snowflakes on his shoulders.

"They expect it now." He shrugged. "I've been feeding them since they were the size of baguettes."

The baker's wife laughed.

"They call him the children's baker," she said.

The baker went behind the counter and poured himself a small glass of brandy.

He looked at Hannah for a long time.

Then he walked over and kissed the top of her head.

The baker's wife stared out through the window – at the world that lay beyond it and the mysterious place beyond that.

When it started to get dark, Hannah and I left the shop. Bicycles were being wheeled home in the snow. Old women left bricks of cake on one another's doorsteps. The butcher was dressed up like Santa Claus.

Children peered out into the night from upstairs windows. And for several kilometers Hannah and I waded through snowy fields, past old gates and fallen trees, laughing and calling out as our bodies disappeared from view.

The shadows remained.

Gifts from the fallen, not lessening our happiness but guiding it, deepening it, and filling us with the passion we would need to sustain our love in the coming days.

A gentle reminder that what we have is already lost.

Tiger, Tiger

WHEN I FIRST SAW Jennifer, I thought she was dead. She was lying facedown on the couch. The curtains were not drawn. Her naked body soaked up the falling moonlight and her back glowed.

Jennifer was Brian's mother. When he frantically turned her over, she moaned. Then her arm flew back, viciously but at nothing. Brian told me to call 911, but Jennifer screamed at him not to. Brian switched on a lamp. He kept his distance and said, "Mom, Mom." Then he asked where Dad was. She moaned again. Neither of us knew what to do.

Brian fetched a bathrobe and laid it across her back. She sat up, then pulled it around herself weakly. The robe was too big and gaped in several places. One of her breasts was visible. I know Brian could see it. It was like an old ashen bird. I made coffee without asking. There was cake in the refrigerator. It said "Tate's Bakery" on the box. I cut the string. With the same knife I cut three equal pieces. We ate and drank in silence. Jennifer swallowed each forkful quietly; my yoga instructor would have called her mindful. She shook her head from side to side. Then Brian and I watched as Jennifer buried her face in her hands as though she were watching a slide show of her life projected across her palms.

On the carpet next to Jennifer's clothes were several brochures for new cars. There was also a wedding band and a glass of something that had been knocked over. The contents of the glass had dried into the carpet and looked like a map of Italy.

We sat in silence; a forced intimacy, like three strangers sheltering under a doorway in pouring rain.

I remembered a childhood dream that went like this: The night before something exciting, such as going on vacation or a birthday party, I would dream of accidentally sleeping through the whole thing. In the dream I would believe I had missed everything – that the event was over; it had taken place without me.

Brian and I had been together for eighteen months when his parents decided they wanted to meet me. I was indifferent. I was thirty-four and settled in a practice with several other doctors. I didn't care about living up to their expectations. I got tired of all that after I entered medical school and started clumsily slicing my way through cadavers. I come into contact with life and death on a daily basis, but not through ailing retirees battling heart disease and lamenting their crumbling bones but through children, who are never to blame for anything that happens to them. I wanted to be a pediatrician from the start.

Countless children have waited outside my office with my secretary, Lauren, a southern redhead with flawless skin. I explain to parents the problem, the procedure, and the risk – in that order. The lone parent never cries, but couples do, even if the prognosis is positive. As they console one another, I often think of the little head swiveling around the waiting room, reading a book about boats, or looking at a plant, or staring at Lauren, unaware of the long and often arduous journey that some force in the universe has chosen for them.

It doesn't do children any good to see their parents upset, and so I sometimes let the child take Lauren out for ice cream.

Several years ago, Brian's parents bought a summerhouse in Hampton Bays. I personally don't like Long Island. It's overpopulated and people find safety through excess. The goal of life seems to revolve around ownership and luxury – just as it did for the English four hundred years ago. It's everything my parents were against in the 1960s. Either America has changed significantly in the last decade or overeducation has left me cynical. So many revere a vehicle like the Hummer and other glorified farm equipment while spending their lives in ignorance of how their own organs work. We plead with God to spare us from disease, while consciously filling our bodies with toxins.

I don't much like the Hamptons either. In the years I have been going out there, it's become a police state – and the police are paid handsomely for what amounts to guarding the estates of a few homegrown aristocrats.

Perhaps you wouldn't think my views extreme if I explained that my parents are from Oregon. I grew up wandering misty fields and sketching cows. My mother knitted clothes and my father built my one and only dollhouse in his workshop. My town is staunchly Democratic and well known as a haven for lesbians – imagine coffee shops and furniture stores run by tattooed women who bake upside-down cake for one another.

They both visited once. My mother feels abandoned by me, her only child. But then she was always strange – somehow detached at key moments. When I was in high school, I put it down to menopause, but now I think it's something that's been long-standing since childhood. My father would never say anything critical to her – he would just rub his chin or rub her hand. My father spent his life rubbing things, like Aladdin.

Of course, my parents didn't understand the Hamptons when they visited, the summer before I met Brian. Especially my father, who became flustered when we were stopped at a beach checkpoint and told we had to pay the town a fee in order to park at the ocean. My father told the teenage attendant that the Town of Southampton was no better than the mafia. But then people behind us started honking. Over dinner at a lobster shack close to where the fishing boats dock, my father said we would have been better off under the British. My mother said that if the British had retained the colonies, the only difference would be that everyone would have bad teeth. The waitress overheard and laughed. She gave my father a beer on the house and told him to cheer up.

On the way back to the city my father looked strangely sad. I think he was going through something painful that he couldn't talk to my mother about. I wish I'd asked. He died last year.

After that long visit, the novelty of upper-middle-class New York life wore off and I appreciated the city for what it was, an indifferent, throbbing pulse with an infinite number of chances to reinvent yourself.

It was sweet of Alan and Jennifer, Brian's parents, to say I was the first of their son's girlfriends to be asked out to their summerhouse in Hampton Bays. But they quickly ruined it by saying they only wanted to meet the ones he was serious about – as though the less serious ones were meaningless. Alan and Jennifer referred often to their summerhouse when they left messages on Brian's machine, which led me to suspect they'd grown up poor. Actually they hadn't. Jennifer was the daughter of a real estate husband-and-wife team from Garden City. Alan was the son of a Jewish tailor from the Lower East Side who knew how to save money and collect secrets while he measured inseams. Brian said his grandfather's knowledge of clients' personal lives helped get Alan into a private school where Jews were not particularly welcomed. When Alan's father died, his few remaining clients on Park Avenue breathed a sigh of relief.

Brian has a younger sister, Martha. I met her once at a concert in Irving Plaza. Perhaps because she isn't pretty, she had decided to be ironic and make her body the canvas for a series of strange tattoos, one of which is an artichoke.

Brian's mother, Jennifer, was once physically beautiful. In the photographs which dotted the living room of their Hampton Bays summer home, she looked perpetually overjoyed – her mouth painted and open like a rose moving its petals.

The night Brian and I arrived in Hampton Bays we kissed in the car before going in. It's something we do. We are always kissing. Brian stopped abruptly when he suddenly noticed the house was in darkness.

"That's strange," Brian said. "There are no lights on." I sensed something was terribly wrong.

Jennifer's eyes were so puffy I felt awkward looking at her. I quietly asked Brian if he wanted me to examine them. He said they always puffed up when she was upset, but he'd never seen them like this.

Alan, Jennifer's husband, had walked out that afternoon. He returned from his tennis match and started packing a suitcase. A woman in a convertible picked him up. She waited at the end of the driveway with the engine turning over. He said he wasn't coming back. He said Ken, their lawyer, would sort out the arrangements. Jennifer chased after the car and threw her shoes at it. Then she walked home. They had been married for thirty-four years. They were married the year I was born.

Brian's father was fifty-seven years old when he left Jennifer. Alan's father, the Jewish tailor, was fifty-seven when he died of a coronary thrombosis. It was a psychoanalytical cliché, but I kept quiet and said nothing to Brian – even intelligent people go nuts around their parents.

I asked Brian again if he wanted me to examine his mother and he said no – that they had a close family friend, a Dr. Felixson, that his mother trusted and who was at his summerhouse in Southampton. I couldn't hide my disappointment. "Let's just get through tonight," he said. "You should meet this guy anyway – he wrote a book back in the seventies on pediatrics or something."

"Really," I said.

As I waited outside in the darkness for the doctor, Brian came out with a copy of Dr. Felixson's book, *The Silence After Childhood*. It was an odd title. I said I would read it. Then Brian told me he'd known about his father's affair. Apparently, Alan had confessed over dinner several months ago. Jennifer had been visiting her family in Florida. Brian thought I would be angry with him for not telling me. But I wasn't.

"What man could resist the opportunity to live twice?" Brian said his father had pleaded. He perceived his son's silence as reluctant approval, but in truth, Brian was disappointed. He finally had to admit his father's cowardice. The marriage to his mother had never been harmonious, but he'd stayed in it. Brian said that if his father wasn't such a coward, he would have hurt Jennifer thirty years ago, instead of hurting her *and* humiliating her after three wasted decades.

"But then Martha wouldn't have been born," I said. Brian was silent for a moment. I thought he was mad at me, but then he said that regardless of his sister, his father had stolen his mother's life.

"But Jennifer let him steal it," I added.

Brian nodded. I think he appreciated my frankness, but I shouldn't have said it then.

The doctor arrived in an old station wagon. A kayak was tied on the roof. He got out and waved. Then he opened the trunk and reached for his bag.

He was a tall, thin man who looked as though he could have been a nineteenth-century Midwestern farmer. His unkempt white hair and strange side-to-side walk gave him the appearance of being drunk. He was born and raised in Stockholm. He'd moved to New York in the 1970s. He wasn't married.

"Brian, my boy, sorry to see you under these circumstances, but we'll sort this out together," Dr. Felixson said quietly. He walked up to me and put his hand on my shoulder. Then he said, "What madness has driven you to retrieve a copy of that book you're holding?"

Before disappearing inside, he turned around and said, "Brian tells me you both went to Stockholm, yes?"

"Yes," I said. "It was beautiful, but it didn't snow."

"Times change, I suppose," he said.

One night, maybe our third date. Brian and I lying in bed. The room sketched by moonlight. The street outside in a deep sleep. Snowing and we didn't even know.

Brian said he and his sister had trembled with fear at his parents' arguments. "They screeched like birds," he said.

Brian said he would never get married. I hesitated. Years of adolescent sleepovers had engraved images of the perfect day. In truth, I hadn't thought about marriage for years.

Brian sensed my fear. He reached for my hand under the blanket. I gave it to him. He was no coward – maybe that was worth a thousand perfect wedding days.

Brian believed that marriage often gives one party the license to behave intolerably without the fear of being abandoned because the state must oversee any separation. He said that with many couples he knew, either the husband or the wife had waited until they were married to really hang out their dirty washing. He believed that marriage was an outdated concept, like circumcision in gentiles.

"But not in Jews?" I said.

"It's more complicated than that," he said, but in a kind way, as if to say I had a point too.

The next day we went to McCarren Park and built a snowman. A young Hispanic boy helped us with the finishing touches. The boy held my hand for a while. Then he said Brian and I should get married. Brian looked at me and laughed, then asked him if he'd settle for a cup of hot chocolate at the Greenpoint Café. The boy said he would. I had wanted Brian all to myself but loved how he was so inclusive. I suggested the boy call his mother and tell her where he was. I gave him my cell phone. Later that night, I noticed there was no new number on my call list. The boy had just held the phone to his ear and talked.

That was one of the nicest days I've ever had with anyone. Later we went to a fondue restaurant and then stayed up all night drinking and listening to Getz and Gilberto. I remember dancing. Brian watched.

A week later when the snow melted, we decided to go to Sweden for a long weekend. It cost more than we thought because you forget to include things like car service to the airport and then the money you happily waste in duty-free. We were both in graduate school, so it took us a year to pay the trip off. I remember we held hands on the flight. You can't put a price on the rituals of love, because you never know what will happen next. I suppose fear is part of the excitement and we can't have one without the other.

Dr. Felixson examined Jennifer in private. We heard her crying. Then we heard Dr. Felixson's voice. It sounded like he was talking to Brian's father on the phone. Before he left, he said that we should call him if we had any questions and that, with any luck, we'd all live through this. I was too tired to get one of my cards from the car, and so I said I would send him an e-mail. Of course, I never did.

Soon after Dr. Felixson left the house, his sedative began to pull Jennifer out to sleep like a tug silently towing a ship out to sea. She mumbled that if Alan showed up or called back, to tell him she was dead. I nodded.

Then she lay down on the couch, and the sedative pulled her under so violently that she began to snore a few moments after closing her eyes.

I was surprised I understood why Jennifer couldn't go into the bedroom and lie down. I covered her up with another blanket. Body temperature drops at night.

Brian came over and put his arm around me. He turned off the lamp and kissed me. Then suddenly I felt strange.

I pulled away.

He sat there for a moment.

Then he kissed my forehead and went outside. I heard him drive away. He wasn't mad, because we understand one another – like two maps pressed together in a book.

It was either the semidarkness of the room or the smell of late summer pushing at the screens – or even the fabric of the couch on my bare legs. All these things in that moment seemed like props arranged by my memory to suddenly transport me to a moment which had long passed.

The exactitude of feeling two years old flickered inside me. I kept very still. I felt like primitive man having inadvertently made fire and wishing, more than anything, to keep it burning just a few moments longer.

It's as if my two-year-old self had been living inside me like the second smallest piece in a set of Russian dolls. It now rose to the surface of my consciousness, and I felt with absolute clarity how it felt to be two years old on one particular day in the 1970s.

My parents had taken me to the park across the street from our house because it was my birthday. There was a party; other children came. The other children weren't my friends; they were just other children. My parents were my best friends, which was why it was so hurtful when they reproached me.

My feet suddenly rose off the floor, pulled up into my shrinking body. I could feel the scabs on my knees like small islands. I pushed my tongue into the spaces where I had no teeth. Dry birthday cake. Juice with crumbs in it. Mild nausea. I pictured the candles, but the feeling was stronger than anything I could visually recall. It was as though I were there but without my eyes or my sense of touch. I remember running through tall grass. I can feel it brushing against my legs like long, thin arms. The other children's high-pitched cries. Presents lowered from large, foreign hands.

The end of the party. I didn't want to go home. I was frustrated that everyone was separating. I wanted the day to rewind itself. Then I remember chasing a boy. My parents calling me. His parents watching us, grinning, encouraging us. He falls, turns over laughing. I'm laughing too. I come upon him. I take his arm and bite into it. Blood appears from nowhere and spreads on his skin. He looks at his arm. He screams and parents scramble. He is scooped up like a bug. I want to say that I am a tiger and tigers bite. I want to remind them I can be a tiger. His face turns red as he is pulled up into the nest of his mother's arms. I sense the tone of crying change from shock to something else. He lifts his arm. His mother kisses it. She rocks him. His father stands erect, on guard, looking around, helpless, pathetic.

I am rooted to the spot by fear. Then suddenly my diaper is yanked down. I recoil but am held in place as my mother's hand clips my bottom. The crack of her hand against my flesh. My little body making forward jerks with each smack. My disgruntled face, my curling lip like a glistening crimson wave.

My eyes are open, but I am almost unconscious with shock and humiliation.

I can feel wind on the exposed flesh of my bottom. My mother walks away. I am burning with emotions too great for my small body. I am undressed in public. There are spots of blood on the grass. People gather around and peer down at me sadly.

I overhear a woman ask if I am a boy or a girl.

I am too scared to pull my diaper up.

My mother has walked away.

My father carries me across the field toward our house. As soon as he pulled my diaper up, I defecated into it. He rubbed my head. My mother stayed at the park with her arms crossed. She had taken off her fancy shoes.

My father said: "You cannot bite – biting is wrong." But there was no passion in his voice. Then we reached the house.

He put me in their bedroom. He closed the blinds, but ribs of light fell through and settled upon the floor as though I were in the stomach of some celestial being. My father stripped me down to my diaper. It was full of feces. I was too afraid to cry. I wondered if I would be killed without knowing what death was. The fabric of the chair stuck to my tiny, fleshy legs. It was my birthday. I was two. Sweat had dried across my body like a veil.

Later, a plate of birthday cake was left outside the door.

"What if she's sleeping?" my father whispered. "She won't be," my mother snapped.

I didn't want the cake. I wanted my mother to forget herself and remember me. Eventually they brought the cake into the room. I ate it and cried and sat between them and repeated over and over mechanically that biting was wrong. But deep down I still loved the boy and would have bitten him again and again, forever. And he knew I loved him. And it was pure and spontaneous.

And so I became a pediatrician. I wanted to be a hand that's lowered to souls dangling off the cliff in darkness.

About two years after Brian and I found Jennifer on the couch in Hampton Bays, I finished Dr. Felixson's *The Silence After Childhood*. I read it in one sitting. It was 3 AM on Monday morning. I picked up the phone and called Brian.

"I have just read Dr. Felixson's book."

There was silence and then Brian said:

"See what I told you?"

"Do you want to come over?" I said.

"Don't you have work in a few hours?"

"Jesus, Brian."

"Okay, okay – I'll bring my clothes for tomorrow."

I was trembling. Dr. Felixson's insights had set off small earthquakes in my body. They were spreading to my memory like soft, warm hands eager to unearth buried things.

When Brian arrived, I sat him down, kissed him, thanked him for coming over, and handed him a glass of whiskey. I opened the book randomly and read a passage.

"Listen to this," I said.

> *To children, parents can seem like blocks of wood – or at best, sad creatures that seem always on the verge of not loving them. Later, we adults learn that our parents are consumed with neuroses they've manifested as seemingly real problems to draw the spotlight away from a more painful reality....*

I closed the book and opened it to another page. Brian leaned forward.

> *There's no going back to childhood unless you're somehow tethered to it and can feel the weight of it against your body like a kite pulling at you from its invisible world; then you will understand everything through feeling, and the world will be at once tender and brutal and you'll have no way of knowing which on any given day. And you'll love everyone deeply but learn not to trust anyone....*

"Wow," Brian said. "Dr. Felixson wrote that?"

"I thought you'd read this?"

He looked up. "It's been in our house for so long. I always meant to," he said.

I turned several pages and let my eyes fall into a paragraph:

> *Childhood is terrifying because adults make children feel as though they are incomplete, as if they know nothing, when a child's instinct tells her she knows everything. But then perhaps the most damaging crimes in a society are committed by most of its citizens and perpetuated unknowingly....*

Jennifer is now living in Florida. She is writing her memoirs. She is seeing someone. He's *Italian* Italian, she says, and he's apparently related to Tony Bennett and has the family voice. Alan lives year-round in Hampton Bays. His relationship fell apart a few months after he left Jennifer. He tells Brian he's "playing the field." He's started wearing cologne. I often wonder if Jennifer and Alan were as close as Brian and I are.

I know Brian has wondered if I've thought about whether he would leave me in the same way. But Brian is not like his father. Brian is a beautiful child, but he's not childish. Children are the closest we have to wisdom, and they become adults the moment that final drop of everything mysterious is strained from them. I think it happens quietly to every one of us – like crossing a state line when you're asleep.

Brian and I may part one day, but it's not really parting – you can't undo what's done. The worst wouldn't be so bad – just the future unknown. Though I would carry a version of him inside me. But isn't every future unwritten? The idea of fate is really only a matter of genetics now. But what's interesting is how so many significant events in my life have come from seemingly random things. Freedom is the most exciting of life's terrors:

I'd decided on whim to walk into a bookstore. There was Brian.

I wonder if I had never met Brian, what I would have thought about all the times I've thought about him. Would my head have been empty of thoughts? Would it have been similar to sleep? Or would other thoughts have been there? Where are those thoughts now, and what would they have been about?

I've thought about these sorts of things since I began editing the unpublished writings of Dr. Felixson. A few days after finishing *The Silence After Childhood*, I tried to call him. A woman renting his old surgery space said he'd died.

I had more than forty pages of questions.

Unbeknownst to Brian, Jennifer had come into possession of some of Dr. Felixson's journals. I discovered this when I called her in Florida. I wanted to find out more about his life. There was singing in the background. Jennifer giggled and asked if I could hear it. I explained the effect Dr. Felixson's book was having on my life. She asked if Brian was there. He was. She asked to speak to him. She then explained to her son how she and the doctor had experienced a brief affair several years before Alan left her. The marriage had never been the same after. Brian was so shocked he hung up. Jennifer immediately called back and said she would have spared him, but she wanted to explain why she had only some of Dr. Felixson's journals. In his will, Dr. Felixson had left Jennifer the journals covering the period of their togetherness.

In a gesture of kindness and courage, Jennifer sent them all to me from Florida via UPS. She said that what little had been written about her was nothing compared with the notes he'd made on his patients and his general everyday thoughts.

"He writes about everyday things like clouds," she said.

She was adamant that they be in the hands of another doctor. I felt truly honored.

When they arrived, I wrote back to Jennifer, asking if she had loved Dr. Felixson and why the affair had ended after only a few weeks. She wrote back almost immediately. She said Blix Felixson was the only man she had ever met who could love unconditionally without having to be loved back. She said it was unnerving because he was never disappointed by anything.

Or he was disappointed by everything. But I didn't suggest this. I had learned my lesson.

December 23rd, 1977

For infants, discomfort in any measure is hopefully met with physical and emotional contact with a parent or caregiver. Could it be then, in the silence and confusion after we falsely perceive childhood has ended, that our experience of discomfort is met with an instinct to seek solace through the same end? An emotional reassurance from another human being bound up with physical embrace? So then, in adulthood, could it be possible that we spend the majority of our lives looking for comfort from strangers?.

Adult fears are idealized to the point where they have become too big to fit through the hole they originally came through.

People's expectations of coupling may be too grand, and thus disappointment, loneliness, and often pain are the inevitable adjuncts of something we thought would be the ultimate answer (an emotional cure-all) to our ongoing fears. Many people who feel an emotional emptiness when alone for long periods look to marriage the way someone financially poor views winning a jackpot.

All wars are the external realization of our internal battles. Humans must learn not to blame each other for being afraid, disappointed, or in pain. We perhaps might learn to view those we have special feelings toward as being our companions rather than our saviors, companions on the journey back to childhood. But there is nothing to find. We must only unravel. And in the meantime -- lower our expectations of each other (and ourselves!) in order to "love" more deeply and more humanly.

It is almost dark now. I can hear rain on the window, but I cannot see it. A car drives past. I wonder who is in it.

I wonder what life would be like if I now were married. Perhaps the smell of cake would fill the house. I think of Mother and Father. I remember launching my model aeroplanes off the hill at Skansen. Visiting my father's office in Stockholm in the bright noon sun. I remember my father's face. My mother's face. If only I could speak to them now. It would be a different story altogether. I would forgive them.

Dr. Felixson died alone and was not discovered for several days. The *Southampton Press* reported that a doctor of many disciplines who was of some note, had passed away from causes unknown at his Shinnecock Hills cottage, and was discovered by a landscaping crew who called local police when they saw an elderly man through an open window lying on the floor, apparently unconscious.

July 7th, 1977

It's true the people we meet shape us. But the
people we don't meet shape us also, often more
because we have imagined them so vividly.

There are people we yearn for but never seem
to meet. Every adult yearns for some stranger,
but it is really childhood we miss. We are
yearning for that which has been stolen from us
by what we have become.

Brian is something in the universe and I am something in the
universe, and our real names are not sounds or marks on a page but
bodies. We meet and then we recede.

We can never truly be one sea, though we are both water.

June 21st, 1978

We are not at home in the world because we
imagine it is as we have become, full of nothing
but yearning and forgetting and hoping for
something so raw we can't describe it. We think
of the world as the place of beginnings and ends,
and we forget the in-between, and even how to
inhabit our own bodies. And then in adulthood,
we sit and wonder why we feel so lost.

It is Sunday afternoon and Brian and I are driving out to Hampton
Bays to see Alan. We've been together almost four years. I have been
editing the journals of Dr. Felixson. They will be published the year

after next by a man I think Dr. Felixson would have admired. I have my own practice now, but eventually I'd like to teach. I have had an article published on Dr. Felixson's methods in pediatric psychology in the *New England Journal of Medicine*. His first book, *The Silence After Childhood*, is being reissued next year by a publisher based in Berlin. Since my article was published, I have received thirty-four letters from doctors across the world.

Brian sometimes tells me anecdotes about when Dr. Felixson examined him as a child. I love these and write them down.

Brian and I have also decided to live together, but we're never getting married.

November 17th, 1980

Today, a woman touched my sleeve in the supermarket as I was trying to pick out good strawberries. She asked if I was the children's doctor from Germany. I corrected her and explained that Sweden is much, much colder in some ways but not in others. She asked me if I had a moment, and I said of course, though I thought to myself, it is an interesting thing to say because one's life is nothing more than a string of moments. Each life is like a string of pearls.

This woman wanted to know why her four-year-old son, when she met him at school, had given his macaroni drawing to another boy's mother and not to her. She said she didn't speak to her son all the way home and even cried. Then she said he cried and locked himself in his bedroom. She was worried that her son didn't love her -- otherwise why would he give his drawing to some other child's mother?

I laughed a little and ate one of the strawberries I was holding. Is that all? I said. She nodded. Well, I explained, you are worrying about the wrong person. I explained that the reason her son had given the drawing to another mother was because he loved her, his own mother, with such blind, unprecedented devotion, that naturally he felt sorry for every other woman in the world, whom he did not love so vehemently.

Then of all things, the woman started to cry. She touched my sleeve again and said, Thank you, Doctor. She said she was going to buy him a toy to make up for it -- but I said to her, Perhaps, Madame, instead of buying a toy, you should simply go home, find your son and remind him of the event, and tell him that you love him with equal devotion, and that you will never again question his judgment when it comes to how he expresses his love for his mother.

When I thought more about the encounter on the way home, I found myself getting depressed. So when I got home, I put my robe on and gave my strawberries to the birds. What a beautiful child that woman has, I thought. What a genius boy, and what a hard life he has ahead of him in this world where beauty is categorized and natural love is negated by flattery.

Toys

Toys are the props by which children share their fears, their hopes, their disappointments, and their victories with the outside world.

The toys parents choose for their children will set the boundaries of their play (fantasy). A heavily representational toy may limit the child's play to those aspects the child associates with the context. For example, a toy based on a television character will determine the way the child plays with the toy and thus limit the fantasy.

Toys that are not representative of some third party (the child and the toy are the first and second party) allow children to develop and explore their own fantasies with less distortion. However, if your child seems unhappy at the idea of playing with pieces of wood or wool shapes, then introduce a few props from nature (leaves from a park or hard vegetables such as pumpkins or potatoes). These will allow your child to set his fantasy in the natural world.

Present your child with a cooking pot, and he will pretend to cook. Give your child a gun, and he will pretend to shoot. It's an easy choice for the thinking parent (unless the child is born into ancient Spartan culture!).

For a child, asking someone to play is an act of trust. And trust helps build love. For the child is eager (through toys) to share her private world with you, and to express through play (with toys as props) what she cannot express through language — either because she doesn't inherently trust language (and why should she? — see Chapter 2, "Everything Is a Metaphor") or because she doesn't yet possess the skills to express herself clearly through the speaking circuit.

Play to a child's emotional development is like food to physical development. Play is a tool for loving. Even the most healthy adult relationships I have studied rely heavily on forms of play.

Conversation with Four-year-old Dorothy

Dr. Felixson: *Why are toys so important?*
    Dorothy: *They are important for kids.*
Dr. Felixson: *Why is that?*
    Dorothy: *Because kids like to play.*
Dr. Felixson: *Hmm. I wonder why they like to play?*
    Dorothy: *I don't know.*
Dr. Felixson: *I wonder why kids want to play with
            grown-ups?*
    Dorothy: *Maybe because they like grown-ups so much?*

Astonishing, isn't it? Dorothy knows she is being questioned, and like most children, she wants to please. She is eager to talk, but perhaps a more effective way to understand children is to do it on their own terms. If I were to play with Dorothy (toys of her choosing) and then study that play, I might understand Dorothy's world more clearly. To question Dorothy as though she were a simple adult as I did above is a great failing on my part. And since writing this, I have changed the way I explore children's perception. To experience an apple, don't eat the apple — become the seed.

Pages 221–223, chapter 8, *The Importance of Toys* by Dr. Blix Felixson, Greenpoint Paperbacks, New York, 1972.

Driving through Riverhead, Brian asks me to unwrap a sandwich we picked up at Greenpoint Café for our trip. He watches me unfold the paper and reaches out to take a half. I slap his hand.

"No," I say. "I want us to share the same half."

Trivial secrets and unspoken pacts keep us going.

We're driving through East Quogue. The road has thinned to a gray strip that slips through a forest. I think of the forest as my childhood.

Brian touches the back of my neck. My concentration breaks like a wave against the shore.

"Remember the champagne glasses?" he says.

I think of the two delicate champagne flutes we left in the Adirondack Mountains a few weeks ago. Brian and I were hiking. There are forests so thick it's like perpetual night – or the subconscious, Brian remarked. The air is thin and crisp. At night, we fell asleep with wood smoke in our hair.

After hiking nine miles up into the white breath of a mountain, we were truly invisible to one world but in the palm of another. Brian heard a river. We followed the sound and then spotted a rock in the middle, large and flat enough for our bodies to sit on comfortably. It had been raining, but it's amazing how quickly the sun dries the earth after it has been washed.

Brian and I lay our bodies on the rock. I closed my eyes. The sound of water was deafening. Brian unwrapped a bottle of champagne and two wineglasses from several T-shirts. I was surprised he would bring such things up into the woods. Then he explained. It was the anniversary of our first date. I told him it wasn't but that I'd help him drink the champagne to lighten his load.

We lay on our backs. The sun in and out of clouds. The silence of the sky intimidating. A landscape of thought.

Then Brian laughed and told me I was right. It wasn't our anniversary. I felt then he was somehow disappointed and so told him that every moment with him is a small anniversary. I don't know what it meant. It just came to me.

We kissed, and that led to us making love. It was sweet and slow. My foot trailed in the water like a rudder.

After, Brian pulled a towel from his rucksack and put it under our heads.

When I awoke, Brian was gazing down off the side of the rock into a deep pool. His bare back was a field of bronze muscle. I had forgotten his male strength. It was late afternoon. The sky had bruised. There was a wind and the trees shook. Wind is the strangest thing. The word describes a phenomenon.

I reached for Brian. I lay my palm on his back. He pointed to the pool beneath the rock. The scent of pine was overwhelming.

While I was sleeping, the champagne glasses had rolled off the bags and fallen into the rock pool below. By some miracle they had fallen upright. The river gushed through the rocks and then into the pool where the glasses stood. Each glass held the weight of an entire river without knowing where it came from and how much was left.

Suddenly, in the car just a few miles from Alan's house in Hampton Bays, I reach for Brian's arm. I dip my head and bite into it. I feel my teeth clamp his warm flesh. He shouts, then screams when I won't let go. The car runs off the road into the woods. There is thumping from underneath. Brian yanks his arm back, still screaming. The front wheels come to rest in a tangle of leaves and branches. I can taste Brian's salty blood in my mouth.

Brian looks at me and then incredulously at his arm. It bears the perfect indentation of my mouth, but the line is blurred by shallow bleeding.

Brian's eyes are full and swirling.

We breathe heavily, as though inhaling one another. Then it starts to rain. Nothing but the sound of drops falling. The rear lights of passing cars break into blood-red bloom through the rain-spattered windshield.

My eyes like leaves, long and wet.

Alan has baked lasagna. He arranges the chairs so that we sit close, so that in the end, as light dims and the curtain falls on another small day, we won't lose sight of each other's eyes, even if everything in-between has been lost or fell away one cloudy afternoon to the sound of passing traffic.

The Missing Statues

ONE BRIGHT WEDNESDAY MORNING in Rome, a young American diplomat collapsed onto a bench at the edge of St. Peter's Square. There, he began to sob.

An old room in his heart had opened because of something he'd seen.

Soon he was weeping so loudly that a young Polish priest parking a yellow Vespa felt inclined to do something. The priest silently placed himself on the bench next to the man.

A dog with gray whiskers limped past and then lay on its side in the shade. Men leaned on their brooms and talked in twos and threes. The priest reached his arm around the man and squeezed his shoulder dutifully. The young diplomat turned his body to the priest and wept into his cloth. The fabric carried a faint odor of wood smoke. An old woman in black nodded past, fingering her rosary and muttering something too quiet to hear.

By the time Max stopped crying, the priest had pictured the place where he was supposed to be. He imagined the empty seat at the table. The untouched glass of water. The heavy sagging curtains and the smell of polish. The meeting would be well under way. He considered the idea that he was always where he was supposed to be, even when he wasn't.

"You're okay now?" the priest asked. His Polish accent clipped at the English words like carefully held scissors.

"I'm so embarrassed," Max said.

Then Max pointed to the row of statues standing along the edge of St. Peter's Square.

The priest looked up.

"Well, they're beautiful – oh, but look, there is a statue missing," the priest exclaimed. "How extraordinary."

The priest turned to Max.

"Why would a missing statue upset you, Signor Americano – you didn't steal it, did you?"

Max shook his head. "Something from my childhood."

"I've always believed that the future is hung with keys that unlock our true feelings about some past event," the priest said.

"Isn't everything something from childhood?" the priest continued. "A scribble that was never hung, an unkind word before bed, a forgotten birthday – "

"Yes, but it doesn't have to be so negative, Father," Max interrupted. "There are moments of salvation too, aren't there?"

"If there aren't," the priest said, "then God has wasted my life."

The two men sat without talking as if they were old friends. The priest hummed a few notes from a Chopin nocturne and counted clouds.

Then a bird landed in the space where the divine being had once stood – where its eyes had once fallen upon the people who milled about the square, eating sandwiches, taking photographs, feeding babies, birds, and the occasional vagrant who wandered in quietly from the river.

The priest looked at Max and pointed up at the statues again. "They should all be missing," he joked, but then wasn't sure if the man beside him understood what he meant.

Max blew his nose and brushed the hair from his face.

"Please forgive me," Max said. "You're very kind, but really I'm fine now – *grazie mille*."

The Polish man sitting next to him had entered the priesthood after volunteering as a children's counselor in the poorest area of Warsaw. He couldn't believe what he saw. He quickly climbed the ranks and was skilled at negotiating the bureaucracy that plagues all men of action. Through his close work with young, troubled children, the priest understood the reluctance of men to share their troubles.

"You can tell me anything," the priest said. "I don't just pray – I give advice too."

Max smiled.

"I simply want to know why a missing statue has reduced a young American businessman to tears," the priest said.

The priest's hair was as yellow as hay. It naturally slanted to one side. He was handsome, and Max thought it a shame he would never marry.

"Just a long-ago story I once heard," Max said.

"That sounds nice, and I like stories very much," the priest said. "They help me understand myself better."

The priest lit a cigarette and crossed his legs. Max stared at him.

"It's the only vice we're allowed," the priest said, exhaling. "Would you like one?"

Max raised a hand to say no.

"Did the story happen here in the Eternal City?" asked the priest.

"Las Vegas."

"Las Vegas?"

"Have you ever been to Las Vegas?" Max asked.

"No, I haven't, but I have seen it on a postcard."

"Imagine a woman sitting on a wall outside a casino."

"A woman?"

"Yes."

"Okay," the priest said, and closed his eyes. "I'm picturing it."

"A woman sitting on a wall outside a casino. It is very hot. The air smells of beer and perfume. The woman's name is Molly. She married quite young."

"A teenage bride?" the priest asked.

"Exactly – very young," Max said. "Molly's parents came from Fayette County but settled in Knox County – that's in Texas. Her father drove school buses, and her mother didn't work. Molly went to Knox County High. The school mascot was a bear. Some of the football players had tattoos of bear claws on their arms. There was a lake near the town. It was very popular with teenagers who liked to sit in trucks overlooking the water.

"From the postcard you've seen of Las Vegas, Father, imagine the ghostly band of neon which hangs above the city, changing the color of all the faces within its reach. The bright, flashing lights that promise children everything but deliver nothing.

"You can see Las Vegas from a distance: Look for the clump of risen metal on the horizon. If you approach at night, lights will beckon you from the black desert like a claw hand in a neon glove.

"Molly's first husband was run over and killed not long after the wedding. Then she met a high school football coach who was married.

"Molly and the coach met intimately once or twice a week for several years. When Molly found herself pregnant, the high school football coach pretended they'd never met.

"Molly's son didn't even cry when he was born in 1985. Molly thought he had an old soul. And for the first four years she raised him all by herself."

The priest smiled and lit another cigarette to show his commitment.

Max went on:

"So Molly was sitting on the wall outside the casino, and she was crying but so quietly that nobody could see – not even her four-year-old son who paced in small circles, following his own shadow. Every so often Molly reached out for him but did not touch any part of his body.

"The trip to Las Vegas was Jed's idea. Molly and Jed had been seeing each other seriously for three months. Jed managed a furniture warehouse. Jed insisted that Molly's boy call him 'Dad.' When the boy saw Jed's truck pull up in the yard, he would run into his mother's bedroom. Under her bed there was a pile of small plastic animals. But it wasn't the best place to wait until Jed left. To the little boy, it sounded like they were taking it in turns to die."

"We're just waiting for your father," Molly said. "He'll be here any minute."

She had been saying it for hours. There was nothing else to say. The first time she said it, her son replied:

"He's not my father."

"Well, he wants to be if you'll let him," his mother snapped.

The sounds of the casino spilled onto the sidewalk. The hollow metal rush of coins played through speakers. Drunk gamblers looked at their hands as ghost coins rushed between their fingers. Their lives would change if only they could hit the jackpot. Those who had loved them in the past would love them again. Every wrong could be righted. A man could straighten out his affairs if he had money – if he had beaten the odds. He could afford to be generous.

A waiter rushed past Molly and her son with a platter of delicious fruit. Then a thin couple in sunglasses holding hands. Then an old woman staggered into the road and was yelled at by a man on a motorcycle who swerved around her. Three men in suits carefully dragged a man with a ripped shirt onto the sidewalk. His feet trailed under him like two limp oars.

"Don't ever come back or you'll be arrested," one of the suited men said.

"Okay," the man said quietly, then picked up the coins that had fallen from his pocket. The little boy helped him. The man said, "Thanks, boy."

There was quiet for a while, and then the boy started to cry. He sat on the ground. He was wearing shorts and his legs were red from the sun. His socks had caterpillars on them. One had rolled into his shoe because they had walked so much.

By 3 AM, the boy and his mother were invisible to the gangs of drunk insurance salesmen, dentists from Orange County, gentlemen gamblers from small towns in Kentucky, and women going to or coming from their work in the casinos and topless bars.

The little boy's throat was so dry he licked the tears from his cheeks. At some point during the early morning, he took a sticker from his pocket and set it on the ground with the glossy cards of naked women that litter the sidewalks of Las Vegas.

A limousine stopped at a light. It was a wedding. The women inside were smoking and singing along to country music. The bride was young. She looked at Molly and screamed.

The boy removed his sandals and set them next to his mother's shoes, which had been shed long ago.

Molly's pocketbook with all her money was in Jed's truck.

"I'll keep control of the money," Jed had said.

The drive from Texas took four days. The boy kept throwing up because Jed smoked with the windows up and the air-conditioning on.

At night they all slept in the back on a mattress. The nights were cool. The sky glowed purple at dawn – then gold poured across the sky as the day was forged.

Molly's son was too afraid to ask his mother for the restroom. The thought of entering the casino made him feel nauseated. An hour or so later his underpants had mostly dried and the stinging upon the skin of his legs had given way to a slight tingling.

Then somebody approached him.

A man stood and watched the boy for some time; then he went away.

Then the man returned with something in his hand.

The boy felt a cold dish pushed against his bare thigh.

Then he noticed a figure standing over him.

"*Mangia*," the man said softly, and pointed to the white, creamy square of dessert in the dish.

The man was wearing black pants with a soft red sash for a belt. His shirt was heavy and long-sleeved, with black and white horizontal stripes.

"Tiramisu," the man said earnestly. "From the Venetian Hotel and Casino, a few streets from here – I just got it for you."

The boy squinted and turned to his mother. Molly eyed the stranger suspiciously through her swollen eyes.

"Don't worry, Mama," the stranger said to Molly. He pointed to himself with both hands. "*Amico* – friend."

Molly had pretty eyes. She had made many "friends" in her life that she would sooner forget.

"No thanks," she replied in a voice loud enough for passersby to overhear. Her voice was cracked with thirst and fatigue.

"Mommy – can I eat this?" her son said, and dipped his finger in the cream. "I think it's good."

Molly held the dish in her hand, inspected the contents, and then put the dish back on the wall. "Eat it and thank the man."

The man sat on the wall a few yards from them and lit a thin cigar. It smelled very sweet. He began to whistle. When the boy had finished the dessert, he slid over to the stranger and set the bowl down gently.

"I really like it," he said.

"We call it tiramisu. It means 'pick me up' in Italian."

Then the man leaned down to the boy's ear. His breath smelled of cigars.

"There's liquor in it too." He winked.

The boy peered down at the empty bowl. In its center were the colors of Las Vegas, held fast in a tiny pool of melted cream.

"Why do you speak like that?" the boy asked.

"My accent?" the man said.

The boy nodded despite never having heard the word "accent" before.

"I'm a gondolier – and the accent is from Italy."

"A gon…"

"Gondolier, *sì*."

"A goboleer?"

"*Sì* – do you know what that is?"

"Goddamn it!" his mother snapped without looking up. "Stop bothering the man."

"But Mom, he's nice."

"They're all nice at the beginning," she said.

The man winked at the boy and then stood up. He took three small oranges from his pocket.

"They were all nice at the beginning, Mama – but could they all juggle at the beginning?" the man said.

The little boy watched the balls rise and fall. He sensed the weight of each orange in his own small hands.

"The magic is in how you catch each ball at the last minute, before it's lost," the stranger explained.

"I want to try," the boy said.

The gondolier stopped juggling and reached down.

Max held the oranges in his hands and looked at them.

"They're too big for me."

"Ah!" the gondolier exclaimed, and from his pocket appeared three kumquats.

Molly laughed.

"Kumquats are the way to every woman's heart, my little friend."

The boy looked at his mother again. He wanted her to be happy. They were on vacation.

"We're waiting for my fiancé," Molly said. "He's just finishing up."

The little boy set the kumquats next to his shoes and said quietly to the gondolier:

"He's lost all our money, mister."

"He'll win it back," Molly said.

The gondolier sat with them and lit another cigar.

"Smoking is bad for you," the boy said.

The gondolier shrugged. "Did my grandmother tell you to say that?"

"No," the boy said. "I saw it on TV."

When Molly woke with a start, it was almost dawn. Her son was sleeping with his head against the gondolier's striped shirt. The gondolier smoked and stared at nothing. Molly wondered for a moment if it was the same cigar.

"You must think we're pathetic," she said.

The gondolier thought for a moment and then said:

"Would you permit me to perform one favor for you and your son?"

"I don't know," Molly said. "My fiancé may not be in a good mood when he comes out."

"Okay," the gondolier conceded. "It doesn't matter — I just thought you might like it."

Two small eyes between them bolted open.

"Might like what?" inquired a little voice.

"Might like to be honored guests on my gondola – through the canals of Venice."

The boy climbed up on his mother's lap.

"We have to do this," he said soberly.

Molly turned to the gondolier.

"I don't know why you're doing this for us – but if you were going to kill us, you probably would have done it by now."

Her son glared angrily at her.

"He's not going to kill us."

As they entered the Venetian Hotel and Casino, the gondolier raised his arms.

"Welcome to the most beautiful country in the world," he said.

The boy looked at the statues perched high up on the roof.

Their white marble skin glistened in the early morning sun, their hands forever raised, the fingers extended slightly with the poise of faith.

"I think they are holy saints, little one," the gondolier said. "They look out for me – and you too."

One of the statues was missing. There was a space on the roof where it had once stood.

"Where's that one?" the boy said.

"I don't know," the gondolier said thoughtfully. "But just think – *caro mio*, he could be anywhere."

"I think I believe in saints," the boy said, and considered how the missing saint might somehow be his real father.

"You truly believe in the saints, boy?"

"Yes. I do."

"Then you are an Italian, kid, through and through – a hot-blooded Italian. Can you do this?" The gondolier pressed his fingers together and shook them at the sky. The boy copied his movement. "Now say, 'Madonna.'"

The boy put his fingers together and shook them and said, "Madonna."

"Good, but louder, *caro*, louder!" the gondolier exclaimed.

"Madonna!" the boy screamed.

People looked at them.

"What does that mean?" Molly asked. "It's not a bad word, is it?"

"No, Mama, it means, simply: I am in love with this beautiful world."

The boy looked up at the saints, his fingers pushed together like a small church.

"Madonna!" he said in that delicate thin voice of all children.

The three of them strolled through the casino without talking.

A few lugubrious souls were perched at the slots. The machines roared with life.

Two black men in suits with arms crossed smiled at the gondolier.

"How you doing, Richard?" one of them said.

"Ciao," the gondolier replied in a low voice.

"Is your name Richard?" Molly asked.

"In another life."

"In Italy?" asked the boy.

"Another life, little one," the gondolier said.

"Actually, can you call me 'big one'?" the little boy asked.

The corridor was a long marble walkway with tall milky pillars. Then they reached a room with a thousand gold leaves painted on the wall. The boy looked up. Naked people in robes swam through color. There were scores of angels too – even baby ones with plump faces and rosy cheeks.

"Madonna!" the boy said.

As they neared the end of the room, they could hear music, a few notes from an instrument strapped to a man's belly.

"*Caro mio*," the accordionist said when he saw the gondolier.

"*Ciao fratello*," the gondolier said. "Let me introduce you to my dear two friends from the old country."

Carlo smiled and moved his instrument from side to side. His fingers pressed buttons and the box emitted its unique croak. The rush of air into its belly was like breathing.

"It's nice," Molly said.

Carlo followed them at a distance of several yards, playing the same three notes over and over again. The little boy kept turning around to smile. He'd never felt so important. When they stopped walking, they were outside on a bridge.

The rising sun was visible through a crack between two towering casino buildings.

"See that, big one?" the gondolier said to the boy. "Every morning can be the beginning of your life – you have thousands of lives, but each is only a day long."

When the sun had passed above them and given itself to the world, a woman in a black dress brought out a tray. She was very tall, and her heels clicked along the stone bricks.

"Good morning," she said, and passed the tray of food to the gondolier.

Molly hesitated. "We didn't order this."

"No, no – it's from your friend," the woman said, then pointed to one of the many intricately arched balconies built into the façade of the casino. An unrecognizable figure from a great height began to wave. When the same three notes bellowed out into the square, the boy waved back.

On the tray were half a dozen Krispy Kreme glazed doughnuts and a small wine bottle with a rose in it.

"Venetian Donetti Rings," the gondolier marveled.

The boy stared at them. "They look nice," he said.

The gondolier sniffed one and handed it to his little friend. "They're fresh – only a few minutes old," he said.

"Like the day," the boy said. The gondolier nodded with enthusiasm.

There were also three very small cups, two filled with black coffee and a third with milk.

"Are these cups for children?" asked the boy.

"Yes," said the gondolier, "because no matter how big sons and daughters get, they will always be children in the eyes of their parents."

Molly laughed.

After breakfast, the gondolier took Molly and her son by the hand and led them to the edge of an enormous swimming pool that ran under bridges and skirted the edge of the main square.

There were strange boats floating, all tied together and bobbing in agreement.

"We should probably get back," Molly said.

"You're right, Mama," the gondolier said, "but one ride won't take long."

"*Jed* will have to wait for *us* now, Mom," the boy said.

"Shit," Molly said angrily.

"Why not?" the gondolier said.

"Come on, Max," Molly said.

Molly started walking away. Her son trailed reluctantly. He felt like crying again and his legs were stinging.

Molly abruptly turned back to the gondolier. "You don't know us."

The gondolier had not moved, as though he hoped she might turn back.

"Yes I do, Lola," the gondolier said without any trace of an Italian accent.

Molly stopped walking.

"Why did you call me that?"

The gondolier looked at his worn-out shoes.

"That was my daughter's name," he said with a shrug.

"Your daughter?"

"Yes – my beautiful daughter. That was her name."

Molly glared at him with anger and pity.

"Well, that's not my name."

"But it could be," the gondolier insisted. "It could have been."

"You're not even Italian, are you?"

"Mom," the boy said.

Molly stood looking but not looking at the gondolier. The boy tugged on her arm. Then the reality of what her life truly was flooded her.

She felt sick and tired.

Several birds blew across a clean sky – unaware of anything but their own tiny lives.

The boy let go of his mother's arm and squatted down.

His head fell limply into his hands. He took his sandals off. In the hot morning sun his legs had begun to sting again.

People walked around them.

Then Molly reached down and fixed his caterpillar sock.

"Put your shoes on if you want to go on the gondola," she said.

At the entrance to the boats there were other men dressed in the same striped shirts. They smoked and drank coffee in little cups. They raised their hands in greeting and nodded without smiling.

Within a few minutes, the gondolier, Molly, and her son were in the boat. The boy said the boat looked like a mustache. He held on to his mother's hand. He wanted her to know she had made the right decision. Hands have their own language.

The gondolier stood like a mechanical toy and pushed against the bottom of the blue water with a long pole. Everyone was watching. Carlo walked alongside them and played his three notes.

"*Buongiorno!*" the gondolier announced to passersby. A Japanese woman started clapping.

Molly marveled at the people on their balconies. The restaurants too were filling up. The sinister cast of characters who had passed them during the night had gone, and the city swelled with a softer, gentler group who rose with the sun and woke only at night to fetch glasses of water.

When they reached a wider stretch of the canal, the gondolier stepped down and opened the trunk upon which he had been standing. He undid the lock and lifted from it a large dark wooden box. He set it down on the bench between the trunk and the emerald seat upon which Molly and her son sat very close together.

"What is it?" asked the boy.

"You'll see, big one."

From the trunk, the gondolier took a thin but heavy black circle and placed it on top of the box. Then he turned a handle quickly and pulled over a thick metal arm with a needle at its end.

At first, Molly and the boy heard nothing but crackling. By the time the strong, sweet voice of Enrico Caruso echoed through the Venetian piazza, the gondolier was back on his trunk mouthing along to the words.

People flocked to the side of the bridge and applauded. Children stared in silent wonder.

The gondolier moved his mouth in perfect timing to the song. People thought he was really singing. But the voice was that of someone long dead.

Molly leaned back and closed her eyes. She had never heard a man sing with such emotion. She put her arm around her son and realized that the love she'd always dreamed of was sitting in the seat beside her wearing sandals and socks with caterpillars on them.

The song ended, but the needle kept going. The box crackled as they returned to where they had begun. The gondolier quickly tied his boat to the line of other boats. His hands were old and beaten like two worn-out dogs.

The gondolier sat down on the bench next to the music box.

"Again," the boy said.

The gondolier wound up the machine as he had done before. At the sound of crackling, the other gondoliers stopped what they were doing and turned to face him. He stood proudly on his trunk, cleared his throat, and began to sing.

The piercing beauty of a lone voice soared determinedly from the canal into the piazza, drawing people from beds and flat-screen televisions to the edges of their balconies.

For a few moments, the voice was even audible in the casino; cards were set down; heads tilted upward.

"What's the song about?" the boy whispered to his mother.

"I don't know," Molly said.

"I do," her son said.

The piazza crackled with applause.

When it came time to say good-bye, the little boy didn't want to let go of the gondolier. They could feel the beating of each other's hearts.

In the Square of St. Peter, the lines outside the tomb had grown very long. Young Italian men in jeans sold water and apples. Tour guides stood still and held paddles. Children fell asleep in carriages. Teenagers tore past on smoking scooters. Restaurant managers heckled passing tourists, who stopped for a moment and then kept walking.

Occasionally, someone looked up and noticed that a statue was missing.

The priest took a handkerchief from his pocket and dabbed his eyes.

"Madonna," he said quietly.

And before parting, the two men thought of a lone gondolier paddling the canals of a swimming pool in the Nevada desert – reeling in the forsaken with the song he had once sung to his daughter on a farm in Wisconsin.

The Coming and
Going of Strangers

WALTER'S JOURNEY
THROUGH THE RAIN

W ALTER WHEELED HIS HOT, ticking motorbike up and down the muddy lane, breathing with the rhythm of a small, determined engine. Fists of breath hovered and then opened over each taken-step. He would soon be within sight of his beloved's house. In the far distance, Sunday parked over the village like an old mute who hid his face in the hanging thick of clouds. The afternoon had seen heavy rain and the fields were soft.

Tired and wet, lovesick Walter thought of the Sunday town streets, hymns and hot dinners, the starch and hiss of ironing; shoes polished and set down before the fire so that each shoe held a flame in its black belly; dogs barking at back doors. Early stars.

He stopped and held his motorbike still. He listened for the sounds of the faraway town. At first he could hear only his own hard breathing. Then a bus growling up the hill; the creaking of trees; and then in the distance – seagulls screaming from the cliffs.

There were scabs of mud on the black fuel tank of Walter's motorbike. Leaves and sticks had caught in the spokes and marked the stages of his journey in their own language. Light had not yet drained from the world, yet the moon was already out and cast a skeletal spell upon the bare branches of trees.

The road sloped downward for several hundred yards. In the distance, cows perched on steep pasture and barked solemnly out to sea. Walter imagined their black eyes full of wordless questions. What were they capable of understanding? The cold country of water that lay beyond the cliffs? Did they feel the stillness of a Sunday?

Walter removed the basket of eggs from the milk crate strapped to the back of his seat. Then he lay the machine down on its side. A handlebar end disappeared into a puddle.

It was the highest point in the county. Looking west, Walter knew from the few books in his uncle's caravan that America lay beyond. He exhaled and imagined how night – like a rolling wave – would carry his breath across the sea to New York. He imagined a complete stranger breathing the air that filled his own body.

Walter removed a glove and rubbed his face. The dirt beneath his fingernails was black with oil. Walter pictured his mother back at home, sitting by the fire with Walter's baby brother in her arms – wondering what her son was doing out in the drizzle. His father would be out of his wheelchair and up on the roof of the caravan, whistling and hammering new panels above the sink where the leak was.

"This country is nothing but rain and songs," his father once said in his Romany accent.

A young Walter had asked if that was good.

"Ay, it's grand, Walter – because every song is a shadow to the memory it follows around, and rain touches a city all at once with its thousand small hands."

Walter loved The Smiths. In the caravan last week, as his mother sat him down for a haircut, Walter showed her a picture of Morrissey.

"Who in the world is that skinny fella?" she'd said.

"Can you cut my hair like that – can you do it, Ma?"

"Why would you want it all on one side?"

Walter shrugged. "It's what I want," he said.

"All right – if that's what you want."

"Thanks, Ma."

"He's a pop singer, is he?"

Walter sighed. "He's a little bit more than that, Ma." Then Walter thought, How could any sane woman turn me down if I looked like one of The Smiths – which in his Romany Irish accent sounded like "The Smits."

One night, long ago, Walter's father sang his own song to seduce a woman he'd just met. She listened with her hands in the sink. She fell in love holding a dinner plate. It was not how she'd pictured it.

Then several years later, he metered softly a different song to baby Walter as rain beat down upon the roof of the wind-rocked caravan.

THE GYPSIES ON THE HILL

W ALTER'S FAMILY HAD LIVED outside the village of Wicklow on the east coast of Ireland for Walter's whole life. Unlike the rest of his Romany family, Walter's had stayed in one place, and contrary to Rom custom, Walter was encouraged to attend the local school and mingle with the people of the village.

Everyone in the village knew who Walter was, and they knew why his family lived on the hill a mile or so outside town.

In 1943, Walter's two sets of grandparents escaped Hitler's murderous dream and came to Ireland. In the early 1960s, at a Rom festival in the south of Ireland, Walter's mother and father met in a sloping field. It was quite dark, but they could see each other's faces. The evening was chilly. She was barefoot. Walter's father asked one of her brothers where they were from. Then later on, he offered her some cake to eat. She took it from his hands and put it straight into her mouth without chewing. They both laughed. Later on she hears a knock on the caravan door. Her brother is reading. She is barefoot at the sink with her sleeves rolled up. Her brother knows who it is. He opens the door and goes out to smoke. The man is holding a guitar. Finally it's happening, and she holds her breath.

Two nights later, they ran away. Then, as was the custom, their families met and laughed and argued in equal amounts. Within a week, bride price was set and Walter's parents (then in their teens) returned home.

Walter's young mother and father journeyed to Wicklow immediately after the ceremony, even though everyone joked about how they'd already taken their honeymoon.

"It's such a fine, wild, and desolate country," Walter's father said to his bride in the car on the drive. He was still quite nervous because she was a quiet girl. He spread a blanket across her knees. She shivered – though it wasn't cold.

Her camp was near Belfast, while his camp was always moving, mostly around Dublin.

Both families made a living from selling used cars, car parts, and scrap metal, sharpening knives, and laying tarmac. The women told fortunes – a craft developed and perfected over centuries and based on the idea that all humans want the same thing: love and acceptance.

After passing through the village, the young couple parked on a hill and began to pitch a marital tent in a field overlooking the sea. The tent was orange, and its sides were hung over cool hollow poles that fit inside one another.

Once it was up, they lay inside under a thick blanket and told stories without trying. Outside the tent, clouds blew across the field and out to sea.

A rabbit hopped up to the tent, then ran back into the hedgerow.

After they were together, her body trembled. She pressed herself against him. He listened to the sounds of night and of the sea wrapping its cold arms around the thick rocks; the white froth of saltwater; a chorus of popping barnacles.

★   ★   ★

In the morning, Walter's father cooked a breakfast with food they'd brought – food that wasn't polluted by non-Romany shadows.

As half a dozen sausages thopped and spat, turning brown on one side, Walter's mother heard a tiny splash. She was washing her face beside the hedge. The water was mouse gray. She turned and looked back at the tent; its tangerine orange sides billowed in the wind against the hard green of the hedgerow. She continued washing. It was such a windy day.

Then Walter's father heard something – a feeble scream in the distance. He looked up from his sausages and saw two specks on the cliff several hundred yards away. He dropped his fork in the grass and ran. Two children stood at the edge beside an empty stroller. The older child was heaving violently and looking down at the water.

Then the young child started to scream.

At least a hundred feet down in the sea, something bobbed.

The water was dark green.

Walter's father kicked off his boots and then jumped.

When he hit the water, several bones in his right foot split.

His wife saw him disappear. She opened her mouth to scream, but no sound emerged.

Everyone thought they were dead because there was simply no trace of either of them. The police launched a boat. Not even a sock or a small shoe. Not a trace.

Walter's mother was taken to the children's house by the police and given tea, which normally she wouldn't have been able to drink because of Romany custom.

The mother of the children sat very close to Walter's mother. Eventually they held hands.

The children sat at their feet.

They were still and their faces were empty.

More family trickled in through the thick farm door. People screamed and then talked quietly. An unmarried uncle sobbed into his hand. Then two women of the family approached the Gypsy in the chair. They touched her shoulders, knees, and then held on tight because it was too late – too late for anything except blind, gentle, wordless touching.

Then the sound of breaking glass upstairs.

Men's voices.

The sound of something heavy hitting the floor.

Time unraveling without notice.

Then suddenly – a miracle.

Almost midnight and the police are pounding on the door.

Lights go on.

People in chairs come to life.

The fire is a dark blood orange.

More screaming, but a different kind as a man and small girl are helped from the back of a police car.

The man is dark-skinned. A Romany. The child clings to him.

They are wrapped in thick blankets. They both have messy hair. The child is too afraid to take her eyes off the Gypsy who jumped off a cliff to save her. His face has never been so still. He's not fully convinced they're alive. Not until he sees his wife will he believe it's not a dream – a fantasy prelude to the life beyond death.

The mother loses a shoe as she runs for the frightened bundle of child. The child reaches out, then once buried in the familiar bosom explodes with tears and shrieks.

Walter's mother slaps her husband across the face, then kisses it all over.

More headlights turn into the driveway.

The rattle of teacups from the kitchen.

Joy fills the house.

Men grab the hair on one another's heads.

Screaming and jumping.

The sound of breaking glass.

Singing.

The Gypsy and the girl were found together walking up the cliff road toward town. They had been swept several miles from the spot where the child had fallen in. The outgoing tide had pulled them away from the rocks.

His arms were raw, burning.

His black eyes blazed with the fury of staying alive.

Soaked clothes weighing them down.

Finally man and child dumped upon a shallow sandbar, then carried up the beach on the spreading foam of a breaker.

Walter's father had lost all sense of time. Perhaps years had passed. Perhaps they were the only two people alive on earth. Perhaps they would live together from now on. Such thoughts entered his mind as he watched the child cough and cough and cough.

Walter's father removed all her clothes and tucked her frigid body under his clothes so that only her head stuck out. As her body sucked the heat from his, she quieted and fell asleep.

She was not dead, he knew that. He could feel her breathing. He could feel her life attached to his.

Finally a car in the distance. Walter's father signaled weakly.

"Fuck off, Gypo," the driver shouted through his window.

More walking.

Then an old farmer with a wagonful of sheep.

He had been in the war and recognized immediately that desolate look of the figure in his headlights.

The farmer saw that the man walking up the dark road was soaked through. Then he noticed a second head. He pulled to the side of the road and hurried them into his wagon, freeing several sheep to make room. Then he drove back to his house without stopping to close the gate.

His wife found blankets. Sugar lumps dropped liberally into china cups.

The farmer watched the fire and wondered if they might stay.

It wasn't until Walter had stopped shivering that he told the farmer how the little girl wasn't his – that he'd simply found her beneath the surface in the swirling black, in the cold, their arms like vines destined to forever entangle.

The farmer looked very serious.

His wife telephoned the police from the hall phone.

The next day, as Walter's father and mother were packing up their orange tent, several old Land Rovers turned in to the field through an open gate. Then several more cars. Even a police car. Walter's mother helped her husband stand. His leg was bandaged. The pain was like fifty wasps trapped inside his foot.

A large group of people walked toward them, headed by the children from the cliff and their parents. They stopped walking several yards off and the little girl's father approached Walter's father. He stood opposite and extended his hand. When Walter's father went to shake it, the young man simply leaned forward and hugged him.

Several people in the group started clapping. The policeman removed his hat. Women made the sign of the cross upon their anoraks.

The man handed Walter's father an envelope.

"For what you done, Gypsy," the man growled. His cheeks glistened.

Walter's father looked at the envelope.

"It's a letter from me to you, and a deed. We're giving you this here land we stand on."

Walter's father had been warned about getting mixed up in the affairs of non-Romanies.

"Take it," the man insisted. "Mary, Mother of Jesus, take it, man."

Walter looked up at the sky and exhaled.

What would his family say if he started deal-making with non-Romanies.

Then the father broke down. Two men stepped forward and propped him up.

Then the sister of the saved child ran over to Walter's father and took his dark hand.

"We don't care that you're Gypsies," she said.

Walter's mother stood by her husband.

"You can bring your whole family here if you like," the girl continued. "We can all be together — it'll be like heaven."

And so the orange tent was never taken down. Instead, the camp was built around it, and they became known as the "Gypsies on the Hill."

And when the father of the saved girl decided to move his family to the safety of Dublin a year later, he made a sign in his metal shop and erected it on the cliff one windy afternoon.

It read:

On this spot in 1963,
An Irish Gypsy jumped off the cliff
To save my daughter.

About the time the sign went up, Walter was conceived.

THE CANADIAN ORPHAN

WALTER LOOKED AT HIS motorcycle on its side in the puddle. He imagined firing up the engine and riding at full pelt toward her house. In the distance waves crashed against the point: the foam, the black rocks – two equally determined forces. Walter felt such forces alive within himself. He thought of his father's daring rescue before he was born.

Walter was headed for the very same farmhouse his mother had been taken to after her husband tossed his body off the cliff into the sea.

After the saved child's family moved to Dublin, a middle-aged man moved in and began to farm the area around his cottage. Now, strangely, it was the home of Walter's beloved. The orphan from Canada.

Walter lifted his bike off its side and continued toward her house. Only a mile or so to go.

He wondered if he might even find out her name – that would be a brilliant start, he thought. He imagined riding his bike off a cliff and screaming her name in midair.

Walter was riding his motorbike the first time he saw her in the village. He veered off the road and almost hit an old woman.

"Dear God in heaven," he muttered to himself as his eyes followed her from shop to shop. "What a beauty, mother of Jesus." The old woman glared at him and waved her stick.

Walter assumed the girl was an American tourist, one of the many who would appear (usually in late summer) with their children and announce themselves in the pub as descendants of so-and-so.

Walter watched her stroll through the village quietly, lingering at shop windows. Then he smoked and pretended not to watch her wait for the N36 bus, which deposited its passengers about the northern part of the countryside every time it pulled to the side of the road.

Walter considered following the bus into the country, but his bike was so noisy it might irritate her, and there was the fear that the bus might end up going faster than he could.

Walter resolved to discover who she was and where she lived from the people in the shops, who between them knew everything that was happening within a twenty-mile radius.

At the newsagent, Walter asked for a pack of twenty Players cigarettes and casually mentioned that he'd seen a stranger in the village – a girl walking alone like a single cloud in the sky – but then his breath shallowed suddenly and he was unable to continue talking.

"You should really think about cutting down," the newsagent said, holding up the cigarettes. "You're only a lad to be smoking so much; look at you, Walter – you can barely breathe."

Before Walter left the shop, the newsagent suddenly remembered what Walter had said and called out.

"Ay, the girl you're talking about, Walter. She's been in, nice girl she is, and very tall, and a bit too old for you, me boy, if you know what I mean – a little too experienced." Then he laughed to himself. Walter shrugged and felt his blood turn cold with embarrassment.

"I'm actually getting on in years," Walter exclaimed.

Just as he was about to step outside, he heard the newsagent add, "And very sad what happened to her and her sister."

Walter poked his head back around the door.

"What's that you say?"

"Very sad, Walter – what happened to her ma and dad."

Walter stepped inside the shop again. It was brighter this time. He reached for a pint of milk and took it up to the counter.

"I bet you didn't know she's Canadian."

"Canadian? That's nice," Walter said, pretending not to care.

"And she arrived in Ireland with her sister sometime last month. Popsy met them at the airport – "

"How does Popsy know them?" Walter asked.

"I heard it was the first time Popsy had been to an airport, and he asked the Aer Lingus girl where exactly on the runway did the people come out."

The newsagent cackled.

"What a daft bugger he is, eh?" the newsagent said.

Walter rolled his eyes.

"So what happened to her family?" Walter said, taking his change and tucking the milk into his jacket.

"Well, me boy – they all perished in a fiery car crash outside Toronto."

"In Canada?"

"Ay. Now all that's left of the family is the tall girl that you saw, her young sister – who's the spitting image of her – and daft old Popsy."

The newsagent sniggered.

"That man's lived alone his entire life – and now he's got two girls to take care of. Jesus, Mary, and Joseph – what next?"

"Ay, it's strange, it is," Walter said.

"But something tells me he'll do all right," the newsagent admitted in a gesture that was particularly Irish – to cajole, mock, embarrass as a prelude to love.

"How's your da?"

"He's fine," Walter said.

"Still in the wheelchair?"

"Ay – but it's grand how he gets around."

"Ay – they don't make 'em like your da anymore. Give him my regards."

"Ay, I will," Walter promised.

Walter slipped from the bright shop and stepped out into the dusk. His motorcycle headlamp was on and cast a web of yellow light across the black concrete.

Walter had never talked directly with Popsy but knew who he was. The man had never married. He lived alone in an isolated farmhouse on the cliffs. He was occasionally seen in the pub – generally in the summer – talking amiably in his soft voice and telling his dog to lie down. Walter didn't know his real name but knew he was a master carpenter. Walter's father had once said that what Popsy did with wood made it stronger than steel.

Walter continued in the rain along the wet farm road with his basket of eggs in the back. A bird dipped alongside him and glided forward, landing on the road ahead to gulp down a worm.

When Walter was seven, he learned to swim on the incoming tide, watched vigilantly by his uncle, who'd come to live at their camp when Walter was a baby. His uncle had wanted to marry a non-Romany girl from Sethlow, but she eventually left him for an Englishman who worked on an oil rig. However, Uncle Ivan didn't seem particularly upset when the girl one day turned up with her new boyfriend at the camp in a brown Rover. In fact, Uncle Ivan had laughed and shaken the new boyfriend's hand vigorously.

Walter (now that he was older) believed the real reason that Uncle Ivan came to live with them was because of Walter's father's accident, which left him partially paralyzed. Walter's father could feel his legs and stand on them (with great pain), but he was unable to walk – or to work. Uncle Ivan had the sort of energy that enabled him to do two men's work in half the time. And he was also a celebrity. Uncle Ivan was the only Gypsy (and Irishman) in history to win a gold medal at the Olympics.

THE TRAMPOLINING GYPSY

U NCLE IVAN HAD ONCE lived in the caravan that now belonged to Walter. Upon the walls, newspaper clippings the color of salt and pepper displayed the impossible: a white figure flying through the air.

As a child, Walter liked to stand very still in front of each clip and study the expressions on his uncle's face. In the grainy prints, Uncle Ivan always wore a white undershirt with a number on it, white shorts tied at the front, thin black socks, and black Brogues.

Walter remembered his own bony white body stretching out in the cold water as he learned to swim. His uncle would call out strokes from the beach. Sometimes waxy slabs of seaweed hung in the water. Walter didn't like it. He imagined other things lurking at the bottom. One autumn day while swimming, Walter was bitten on the thigh by a conger eel. At first it felt like something was scratching him – maybe a dumb jellyfish washed in from deep water – then Walter looked down and saw a black head and an impossibly thick body writhing about his legs. Walter remembers his uncle's shirt tied around the wound. Watery blood running down his thigh, dripping off his big toe.

His uncle carried him a mile up the hill at a jog, and then the local doctor came. The doctor was from the north of Ireland and drove a Mercedes Estate. He looked at everyone from under his glasses. He balanced a mint imperial on his tongue during the examination. Several days in bed with the black-and-white television brought in from the living room, and anything he wants to eat, was the doctor's advice.

His uncle sat faithfully at his bedside the whole time, smoking, feeding him sausages, and telling him what a man he was, to have been bitten by a conger and survive – it was unthinkable. Walter still had the scar; a white line, jagged but no longer raised.

Then Uncle Ivan would fry up a dozen pieces of black pudding and they'd eat in front of the television.

His uncle had loved cold weather and kept fit by running in singlet and shorts on mornings too cold even for school.

BROKEN EGGS

T HEN THE RAIN STOPPED.

The landscape stretched before Walter like in a painting — lines of dark green hedgerows, a cluster of bare trees, an ancient gate hung during harvest, dots of hill-sheep and then the fabric of sea.

The morning Walter found Uncle Ivan stiff in his bed, snow had blown in through an open window and covered his body. In his will, Uncle Ivan had left his caravan, the motorbike, and his Olympic gold medal to Walter.

Walter watched the thread of smoke rise up from his beloved's farmhouse in the distance. The medal lay flat upon his chest, inside his shirt. He could feel the weight of it pulling on the back of his neck like an omen of hope and success.

The cake at Uncle Ivan's funeral was in the shape of a trampoline. The baker had made a frame of drinking straws over the cake from which dangled a marzipan figure.

At the burial, someone read a newspaper story written about the deceased in 1972. The story was called "In Mid-Flight an Irish Gypsy Soars."

Walter was almost at the farmhouse. He repeated the headline over and over to himself, with the voice the priest used when he read from the Old Testament in assembly.

"In mid-flight an Irish Gypsy soars."

"In mid-flight an Irish Gypsy soars."

Then Walter thought of his own headline.

"In love with a Canadian girl, a Romany hero soars."

Walter's leather jacket and trousers were heavy with water. He could feel the last few drops of rain bouncing off his helmet. He'd ridden twenty miles through plump green valleys. Sheep raised their curly heads to see him speed noisily by. The long lane down to the cold farmhouse was full of deep puddles, the moon in each puddle like a small white anchor, and the pale honey of windows in the distance.

Walter imagined her walking around the house, like a beautiful thought wandering around someone's head.

Walter pushed his bike through the gate. He could sense her breathing beneath his, and he felt her hands reach out from the handlebars and curl around his black gloves. He imagined how she would throw aside the basket of eggs and by the time they smashed against the stone floor, she would be kissing him wetly on the lips. In the dark, he might look even more like Morrissey.

By wheeling his motorbike instead of riding it, Walter might have a chance to sit and watch her through the window before knocking on the door and asking her uncle Popsy, quite innocently, if he might want some of the eggs left over from the morning's collection.

Walter had spent the early part of the day picking out the best eggs from the chicken hatch and reciting William Blake's *Songs of Innocence* to the hens, which stared at him angrily, then clucked away in panic.

After laying each egg out by his caravan, Walter found an old toothbrush and filled a bucket with warm soapy water.

As Walter scrubbed the feathers and burnt yellow feces from the shell of each egg, he noticed that his mother, father, and baby brother were watching him through the low window of their caravan.

Walter's father was sitting in his wheelchair with the baby on his lap. His mother was standing up in her fluffy slippers. She knocked on the thin pane of glass with her knuckle.

"Walter, you cleaning the eggs now, is it?"

"Do you want a cup of tea?" his father shouted from his wheelchair. After reaching for something too heavy, he'd fallen the wrong way. He lay there for several hours wondering what his life would be like.

Birds filled the sky before anyone came. Then a coworker discovered him.

A doctor in Limerick believed that within ten years, they'd have the technology to fix him. He wasn't paralyzed, they said – it was something to do with nerves. Everyone said it was the fall from the cliff – that his back had never been the same.

Walter liked to push his father along the road. The thin black tires glistened after rolling through thin puddles. Cars would slow down at the sight of them, and each face would stare blankly out.

The last time Walter had pushed his father to the new supermarket a couple of miles from the caravan, Walter noticed how the hair on his father's head was very soft. On the way back from the supermarket after a lunch of doughnuts and strong, sweet tea, his father's thinning crown made Walter want to cry; the vague idea that the seated figure before him – the king of dads, hunched in his chair – was not Walter's father but his son or his brother; and that life was a lottery of souls.

Walter took his business with the eggs into his small caravan and continued his work earnestly. When each egg was so shiny that it balanced a smaller version of the caravan window upon its shell, Walter sat on his Honda 450, which he kept inside next to his bed (a very un-Romany thing to do), and smoked one of his Players cigarettes. He liked the way his motorcycle looked under the single hanging bulb.

The corners of the ceiling were softened by thick cobwebs. The caravan had once been Uncle Ivan's. It now belonged to Walter, and Walter loved it, as he would love no other house for the rest of his life, no matter how grand or expensive or unique.

Walter was nine when Uncle Ivan decided he wanted electric lights.

Walter's eggs sat in a line upon the table, touching one another so as not to roll away. The table had once supported the weight of his uncle's elbows as he studied the lightbulb on that long-ago afternoon.

After hours of wiring and cursing, Uncle Ivan slowly screwed the bulb into its neat socket. Walter's mother and father were summoned from their caravan. Ivan had wanted Walter to push the switch that would bring it to life, but in the end he was not allowed. Uncle Ivan was an Olympian, not an electrician, Walter's mother had said.

They all cheered as the bulb suddenly glowed with the push of a button.

"What a miracle," said his uncle. "It's like there's a slither of sun in there."

"It's about time you got the electric in your van, Ivan," Walter's mother had said.

The four of them sat under it for some time without a word until his mother finally said:

"Look at us sitting here like idiots."

Uncle Ivan stood up and turned the switch on and off several times before they all went down to the pub for an early drink from glasses the barmaid was happy to keep away from the other glasses. You must understand that the Romany rituals of cleanliness are symbolic, not practical.

Walter wondered why he had thought of the lightbulb. And then he realized that his heart was also small and bright and hot. He would deliver the eggs that very afternoon, lest the bulb mysteriously flicker and die.

Walter turned around and saw his mother standing in the doorway.

"So who are the eggs for?"

"Nobody," Walter said.

"A girl, is it?"

Walter nodded.

His mother kissed him on the cheek.

"Your dear father was the same way for me," she said. "But he never polished me an egg a day in his life."

She handed Walter a cup of tea.

"Just don't start that thing up unless you've strapped your helmet on. I don't know why you keep it in here – your Romany ancestors would turn in their graves."

As she shuffled back past her small garden in her slippers, she stopped to unpeg several socks hanging on the line. Walter saw his oily handprints on the back of her blouse.

A few moments later, Walter heard laughing from their caravan.

Then Walter imagined his mother lying down with her husband and closing her eyes, the baby in a soft sleep in the back bed. Everything warm and dark. Raining again outside. The tapping of it against the window.

Then later, the baby quietly awake in his crib, playing with his feet and watching clouds move like gentle friends.

*　　*　　*

Walter leaned his bike against a tree and crept up to the kitchen window. He slowly lifted his head to see inside.

"Oh, my love, my love," he gasped, and his gaze like a net reached over her.

Walter pressed himself against the cold stones of the house as close to the glass pane as he dared. In her outstretched hand was a half-eaten apple. The white flesh glistened. She chewed slowly, occasionally touching her hair.

Walter longed for something to happen – a fire, a flood, some biblical catastrophe that would afford him an opportunity to rush in and rescue her.

Her uncle tended the fire dispassionately, and then sat down again. They were watching a black-and-white television and not talking. With their eyes safely fixed upon the screen, Walter wiped the window with his sleeve, but the mist was on the inside.

His body went limp as he let his eyes explore the length of her body. Her legs were so long, they stretched out almost the length of the table. Her young sister was nowhere to be seen – perhaps in her bedroom playing with dolls, Walter mused. Walter imagined her talking to them, smoothing out their clothes with her small fingers and setting them down at a table of plastic plates and plastic food which she held to their lips encouragingly.

Then a gentle but powerful feeling took Walter, and the boy immediately understood the obsession of the portrait artists he'd read about in his uncle's books; the troubadour poets and their sad buckled horses; the despairing souls who rowed silently at dusk in a heavy sea; the wanderers, the lost, those dying blooms who'd fallen away.

Walter's young mind reeled at the power of his first feeling of love. He would have walked to America if she had promised to meet him there.

From where had these feelings come? Walter thought. For he had not swallowed anything created by her body; neither had there been any physical contact, not even the brushing of sleeves in a crowded market. So these feelings for her – like fires lit in various parts of his body – must always have been within him, waiting to be lit.

And then Walter thought of something else. Could it be that first love was the only true love? And that after those first fires had been doused or burned out, men and women chose whom they would love based on worldly needs, and then reenacted the rituals and feelings of that first pure experience – nursed the flames that once burned of their own accord....

Walter declared in his thoughts that his virginity was spiritual and that he had already lost it to someone he was yet to meet. The physical act, should it ever occur, would be nothing more than blind and fumbling reassurance that man's mortality could be celebrated with the division of spirit through flesh.

Walter wondered what else he was capable of – what other emotions, talents, even crimes might suddenly erupt under certain conditions.

He remembered all those mornings as a child out in the field beside his caravan, watching storms move across the fields below. Eyes glued to the sky until a fork of lightning hit the earth; wind ripping trees from soggy riverbanks; an early morning blizzard like pillows ripped open. Walter suddenly felt that such things were part of his very being. And that for his entire life, the countryside he'd grown up in was a form of self-portrait.

And with his mind churning experience to understanding like milk into butter, Walter thought of Adam and Eve, the inevitable fall – their mouths stuffed with apple; their lips dripping with the sweet juice of it; the knowledge that life was the fleeting beauty of opposites, that human existence was the result of conflict, of physical and spiritual forces trapped within a dying vessel.

Every change in his behavior started making sense to him.

The days after seeing her, Walter took long rides on the roads he imagined she might be out walking. He dreamed of stopping to offer her a lift.

Walter would ride for miles and miles, as far as he could on a full tank – through the wind and pelting rain which lashed his face. Then he'd find a petrol station in the twilight and fill his tank while being watched suspiciously by the cashier from the bright kiosk that sold crisps, chocolate, Pot Noodle, magazines (dirty ones on the top shelf), birthday cards, cigarettes, maps, and black pudding.

The greatest hazard to riding a small motorcycle through the countryside of Ireland was the wildlife – sheep in particular, who when they spotted Walter rattling along would hurl themselves into the road.

The evening matured into night. Walter shivered. It had stopped raining, but his clothes were wet through. Standing at the window, he began to feel cold.

When she laughed at something on the television, Walter laughed too. There was a moment when she turned and peered through the glass, failing to notice the face of a boy upon the pane like an unfinished painting.

What he'd read in books was not right – man did not love with his heart but with his whole body. Every piece of him was involved somehow – he could feel her in his legs, in his fingers, the imagined weight of her shoulders upon his, her head upon his bare white chest. Walter knew he would die for her. And he thought of all the old songs he'd heard, the ancient ones from the days of horses, candles, and hunks of meats spitting on open fires. The songs composed for men at sea, the sweet high voices of girls imploring the Lord to bring home their loves. Walter imagined himself one of these men, called from the frosty woods to her cottage by singing, his horse nodding through the marsh, hands blistered from wet reins, breath in the cold like white fire.

Walter knelt and coughed into the patch of wet grass at his feet. Then he sat down knowing that on the other side of the wall was his eternal love. He could sense the weight of her body in the chair. He wanted to touch himself in the way Father McCarthy had forbidden all young boys to do in assembly – and he would have but for the sense that in some way it would have defiled his pure love for her.

His fingers dug into the soil as he imagined the vibration of her voice touch his body. He stiffened. His mouth hung open. And then he sprang back at the shock of seeing a figure standing a few yards from him.

"Mary, Mother of Jesus!"

"What are you doing out here?" a small, trembling voice said. It was a little girl. The younger sister, wearing an overcoat and orange Wellington boots that were too big for her. A plastic hairless doll hung down from one of her hands.

"Don't you have a television at home?" she said.

"What? A television?"

"Is that your motorcycle by the tree?"

"My what?"

She turned and pointed.

"Oh, my motorcycle – yes, it's mine."

"Can you take us for a ride?" she asked.

"Us?" Walter said, suddenly hopeful. "Us?"

The girl held up her doll.

"Ay," Walter said. "I'll take you and your dolly for a ride."

The girl's eyes widened with excitement. She said something in her doll's ear.

"But you have to tell me something first," Walter said quietly.

"Okay."

"Does your sister have a boyfriend in Canada?"

The girl looked back at his motorcycle.

"Are those eggs for us?"

"They might be – but first you have to tell me if your sister has a boyfriend."

"A boyfriend?"

"Some awful, boring fellow who tried to impress your sister but who just ended up being a nuisance without even realizing she was beyond him in every way imaginable. Did you notice anyone like that at all?"

"I don't think so," she said, unsure as to whether it was the right answer. Then in a voice loud enough to be heard from inside, she said, "Are you in love with my sister – is that why you've brought us a basket of eggs?"

Walter felt the tingling of embarrassment.

"It's more complicated than that, you know – you're too young to understand."

"Are you going to marry her?"

"Is that a serious question?" Walter said.

The girl nodded.

"Do you think she'd like me?"

She nodded enthusiastically. "I think she would."

"Well, that's a brilliant start," Walter said with pure joy. "I'm Walter, by the way."

"I'm Jane," the girl said, with the embarrassment of all children when talking to someone older.

Walter didn't care that he was speaking to a girl of eight or nine. Through the cold autumn night, he could hear the bells of the church casting their notes upon the village like seeds. He could see Father McCarthy's serious face as they approached the altar. The Canadian orphan in white like the queen of swans, her eyes like tiny glaciers that held him, the church, the congregation, the whispering smoke of incense; old women's heads in colored hats, bowing like yesterday's flowers. He would wear his motorcycle jacket and Uncle Ivan's Olympic medal.

"What should I do, Jane?"

"It's a bit cold out here," Jane said.

"Well, go on in," Walter said. "You'll catch your death."

Then he regretted saying it as he remembered what had happened to her parents only several months ago.

"I'm sorry about your ma and dad."

Jane set down her doll.

"Don't worry, Jane – they're up in heaven, and when you've had a long life and your own babies you can see them again, so don't worry now, they're not really dead, they're just not here."

Jane went back into the house with her doll.

Walter listened for the sound of the latch and considered for a moment that she might tell the uncle, and then he'd be discovered and would have to explain what he was doing.

He imagined her uncle coming out in black boots. His kind face quickly turning to scorn. Jane pointing at the hot, wet ball of boy in the thicket beneath the window. Then his beloved – ashamed and disgusted, surveying him from afar; a shawl over her shoulders like closed black wings.

What would he say? By the next Sunday, the entire village would think him a Peeping Tom.

But you can't explain love, Walter thought to himself, and with the breathless ambition of youth, he believed, in his young heart, that those five words would be enough to shield him.

"You can't explain love," he said out loud. "That's how it gets ruined."

Without daring to look in again, Walter decided he had to go – but that he would allow himself to return. He would leave the eggs at the door with one of his gloves – then he'd have to return to pick it up. He'd started to rise when he heard the latch of the front door.

His heart rolled like a stone ball into his stomach.

"It's just me," Jane whispered. She handed Walter a lukewarm mug of tea.

"Jesus of Nazareth," Walter said, gulping back the tea in gulps. "You're a little star, Jane – but you bloody well gave me fright."

Inside the house, Uncle Popsy searched in vain for the tea he thought he'd set on the hall table only moments ago.

When the mug was empty, Jane pointed past the cottage and into the night.

"We have to go down to the sea now," she said, and Walter noticed that in one of her small hands were two red buckets, the kind children used to build sand castles.

"The sea? Why, Jane?" Walter asked.

"Because," she said, "I'm not allowed to go by myself."

"But you don't know me."

"Yes I do," she said emphatically.

Walter sighed. "You want to go there now?"

Jane nodded.

"In the dark?" Walter said.

Jane nodded. "It has to be now," she said, and pointed up at the moon.

"What about your uncle?"

"He's watching TV with my sister," Jane said. "Can we go on your motorcycle?"

"No."

"Please?"

"Absolutely not."

Jane stood and looked at him. She lifted her doll up to Walter's face, so they were at eye level.

"Please," the doll said without moving its mouth. "Don't be boring."

"Jesus, Jane – it's too feckin' loud."

Jane looked at her feet. Her bottom lip protruded slightly from the rest of her mouth.

"All right, " Walter said. "But if we go, we go on foot."

Jane clapped her hands and said something to her doll.

"C'mon then," Walter said. "Are you sure you're warm enough?"

But Jane was already five paces ahead, her small body buckling with the flood of desire and the breathlessness of grief.

The journey would not be an easy one, for the path down to the sea was treacherous; they would have to hold hands for part of the way, stepping with more courage than faith.

JANE

S HE SAT ON A red towel, looking out to sea. People laden with bags and beach chairs passing slowly across the surface of her Wayfarers. It would soon be time to go home.

The sand beneath her towel had molded to the shape of her body. She glanced down at her legs. They were not as she would have liked them to be, but for her age, she felt she was still attractive. In the deli below her apartment, the Spanish men sometimes flirted with her if they weren't too busy. At the office, she realized that the young girls – the assistants and the interns – probably looked at her as being old. She didn't feel old. Although her feet ached sometimes. Her enthusiasm for life had turned to appreciation for life. And she could feel life getting quieter. *Her* life getting quieter, like the end of a party where only a few people remain at long messy tables, staring at their glasses, at the absent chairs, and at each other.

It was the end of summer and families were migrating back to New York from East Hampton. The lines in the cafés were shorter, and it was no longer difficult to park on Main Street.

In the distance, Jane's teenage daughters sat at the water's edge discussing boys and the secret things known only to siblings.

Jane had been close to her own sister.

They looked very much alike.

And while Jane's accent became unmistakably Irish, her sister had never lost her Canadian twang. They both had blond hair and would take turns twisting braids for one another in the garden on summer days, as their uncle Popsy picked lettuce and whistled.

Jane's daughters were close too.

They were both at the Waldorf School and always ate lunch together. Jane could sense how the world was opening up to her children. The telephone in the kitchen rang all the time now, and their doorman had got to know several boys quite well. Jane approved only of the ones who were nervous when they met her.

Her daughters' lives were very bright; everything felt for the first time.

The roots of her own life had found deep soil – holding her in place. Jane felt the strength and poise to give her children a safe and stable shelter. A place to rest when they sat at the kitchen table and said things that made them cry.

Her children meant everything to her.

The shelter of a mother's love was something that Jane thought of very often, for her own parents had lost their lives in a car accident when she was very little. Then her older sister died of cancer in London two years ago. Jane's husband experienced a breakdown at the funeral and was taken to a hospital in Kings Cross. He had been very fond of her sister.

In Jane's opinion, her sister had never been able to get over the death of their parents, as though a part of her had died too on that long-ago morning when charred debris lay scattered across the freeway outside Toronto.

The first car to come along saw several small fires: Something completely wrong. No trace of people. It was an image Jane conjured daily. Age is a plow that unearths the true nature of things. But only after the moment has passed and we are powerless to change anything, are we granted wisdom. As though we are living backward.

Jane knew her daughters must learn this for themselves, and so there was only one piece of advice Jane wanted to pass on to her girls.

She watched them at the water's edge.

Laughter.

Seagulls swooping down in their endless pursuit of scraps.

The billowing sail of a faraway boat holding the last of the day like a nugget of gold.

One day, Jane thought, this moment will be a long time ago.

For Jane knew that wisdom means knowing when to give everything, knowing exactly the right time to give everything and admit you've done it and not look back. Loving is the path to eternal life, Jane thought, not worship, as she was taught in Ireland.

And she sensed that everyone she had ever touched – whether deeply over years or for only a brief moment in a crowded elevator – might somehow be the whole story of her life.

Jane wiped her eyes and noticed a small child standing at the edge of her blanket with a red bucket.

The girl had lovely eyes. Her belly lunged forward. Her red bucket was full of water. Jane reached out to the girl, but she turned and ran away.

Above her, the sky held on to a few clouds. They hung far out at sea – watching the lives of people who'd gathered at the edge of land.

The red bucket reminded Jane of Walter, calling to her as she reached the edge of the field long ago in Ireland. And then his large, rough hand, which although she didn't know it then, was a young hand.

The beach was dark, and the sand had been packed hard by the outgoing tide. Rain lingered; like something said but not forgotten.

Walter ran to the water's edge, and Jane remembered a moment of panic when he disappeared from her sight – but then he was upon her again. He had found shells and he unloaded them into her small arms.

She told him about her mother and father, and he listened and kissed her once on the forehead, telling her that they would never truly leave her behind – that people, like little fish, are sometimes caught in the cups of rocks as the tide sweeps in and out.

Jane wondered what he meant; whether it was she or her parents who were trapped.

"And should you ever feel too lonely, Jane," Walter said as they carried the moon home in buckets, "listen for the roar of the sea – for in it are all those who've been and all those who are to come."

Jane remembered his words during the long nights in the cottage where she would spend the next fifteen years.

Some nights, she believed that if she listened hard enough, she might hear the voice of her mother and father calling to her from wherever they were.

Some mornings, the moment before she opened her eyes, she had forgotten they were gone; then like all those left behind in the world, Jane would have to begin again. For, despite the accumulation of experience, one must always be ready to begin again, until it's someone else's turn to begin without us, and we are completely free from the pain of love, from the pain of attachment – the price we pay to be involved.

As the sun dropped lazily in the sky, Jane stood and removed her sunglasses. She brushed the sand from her legs. Her eyes were swollen with crying. She stepped across the warm beach down to the water where her daughters were huddled.

When they saw her coming, they made a space and she sat between them – excited and afraid to tell them how the very best and the very worst of life will come from their ability to love strangers.

And they would think she was talking about Dad, about Walter, who grew up in a Gypsy caravan on a cliff, and who every Christmas without fail gives their mother a dozen eggs which he cleans in the sink on Christmas Eve, while they – his two daughters – talk to their friends on the phone, help string the tree with tinsel, or stare out the window at fading shadows, at the happy sadness of yesterday, the promise of tomorrow.

The City of
Windy Trees

I

ONE DAY, GEORGE FRACK received a letter. It was from very far away. The stamp had a bird on it. Its wings were wide and still. The bird was soaring high above a forest, its body flecked with red sparks. George wondered if the bird was flying *to* a place or away from it.

At first, George thought the letter had been delivered to him by mistake, but the name on the envelope was his name and the address was where he lived.

Then he opened it and found a page of blue handwriting and a photograph of a little girl with brown hair. The girl was wearing a navy polyester dress dotted with small red hearts. She also had a pink clip in her hair. Her hands were tiny.

The handwriting was full of loops, as if each letter were a cup held fast upon the page by the heaviness of each small intention.

When George read the page, his mouth fell open and a low groaning resounded from his throat.

★　★　★

He held the paper very close to his eyes and read it again several times.

Then he dropped the page and looked around his apartment as though people were watching him from every dusty corner.

On the mantelpiece was the only photograph of his great uncle, Monsieur Saboné, who like George had lived alone in a quiet part of the city where he was born.

George wandered from room to room without knowing why, balancing the words of the letter in his mind; trying to make sense of them.

When George found himself standing in the kitchen, he automatically reached for the teapot. Perhaps because he wasn't himself, he somehow managed to knock it to the floor. When George tried to pick up the pieces, he realized he could not control his shaking hands and he cut his fingers in several places.

Blood dripped onto the broken pieces of china; large spots fell upon the white sink.

George sat on the edge of the bathtub and wrapped his hands in old bandages. He imagined writing out the story of his life across each length of white. What words would he choose; would there be things he wrote that weren't true; would there be spaces for things he wished he had done, people he wanted to meet, but who never came?

George sat on his toilet with the lid down. He remained there for two hours looking at his bandaged hands. When he felt faint, George removed his clothes and slipped into bed. Blood soaked through the bandage and left spots on the sheets.

Outside, a fire engine wailed, changing pitch as it passed: one sound for coming and one for going – the moment in between, indistinguishable.

George was asleep by the time it was dark. Lights went on in kitchens across the city as people arrived home. As George entered his first dream, the unknown world carried on. Men in heavy coats walked dogs outside his front door. Women fell asleep in front of television sets; others stayed up without any good reason. And as in every city, a handful of children gazed gently from windows upon the roads and passageways of their childhood, small questions falling in their minds like a rain that disappears by morning.

When George opened his eyes the next day, they were wet. His body was also very stiff. He unfurled his limbs as though waking from hibernation.

The sky outside his window was very bright. Yellow light fell through holes in the curtain and made patterns on the bed. The patterns came and went with the journey of clouds.

George's first thought was that the whole thing was a dream, but life soon poured over him. On the desk he noticed the tip of the envelope. The photograph of the little girl would be lying next to the letter.

Along the rim of the kitchen sink, George's blood had dried in crimson circles. Pieces of broken teapot on the floor had not moved, like small ruins of an ancient civilization.

George didn't go to work and no one telephoned to see if he was ill.

Every so often he checked the address on the letter to make sure it had been delivered to the right person. Then he looked at the photograph. Then he read the letter again.

He stayed in bed until it was dark and did the very same thing the next day, swallowing mild sleeping pills every few hours and drifting in and out of a slumber heavy with memories from childhood.

In the middle of the night, George woke up sweating and gasping for air. For a few moments, the residue of the dream convinced

George he had died and was reliving life all over again – but with the memory of everything that had happened before and all that was going to happen. What would it be like to know every detail of every event that would ever happen? The thought carried him in its arms to another dream.

When George finally woke at noon the next day, he sat up for an hour trying to piece his thoughts together like jigsaw pieces from different puzzles.

When he lay back down and drifted into a snooze, pieces came together by themselves, and the book of his childhood blew open. George heard the sound of his father's key churn the lock of the front door. Home from the office. His suit would be creased from the office chair. A small George sat very still in a room that glowed with the spell of television. He wanted to be found. He wanted to be scooped up like a rock from a river and found precious. And every evening his father returned home, George held his breath, like an understudy watching from the wings. George lived always on the verge of his greatest performance.

Then in the dream, George felt himself reaching for the television, turning up the volume as the shouting got worse. If only they had got divorced. Children at school ripped to pieces by their parents' lack of love, shells of their former selves – and George burning with shame, wanting only to have his parents by themselves in the park on dull afternoons at the duck pond.

Instead, George spent his childhood like a small satellite orbiting their unhappy world.

Then he left home. His parents remained together, until one day his father jumped off the office building where he worked. George imagined his raincoat flapping, then the impact; strangely bent limbs; people circling in disbelief; somebody's ruined day.

George wept at the funeral, not because his father was dead but because he'd never known him. If grief has levels, this was the one below guilt.

On the third day after receiving the letter, George lay on his back and followed the cracks in the bedroom ceiling with his eyes. He imagined he was on a journey across a tiny Arctic plain.

And then he fell asleep and dreamed it.

At the end of his journey across the snow was the little girl from the photograph, waiting for him in the dress with hearts on it. In the dream, all the hearts were beating. When George drew close, he noticed she had butterfly wings. Whenever he tried to reach her, she fluttered away laughing. The sound of her laughing filled him with joy. George managed to cup the feeling and hold on to it for a few seconds after waking up. In his heart, some tiny piece of what hadn't happened would lodge.

In the afternoon George drank tea in the quiet of his bedroom. He wiped away his blood and took a series of showers, concentrating on a different body part each time. He swept his apartment and threw out many things that at one time had been valuable to him.

On the fifth day, George stared through his bedroom window into backyards of bare trees, children's toys, and half-filled plant pots.

Although he lived on a city avenue, the back room where George spent his evening hours was very quiet. Sometimes a neighbor's dog could be heard barking and scratching weakly at a back door. For some reason, George found these to be comforting sounds – while the mean grinding buses that passed his front room irritated and depressed him.

After graduating from university about ten years ago, George had gradually lost interest in the lives of his friends. He dreaded the blinking red light on his telephone that indicated messages waiting to be heard. He stayed away from gatherings, and he purposefully forgot birthdays. Life had not turned out the way he thought. He had not stayed with the woman he truly loved (she was married and living in Connecticut). His mother died one day at the kitchen table before she could drink her tea. He developed a mysterious pain in his hands. His sister became a single mother to a boy (Dominic) with Down syndrome. His job was uninteresting and he felt that his life was nothing more than a light that would blink once in the history of the universe and then be forgotten.

George had lived for several years without a television. Television made him feel lost and lonely. George's local post office had recently attached one to the wall – an attempt to calm people confined to wait in massive queues. George bought his stamps elsewhere and avoided the voice he felt knew absolutely nothing but refused to stop talking.

George's neighbors were very fond of him, however. His apartment was situated on the top floor of the Greenpoint Home for the Agéd, and George occupied the only dwelling that wasn't part of the "home." It had, of course, originally been built for a live-in nurse, but thanks to a cocktail of modern drugs, the residents had little need for any professional assistance. George could even hear them being intimate, and sometimes the occasional fight, and sometimes sobbing – if he listened with a glass against the wall.

The previous tenant – still discussed in the hallway from time to time when a letter came for him – was a Polish carpenter who punched holes in his walls, then spent half the night repairing them with cutting, sawing, and sanding.

★   ★   ★

George Frack was not without interests. He liked:

1. Large Chinese kites
2. Sitting beside the window in his bathrobe with a box of Raisinets
3. New-wave European films (viewed only at Eric and Burt's small movie house in Greenpoint)
4. Horoscopes
5. Velvet loafers
6. Drinking coffee in the park from a thermos when nobody was around
7. His collection of world Snoopy figures (Chinese Snoopy, Arctic Snoopy, Russian Snoopy, Aussie Snoopy, etc. etc.)
8. David Bowie songs
9. A cat called Goddard (pronounced God-AR) now deceased
10. A heavy fall of snow that ruins everyone's plans

George's last serious relationship was with Goddard, a stray cat who one day appeared outside the building and threw himself at everyone who passed. They slept together under the same blanket, and George sometimes awoke to Goddard's paw upon his hand. After almost a year at the Greenpoint Home for the Agéd, Goddard escaped one Sunday morning while George was out buying oranges and sardines. He had squeezed through an open window and carefully stepped down the fire escape.

A few minutes later Goddard lay squashed under a bus. Someone put him in a shoe box; his limp body was like a sack of broken parts.

The evening Goddard died, George stood naked on the edge of his fire escape until it got dark and lights came on one square at a time. Then some neighbor spotted a bare human figure on a fire escape and shouted. Suicide was one thing – but confrontation was out of the question. George climbed back inside. Then he went to bed. His usual supper of Raisinets went untouched. The oranges lay on the floor where they had rolled.

George held the letter and the photograph of the little girl in his hand and sat very quietly in a wooden chair beside his bedroom window. He remembered the feeling of Goddard's head brushing his legs.

After almost a week in his apartment without any human contact, a storm built slowly on the edge of the city and then broke open. George watched from his window as a seamless band of clouds rolled toward him. Trees bent, as if leaned on by invisible hands. The streetlight fell in perfect columns of raindrops.

Cars pulled to the sides of the road. Umbrellas blew out like escaping squid.

George got up from his chair and went to the closet for a blanket. The kitchen light felt good against the darkness of the afternoon. He walked halfway into the kitchen, but then decided against making tea and went back into his bedroom, where he planned on settling down for the night. It was six o'clock.

He sat down and spread the blanket across his legs. He was wearing his velvet loafers and a bathrobe. The rain tapped gently against the window, magnifying the backyards in long watery lines. The roofs of the buildings glistened black, and a tiny alphabet of birds hung motionless in the sky.

George looked at the photograph. The girl in it would smile forever. Every photograph is a lie, he thought – a splinter from the tree of what happened. Clouds moved from one side of the sky to the other. The darkness would be upon them sooner than ever. George pressed the photograph of the girl to his cheek. In his mind, he could feel her gentle fantasies. Then her heart began to beat within his and he was suddenly full of yearning for this child, a daughter who came in the mail – in a dress of tiny hearts, from a city of windy trees: a place where he had been conjured ten thousand times from a pillow of alternating hope and disappointment.

II

A FTER THE STORM, NIGHT filled the wet city.

George had been still for such a very long time that evening had etched his face into the window before him. It was a face through which city lights twinkled in the windy distance. George leaned forward. The figure before him also leaned, as if ready to hear the whispering of a secret. George imagined his daughter's hands upon his face, like someone blind trying to feel his way around. He wondered what she would make of it.

Would she touch it?

Would she wonder what stories swirled behind the eyes?

Would she find it handsome?

Perhaps she might see herself.

And, then, perhaps in time, it might be a face that she cared for, that she was pleased to see, that gave her comfort in the night when she surfaced on the back of a nightmare.

George ripped open a box of Raisinets and chewed each one carefully. He decided to write a letter to his sister. Since he'd received the photograph of the little girl in the mail, the old love for his sister had stirred; a love that had become buried under the rubble of his life. Growing up, they hadn't said much to one another but sometimes held hands in the car and sometimes cooked together listening to

David Bowie after their mother had passed out on the couch, still clutching the neck of a bottle.

One Easter, George left several drawings of rabbits outside her bedroom door. When he found them in the trash can in the kitchen that afternoon, George stormed into her room, grabbed the egg that she was decorating, and stamped on it.

Not until she was a woman did George's sister realize how much her younger brother had looked up to her, and how lonely his life must have been without her friendship. But by that time George had disappeared from her life completely.

George wondered what he would say to her in the letter. He found a pen and some paper from a drawer and sat down at his desk. He went to switch on his lamp, but there was no bulb in it. Then he remembered two boxes of bulbs in the cupboard under the stairs. He went to fetch one.

Several weeks ago, while walking home from work, George passed what he thought was a shop. In the window were packs of diapers, dusty toys in sun-bleached boxes, a pile of women's clothes, and three dirty boxes of lightbulbs, which reminded George that he needed some.

When he tried to enter the shop, however, he found the door locked. As he stepped back to see if the opening times had been posted, a panel opened in the door and a face appeared.

"Yeah?" the face said.

"How much are those lightbulbs?" George asked.

The face eyed him suspiciously.

"What lightbulbs?" the face said.

"The lightbulbs in the window – how much are they?"

The face tightened as if agitated and then disappeared, leaving the panel open.

A moment later, the face returned. It stared curiously at George Frack.

"So how much are they?" George asked.

The face laughed.

"A dollar," the face said.

"Each or for the pack?"

"For the pack."

"Great," George said. "I'll take two packs."

"Okay," the face said, "that's two dollars."

"What about tax?" George asked.

"Okay, that's two dollars and nineteen cents," the face said, and laughed again.

A week later, the shop was raided by the police and then boarded up by city workers with cigarettes in their mouths.

George found the two boxes of lightbulbs in his closet under the stairs where he had set them. He put one in the lamp on his desk.

It came to life before he had finished screwing it in.

Then he began the letter to his sister.

She was a single mother to a boy named Dominic with Down syndrome. George had not spoken to her since Dominic was born. All George knew was that his nephew was conceived one night on a skiing holiday in Canada with a man who had another family. As George wrote his sister's name, he realized that Dominic would have no idea who he was.

Dear Helen,

I know I haven't written to you before like this
~~before~~- but I wanted to tell you that I'm going to
Sweden. I also want to explain that the reason I
haven't kept in touch is because I felt sorry that
your life was ruined.

This afternoon I sat by the window and watched
the rain. I was thinking about my life--but not in the
usual way. I don't think I feel sorry for you anymore,
Helen, or for us for that matter.

While I sit here*-life is going on without me.

If not for something that happened to me a few
days ago, I would not have realized that your life with
Dominic--while being hard at times--is probably full of a
joy we never had as kids.

One day soon I will come and visit you.

Is this okay?

You will see my headlights in the driveway. I will
bring food in white plastic bags from the supermarket.
Perhaps the three of us might cook something together,

...the way we did when we were little. I can't say
it tasted very good, but that ~~want~~ wasn't the point,
and don't you think the quality of food is higher since
the advent of those automatic sprinkler systems in the
produce aisle?

I can't tell you when I will see you, but it will
be before the end of the year.

There's something I have to do first--somewhere I
have to go, someone I have to meet, and someone I have
to become.

I am the most important person to someone I didn't
even know existed.

Wish me luck...
Your Brother,

-~~George~~- MAJOR TOM

   p.s. for some reason I think my passport is in the boxes of
      Mom's things that you have. Would you send it to me as
      soon as possible? MORE THAN ONE LIFE DEPENDS ON THIS.

   p.p.s. I had a cat--but it was killed by a bus. I wish he
      had met Dominic--they could have played together.

   p.p.p.s. I regret things I haven't done--rahter than thing[S]I
      have--strange eh?

--~~p.p.p..p.p~~- FINAL NOTE: Do you still like David Bowie?

    ENCL: Two Boxes of Raisinets

Then George crossed out his name, and wrote "Major Tom."

A few days later, Human Resources from George's office called. They kept calling him Mr. Frack. George asked them to call him George, but they wouldn't. There were two people talking on the same line, and at various points in the conversation, nobody knew who was talking to whom. George kept looking down at his velvet loafers. After ten minutes, George's boss came on the line. It sounded like he was chewing. He was a boorish man from the suburbs who picked his nose when he didn't think anyone was looking.

George said he didn't understand why they had called. His boss asked George if he was kidding. Then he told George that he was being fired. George sighed.

"Well, that's fine," George said, "because I'm going to Sweden for a while."

There was silence, and then his boss said:

"Where the hell is Sweden?"

"It's like Scandinavia – or something," George said, looking for an open pack of Raisinets.

A week later, his passport arrived. In the package was:

1. A pair of adult-sized mittens
2. A kid's drawing of a whale with "Good Luck!" written on it in blue and yellow crayon
3. A letter from his sister
4. A list of things they had cooked when they were children

5.   One of three drawings secretly rescued from the trash after the egg incident

The letter from his sister was addressed to "Major Tom" and signed "Ground Control."

A short P.S. read: "You've really made the grade."

G EORGE'S TAXI BROKE DOWN on the way to the airport. The driver cursed in Hindi, then ripped a tiny plastic deity from the dashboard and yelled into its face.

George leaned forward and explained to the driver that he had a daughter he'd never met, that she was waiting for him, that he had only one chance to find her. The driver replaced the deity with a kiss, then threw open his door and ran out onto the Brooklyn-Queens Expressway, waving his arms. George noticed that he was wearing loafers – patent leather.

Several cars skidded, almost hitting a Wonder Bread truck. The bread truck driver jumped from the cab and stood with his chest against the taxi driver's face. The cars behind suddenly stopped honking. Just when it seemed the truck driver was going to punch the taxi driver, the two men shook hands. The cars behind started honking again.

George climbed into the bread truck. A small Puerto Rican flag dangled from the rearview mirror. The driver swerved in and out of traffic as though sewing up the highway. He smoked one cigarette after another. A can of Red Bull fell from the cup holder and spilled all over George's velvet loafers. The driver laughed. George could hear the bread flying around in the back, hitting the sides with dull thumps.

When they arrived at Newark International Airport, the driver looked at George and shouted, "Go, motherfucker, go."

George grabbed his bag and fell from the cab, then sprinted through the doors into the terminal.

The woman at check-in had a glass eye. She told George he had five minutes to get to the gate. Then a large African-American man in gold-rimmed glasses studded with fake diamonds appeared on an airport golf cart. He told George to climb on, and they beeped their way to the gate, scattering passengers on all sides.

Once at a cruising altitude, the passengers around George began to sleep – like people falling into pools of their own lives.

George thought about his journey to the airport. He'd never see those men again. Love between strangers takes only a few seconds and can last a whole life.

Then he thought back six years to the night he'd spent with the Swedish hotel clerk at a truck stop in upstate New York; it was the night of beginning, because it was the only night they were together. To think that one unplanned night with a stranger in a strange place could create the most precious person who ever lived.

Six years ago, George had a sort of nervous breakdown. Instead of calling an ambulance and waiting on the couch in his underwear, George decided he was going to drive to his ex-girlfriend's wedding in Massachusetts and then charge the cake as it was brought out. He pictured himself being arrested and then institutionalized. He imagined the pleasure of sitting in a bathrobe on a bench beside a rose garden, nurses gliding past like swans.

The wedding was to take place on a Saturday morning. George left on Friday and drove until his nerves could no longer handle the traffic. He took the next exit and followed the car in front. He wondered who was in it, what sort of life they were having. He knew he would never see their face and that their lights would soon disappear along the road to somewhere he could not imagine.

Then George spotted a red neon sign:

RED'S, SINCE 1944.

He parked and went inside.

The waitresses wore white shirts with frilly collars and black vests. There were plastic flowers on all the tables. The wind howled against the windows.

Opposite the diner, about half a mile in the distance, burned the lights of a correctional facility.

There were photographs of 1950s baseball players on the walls. Snow blew around the parking lot. A storm had been predicted, and the waitresses kept looking through the windows and pointing.

The silverware was flimsy. George bent his spoon with one hand. The spoon reminded George of a child's hand.

The lamp shades hung low over each table. George asked for the special. When he finished his glass of Diet Coke, the waitress brought another, but George's mouth was so full of bread, he could only nod when she set it down on the table before him.

A man walked his little son to the bathroom. They were both wearing neckties. The boy kept touching his. Near the entrance was a lobster tank with only one lobster in it. George wondered what the lobster was thinking; perhaps wondering when the others were coming back.

When George returned from the bathroom, his food had arrived. The lobster tank was empty. George ate a few mouthfuls painfully, and then concentrated on the coleslaw which lay in a sad heap half off the plate.

Outside, snow lay thick upon the picnic tables. A couple at the next table was eating dinner. They were about George's age. They were wearing scarves and laughing. They ordered a bottle of wine, and it arrived with a napkin around its neck. Why did everyone else's life seem perfect?

At the other end of the restaurant, a father held his daughter aloft, as though he had just pulled her from the ground. George felt dizzy. There were plastic snowflakes hanging in the windows.

George tipped the waitress the year of his ex-girlfriend's birthday, $19.72 – more than the meal itself.

He knew he was only twenty minutes from where the wedding was being held the next day, so when George saw a sign for lodging not far from the restaurant, he followed the flashing arrow. The hotel was a line of connected chalets, each with the same color door. Lines of trucks filled the parking lot, their engines like snouts gleaming and puffing in the moonlight.

Drivers milled about, smoking and stomping the snow from their boots.

The check-in desk was lit by a long fluorescent bulb missing its cover. An ashtray on the counter was full of ash but no cigarette butts. There was also a calendar with a glossy photograph of a Mack truck.

George rang the bell and waited. Nobody came.

As he turned to leave, a woman with short black hair appeared.

"Sorry," she said.

"It's okay," George said.

Her skin was pockmarked, but her eyes were very beautiful. Her hair was uneven, as though she'd cut it herself. She also had an accent. When she spoke, it sounded like she was singing.

"A room?" she asked.

"Yes, please," George said.

"Are you a driver?" she said, looking at her book.

George thought for a moment and remembered all the rigs parked outside.

"No," he said, "just a regular person."

The woman laughed.

"245," she said. "It's on the second floor. How do you wish to pay?"

George handed her his credit card.

"Nonsmoking – is that all right?"

"I don't smoke," George said.

The woman looked at his credit card and said his name aloud.

"George Frack."

"Yes," George said.

"That's a funny name."

"Is it?"

"It sounds like it's made up."

"Well, it's not made up," George said. "I've had it for years."

"Well, here's your key, George Frack."

George took his key and thanked her. Then, for some reason, instead of going immediately to his room and getting into bed as he'd planned, he turned to her and said:

"Where are you from – I like your voice."

The woman stared at him closely.

"Sweden."

"Oh," George said, "so you're happy about the snow."

"I am," she said.

"What are you doing here?"

"You mean, working at a truck stop in Nowhere, New York?"

"Yes."

"It's a long sad story, George Frack. Why are you here?"

"It's a long sad story also."

A trucker passed through the lobby and disappeared into the bar, leaving a trail of cigarette smoke.

"Do you want to watch TV with me in my room later?" George said.

"Okay," the woman answered without looking up. "I'll be over in two hours – shall I bring anything?"

"Orange juice, please."

"And how about some Raisinets?" she said.

"Candy?" George said.

"You'll see."

An hour later, Marie sat with George on his bed. The room was quite sad. Cigarette burns in the carpet, a ball of sweatpants in a drawer, dirty ashtrays, the cap from a bottle of something under the bed.

Instead of watching television, Marie told George about how she'd come to New York to find her father. Her mother said he was a truck driver – at least he was in 1978.

"You picked a good spot," George said.

"I suppose so," she said.

"How long have you been here?"

"Almost three months – but I'm going back next week because my visa runs out."

"You didn't find him then?"

"I hoped I'd recognize him."

"At least you tried."

Marie shook some Raisinets into George's hand.

"My father is dead," George said.

"Is that why you're so unhappy?"

George thought for a moment. "Actually yes," he said.

"But why are you up here, George Frack?"

"I don't think I know anymore," George said, moving deeper under the covers. Then Marie kissed him.

Afterward, they lay in each other's arms without saying anything.

When George woke up the next morning, Marie was gone. The bed was full of Raisinets. He'd missed the wedding. The television was a reflection of the room. He took a shower, then got in his car and drove home. The traffic was very light.

IV

WHEN GEORGE'S PLANE TOUCHED down in Stockholm, it was
still dark. Orange Volvo wagons idled within yellow lines
painted around the docked aircraft.

A group of men stood about a luggage cart looking up at the faces
that peered out from the small windows of the airplane. Some of the
men wore blue headsets around their necks.

A child started to cry.

George thought the man next to him was asleep, but then he reached
up and touched his mustache, as if to check that George hadn't stolen it.

As people made their way lugubriously to passport control, George
noticed that the man who'd been sitting next to him was limping
badly. He was soon passed by all the other passengers. Three mechanics
glided by on small scooters.

The woman in the passport booth hardly looked at George's passport. Then he was suddenly waiting for his luggage. He recognized
a few faces from the plane. Most of the passengers were Swedish and
talked quietly in singsong voices.

He couldn't believe he'd done it, that he was a father – that he was
in Sweden. A situation George would have thought nightmarish if it
had been put to him hypothetically was now the single most important
thing that had ever happened to him.

Life had called his name, and without thinking, he had stepped forward. He wondered if perhaps he was becoming the person he had always wanted to be.

On the plane, George had made a list of the different jobs he might enjoy and that might earn him enough to travel back and forth to Sweden. Maybe he might even live in Sweden. He liked snow, after all, and he owned a green Saab.

A little girl sat on the edge of the baggage car, dangling her feet as though she were on the edge of a pier on the last day of her family vacation. Her eyes kept closing and then opening. Several more children arrived and did the same thing – sat on the edge of an empty baggage cart and dangled their legs off.

The baggage area was bright but desolate. People watched the pushing belt of suitcases and boxes. George sat on his briefcase as though it were a very small horse. The only things in it were the photograph of the little girl, a photograph of Goddard, the stuff from his sister, plus several boxes of Raisinets.

For the first time, George wished he'd held on to the money his mother left him when she died. What wasn't used to pay off debts, George had spent on thirty pairs of velvet loafers and delicate kites from China – of which not a single one remained. Of the thirty-seven kites he'd bought through the mail, about two dozen had ripped when George launched them from the New Jersey cliffs. Others had broken in mid-flight and dotted the trees of McCarren Park.

It had occurred to George that if his plane crashed, one reason might be that one of his missing kites had landed on the windshield as they tried to take off.

Everyone had collected their luggage and seemed to be walking in one direction. George followed. If there was a customs, George wasn't aware that he'd walked through it. He followed several knots of passengers down an escalator to a train platform. He felt as though he was quite deep underground, as above the tracks the ceiling seemed to be natural rock. There was not a single piece of litter on the platform, and George could hear the low buzzing of the neon sign that announced the time of the next departing train. The announcement was made in Swedish, then English.

At the station in central Stockholm, George got some money from an ATM, called a Bankomat.

With thousands of kronor in his pocket – and knowing nothing about how much meant anything – George joined the line of people waiting for taxis. There was a large man in a yellow jumpsuit directing people into cabs, which were all Volvos. There was a woman in a wheelchair in front of George who had to sit to one side while the dispatcher waited for a different kind of taxi. George wondered why someone couldn't pick her up and carry her into the car. He even thought of volunteering, but perhaps the only man allowed to carry her was her husband.

The taxi driver had a large head and thin white hair. He wore a black leather jacket that read "Taxi 150000" on the arm. He also had thick silver hoops in both ears.

At the hotel, the woman at reception informed George that he wouldn't be able to check in until 2 PM. When he sighed, she asked if he wanted to leave his luggage and go for some breakfast. It was about ten o'clock, and the sky was beginning to brighten.

As he walked along the street, it started to rain. It was light and refreshing, but then it got heavy and George was soon quite wet. He walked and walked, looking for somewhere to have coffee but passed only offices.

He wished for someone to stop him and talk. He wanted to say that it was his first day in Sweden and that he had come to see his daughter.

George wondered if it was a custom for offices at street level to have large clear windows, because they all did.

Every so often, George stopped and looked in on a board meeting or a secretary who had changed under her desk from heels to flats. Through one large window, George stood for some time in the pouring rain and watched a pretty woman with her hair tied in a bun. She was brushing the frame of an old mirror. On a shelf behind her was a small microwave with black finger marks, heaviest around the door.

When George saw a woman with a shopping bag that read "NationalMuseet" on the side, he walked in the direction from which she had come, hoping that he might find a museum where he could dry off and sit down for a while. Everything seemed to be closed.

For several hours, George simply walked around in the rain. He had never been so wet and so cold. When he finally checked into his hotel room, he took a hot bath, then sat on his bed in the hotel bathrobe. He dried his feet and held his velvet loafers under the hair dryer for half an hour.

He took the letter from his pocket and looked at the address. The area of Stockholm where she lived was called Södermalm.

He picked up the phone and dialed the number as it was written on the letter. A child answered.

"Hello?" George said.

"*Hej,*" the small voice said.

Then a few seconds of silence.

"Ma-ma," the voice said, and George heard the echo of footsteps. The woman on the other end of the line repeated her phone number in Swedish.

"It's George," George said.

"George?" the voice said.

"George Frack."

There was a faint gasp and then silence.

"Was that her?" George asked.

Just when George was about to repeat the question, he realized the woman was crying.

He heard the child say something gentle to her mother in Swedish.

"I didn't expect you to come to Sweden," Marie said.

"I know," George said.

Then Marie said something to the child, which met with a few words of protest.

"I just told her to go and wait for me in her bedroom," Marie said quietly, "because I'm going to beg you, George Frack – don't come here if it's only to see what she looks like."

"I know what she looks like," George said, glancing down at his briefcase.

"Oh," Marie said.

"Does she know who I am?"

"No," Marie said. "Though she asks me every day why she doesn't have a daddy."

"And what do you say?"

"I said nothing, until two weeks ago, when I said that you worked in America."

"Is that when you wrote to me?" George asked.

"Yes, George Frack – do you remember why?"

"Yes," George said. "Funny how we do what was done to us."

Silence again.

"After I told her, she began putting up pictures of President Bush all over her bedroom, and I realized that I had made a terrible mistake. I should have told you at the beginning."

"I'm not mad," George said quickly.

"Her name is Charlotte."

"I want her to know me," George said.

"She doesn't know you," Marie said. "And she already loves you."

Then she started crying again.

"Are you married, Marie?"

"I'm engaged. And you are married with kids I suppose, George Frack?"

"No," George said. "But I had a cat."

"You'll meet my fiancé. He's nice, quite a bit older than me – twenty years, actually. He was the one who encouraged me to write to you."

"Really? What's his name?"

"Philip."

"He sounds nice," George said.

"Can you give me a few hours to think, George? I know it's a lot to ask, but – "

"Sure. I'm staying at the Hotel Diplomat – call me when you're ready."

George hung up and lay back on his bed. He took a box of Raisinets from his briefcase and ate a handful. He then found a large envelope with the hotel name on it. In the envelope, George put his boarding pass, the chocolate he'd found balancing on his pillow, a feather that had been in his jacket pocket for years, a small thin bar of soap from the bathroom, and a drawing he'd done on the plane – of the man with the mustache.

Then George took a blue pen from the desk and wrote "Dominic Frack" on the paper. Then his sister's address.

He sat on his bed and turned the television on. Then he turned it off again.

He picked up the phone and dialed his sister's number, making sure he pressed the country code in first.

It rang and rang and rang.

George wondered if Helen was giving Dominic a bath. He imagined himself standing next to her with a towel. Dominic's shiny face. Clouds against the window. Trees outside too, and the sea not far away.

A few minutes later, the phone rang of its own accord.

"George," Marie said, "I don't want to wait because I'm afraid you'll change your mind and it will be my fault."

"Good," George said.

"Meet us at Skansen in two hours – it's a park with animals, not far from your hotel."

"Is it still raining?" George said.

"No, George, look outside."

Outside, flakes the size of buttons drifted down and settled upon the earth. People on the sidewalks had slowed to look.

Then in the background, George heard his daughter scream something in Swedish.

"Did she just say it's snowing?" George asked.

Within a couple of hours, the snow had stopped, leaving a thin layer of white across the city – just enough to catch footprints and bicycle tracks.

★   ★   ★

George took a shower. Then he shaved and brushed his teeth. He slowly dressed in his finest suit. Then he put on a brand-new pair of velvet loafers he'd brought with him. There were balls of tissue paper in the toes.

George left his hotel and walked east along the Strandvägen toward the bridge. After crossing the busy road, he came to a fork. One path held the painted outline of an adult and child walking hand in hand; the other had the painted outline of a bicycle.

It was very cold outside, and each time George exhaled, he passed through a cloud of his own life.

Skansen was a park within a park. The Djurgården, in which the park was situated, was once the king's private hunting grounds. Joggers passed in yellow spandex and thick hats. Along the water there were many boats. George guessed that they took tourists to the small, uninhabited islands around Stockholm. Most were closed for the winter, though one boat had lights on around its deck. As George approached, he saw several men working on the deck with their tools laid out next to them. As he passed, one of the men said something and waved. George smiled and waved back.

George entered the park through a blue iron arch with gold deer heads carved at the top. Birds swung from tree to tree. The path took him along the edge of another small lake. George checked the trees for the wreckage of kites. He wished he'd brought one. Ducks glided along the banks, while farther out, tall white birds cried out in the mist that lingered upon the surface of the lake.

When he reached the entrance to Skansen, George found that he was the only person there. A man with silver-rimmed glasses waved to him from the ticket office. George approached.

"One adult ticket?" the man asked.

"No, three tickets," George said. "I'm expecting a woman and a girl in an hour – and I'd like to pay for them too."

The man looked a little confused. "How will I know if they're the right people?"

"I don't know," George said.

"Is it your family?" the man said helpfully.

George nodded.

"Then I'll look out for a girl who looks like you."

George nodded and grinned a little.

"There are also two other entrances," the man added, "so if they don't come through my gate, come back before we close and I'll refund your money."

"Okay, I will," George said.

"Where are you meeting them?" the man asked.

"Somewhere, I guess." George said.

"Very good," the man said. "Well, I should tell you that Skansen was founded by Artur Hazelius in 1891."

"1891?" George said.

"I think you're going to be surprised."

"I think I'm already surprised," George said.

"That's what we like to hear," the man said. He was a cheerful sort of person.

George walked through the deserted model town that was supposed to be a miniature Sweden. There were empty workshops, empty schools, empty shops that in summer would be full of employees in period costume and Swedish children licking ice creams.

In the middle of winter, Skansen was like George's life: a world that quietly waited for people to fill it.

After a few minutes, George's loafers were covered in snowy mud. Birds circled high above the park. As he passed a plowed square of soil with a sign that read "Herbgarden," George found himself on a ridge overlooking the city of Stockholm. The sound of cars and trains echoed through the cold air as a continuous hum, broken only by the occasional call of a bird from faraway trees.

When George approached the aviary, he noticed an empty stroller. A few yards away, a small woman was holding a girl up to the bars so she could see. George looked at his watch. He wasn't supposed to meet them for another hour. As he approached, the little girl turned around as if she sensed him.

George stood still.

He looked at the girl and she looked back at him. She was the first to smile. It was the face from the photograph.

Then her mother turned and looked at George. She slipped a handkerchief from her sleeve and wiped her eyes.

"Hello," George said. But though his mouth moved, the word came out so quietly that only he heard it.

"Hello, George Frack," Marie said.

She looked much older than George remembered. Her body sagged in the middle, and her hair was flat and thin. But her eyes were still beautiful.

"*Vem är han?*" Charlotte said to her mother.

"*Han är George,*" her mother said. "*Talar engelska, Lotta.*"

"Hello," Charlotte said, turning to George. "My name is Lotta."

"My name is George."

"Would you like to come with us, George?" Lotta said.

George fought to control the trembling in his throat.

"I'd like that," he said.

And so, as Marie watched from a little way off, Lotta took

George's cold, shaky hand into her little hot hand and led him through the aviary.

"The houses here are from all over Sweden," Lotta said. "There are many wild animals too and an owl – two owls."

"Really," George said.

"What's your favorite animal, Mr. George?"

"Cats."

"Me also!" Lotta exclaimed.

Before they reached the owl enclosure, George felt dizzy. Then his legs crumpled beneath him, and he lay motionless in the mud looking up at clouds.

Lotta stood and watched, unsure of what to do. Marie rushed over. The sound of footsteps on wet earth, then George sobbing so loud that some of the animals turned to see from their cages.

After that, Lotta kept her distance from George, though every so often she would hand him a piece of candy covered in pocket-dust.

Later on, as a family of bored elk chewed straw, Lotta took George's hand again.

"Are you okay, Mr. George?" she said.

"No," George said. "I'm actually pretty freaked out."

Then Marie knelt down and held Lotta by her shoulders. The elk continued chewing behind them.

"*Lotta, George är dina pappa.*"

Lotta looked up at George.

Then her face broke apart.

"*George är dina pappa, Lotta,*" Marie shouted, shaking Lotta as if she were a lifeless doll.

George looked down at his fingers.

Lotta screamed and ran away.

Her mother shouted for her to come back.

Then George, without consciously deciding to, began to chase her. He could feel the mud splashing up his legs. He felt dizzy again, but his legs moved faster than he'd ever imagined. In the distance, a small figure rounded a corner. George followed it. He caught sight of her again, her brown hair tossed with each desperate stride. When he caught up to her, he reached out for her shoulders and they both fell into the snowy mud.

George grabbed her and held her close. He rocked her back and forth and their bodies dug a small space in the earth to cradle their weight.

An employee feeding the animals watched and then turned away with a sigh.

When Lotta reached her arms around George's neck, he could feel the heat of her mouth against his cheek. It was the weight of the entire world pressed against him in two small lips.

Even when Marie appeared, breathless – they wouldn't let go of one another.

Lotta's hair smelled like apples.

And her hands were so very small.

They left the park in darkness. The moon hung above the city like a bare knuckle. Water clapped against heavy boats and then, encircling Stockholm, re-created a city of no consequences.

Lotta was singing loudly in her stroller. She held the flag George had bought her at the museum shop. It had a cat on it.

Lotta kept turning to look at George; but her small face was hidden by shadows. George imagined her blinking eyes, her small hands under the blanket, hot breaths, the feeling of being pushed along the muddy path home.

V

A FEW DAYS LATER, ICE-SKATING at the Kungsträdgården.
Lotta is doing pirouettes on the ice. It is late. They ate dinner
at Max – Lotta's favorite hamburger restaurant. After eating a third
of her burger, Lotta had a Blizzer. She said it was very sweet, and
she made George try a few mouthfuls with a flimsy spoon. Marie's
boyfriend, Philip, joined them when he finished work. He sells
home appliances. Philip's wife left him in 1985 for another man with
whom she now lives in Gothenburg. Philip's daughter is grown up
and goes to university. Lotta likes to tease Philip by running away
with his hat.

The man who served them at Max Hamburger was cross-eyed,
so no one in the line knew whom he was talking to. Lotta thought
this was funny, even when the man glared at her (if he was glaring
at her). The restaurant had orange doors. Tired fathers drank coffee;
shopping bags balanced on the end bars of strollers. On the wall
were photographs charting the pictorial history of Max Hamburger.

The outdoor ice-skating rink was not far from the restaurant.
Clouds rubbed faintly against an early evening sky. In the distance
burned the bright neon letters of the Svenska Handelsbanken.

The streetlights were a cluster of white balls, with a single dome
of light held aloft. Many of the buildings were painted yellow.

George had never ice-skated before. Lotta pulled him around the statue that stood in the middle of the small rink watching over everything but seeing nothing.

"We're on the top of the world," Lotta shouted. "This is the North Pole!"

Marie and Philip watched from the side, their arms locked.

Then George broke away and began to skate clumsily but without falling over.

"Look at Pappa," Lotta shouted. And George knew that he had to keep going, despite the feeling that at any moment he might slip or the ground under his feet might suddenly be taken away – he had to stay up, he had to keep moving, and in time he would learn how to do it.

VI

W HEN THE COLD AT the ice rink became too much, George and Lotta changed back into their shoes, and they all found a café in which to warm up.

The city was cold and quiet but with lights everywhere.

There will be many things to sort out. George, Philip, and Marie will spend many nights drinking schnapps talking about arrangements. The four of them are convinced things can work out.

Lotta has stopped wetting her bed. She wonders what New York looks like. She wonders if she will ever look down from a skyscraper at all the people. She has put a photo of Goddard next to her bedside lamp. Her favorite David Bowie song is "Life on Mars?"

On the subway back to Lotta's house in Södermalm, Lotta tells George about the old boat that was found in Stockholm harbor.

She tells him how in 1628, the most beautiful ship ever made sank before it could get out to sea. And then over three hundred years later, somebody decided to find it and bring it back to life.

Lotta wants to know if they have museums in New York. George tells her there are many. She asks if there is a cat museum. George tells her that he wishes there were one.

Then he thinks about the idea of a museum: the physical record of things; the history of miracles; the miracle of nature and the miracle of hope and perseverance, arranged in such a way as to never be forgotten, or lost, or simply mistaken for everyday things with no particular significance.

Part Two

The Secret Lives of People in Love

To Maddie

… we could all be rejects in a rejected world and never know or dream that simultaneously the chosen flourish elsewhere in a perfect world.

JANET FRAME

The Carpathians

Little Birds

THIS MORNING I WOKE up and was fifteen years old. Each year is like putting a new coat over all the old ones. Sometimes I reach into the pockets of my childhood and pull things out.

When Michel gets home from his shop he said we are going out to celebrate – maybe to a movie or the McDonald's on boulevard Voltaire. Michel is not my real father. He grew up in Paris and did a spell in prison. I think he was used to being alone, but we've lived together so long now, I'm not sure he could survive without me.

We live in Paris, and I think I was born here, but I may never know for sure. Everyone thinks I'm Chinese, and I look Chinese, but Michel says I'm more French than bread.

It is the afternoon of my birthday, but still the morning of my life. I am walking on the Pont des Arts. It is a small wooden bridge, and Americans sit in colorful knots drinking wine. Even though I'm only fifteen and have not had a girlfriend as such, I can tell who is in love with who when I look at people.

A woman in a wheelchair is being pushed across the bridge by her husband. They are in love. Only the back wheels move across each plank. He tilts the chair toward him as though his body is drinking from hers. I wish he could see her face. She clings to a small cloud of tissue. They look Eastern European. I can tell this because they are well dressed but their clothes are years out of style. I'd like to think this is their first time in Paris. I can imagine him later on, straining to lift her from the chair in their gray hotel room with its withering curtains swollen by wind. I can picture her in his arms. He will set her in the bed as though it were a slow river.

A filthy homeless man is squatting with the American tourists and telling jokes in broken English. He is not looking at the girls' shaved legs but at the unfinished bottle of wine and sullen wedge of cheese. The Americans seem good-natured and pretend to laugh; I suppose the key to a good life is to gently overlook the truth and hope that at any moment we can all be reborn.

The Pont des Arts is wooden, and if you look through the slats, you can see boats passing beneath. Sometimes small bolts of lightning shoot from the boats as tourists take pictures of one another, and sometimes they just aim the cameras at nothing in particular and shoot – I like these kinds of photographs best, not that I have a camera – but if I did, I would randomly take pictures of nothing in particular. How else could you record life as it happens.

Michel works in a shop on the place Pigalle. Outside the shop is a flashing arrow with the word *Sexy* in red neon. Michel has had the shop since I can remember. I am forbidden to visit him there, though sometimes I watch him at his desk from the street corner. He likes to read a poet called Giorgio Caproni, who is dead, but Michel says that his words are like little birds that follow him around and sing in his ear.

If you saw Michel, you might cross the street because he has a deep scar that runs from his mouth all the way across his cheek. He told me he got it wrestling crocodiles in Mississippi, but I'm fifteen now and just humor him.

He has a friend called Léon, who sometimes stays the night with us because if he drinks too much, his wife won't let him into the apartment – though he always makes an effort to explain how his wife has beautiful dreams and that he doesn't want to wake her with his clumsiness. One night, while Michel was in the bathroom, Léon told me how Michel's face came to be scarred.

"Before you lived with Michel," he said breathlessly, "there was a terrible fight outside his shop. Naturally Michel rushed outside and tried to break it up." He paused and slid a small bottle of brandy from his shirt pocket. We each took a sip, then he pulled my ear through the brandy fumes to his mouth. "He was trying to save a young prostitute from being beaten, but the police arrived too late and then the idiots arrested Michel – she choked to her death on her own – " But then we heard Michel's footsteps in the hallway and the words disappeared forever, lost in the wilderness of a drunk.

Michel would throttle Léon if he knew that he'd told me this much, because he tries to pretend that I don't know anything and that when I get into the Sorbonne, which is the oldest university in Paris, I'll leave this life behind and visit him only at Christmas with gifts purchased at the finest stores on avenue Montaigne and Champs-Élysées. "You don't even have to wrap them," Michel once marveled. "The girls are happy to do it right there in the shop."

I like to stroll around Notre-Dame, which is on its own private island. I like to see tourists marvel at the curling beauty of the stone frame. It reminds me of a wedding cake that is too beautiful to eat – though perpetually hungry pigeons know the truth, because hundreds of them drip from the dirty white ledges, pecking at the marble with their brittle beaks.

Sometimes tourists go in and pray for things. When I was very young, Michel used to kneel at my bedside when he thought I was asleep. I would hear him praying to God on my behalf. He referred to me as peanut, so I'm not sure if God knew who he was talking about – but if there is a God, then he probably knows everything and that my real name is not peanut.

After smoking on the steps of Notre-Dame and making eyes at an Italian girl posing for her boyfriend, I am now in the Jardin des Plantes. Michel and I have been coming here on Sunday since I can remember. Once I fell asleep on the grass and Michel filled my pockets with flowers. Today I am fifteen and I'm taking stock of my life. Even though I want to go to university and eventually buy Michel a red convertible, when I think of those Sundays in the Jardin des Plantes, I want to do things for people *they* will never forget. Maybe that's the best I can do in life. It is cloudy, but flowers have burst open.

It's amazing how they contain all that color within those thin, withering segments.

Michel's shop sells videos and now DVDs of mostly naked women having sex with all and sundry. Michel said that sex is sometimes different from love, and he never brings anything home; he said that what happens on the Pigalle, stays on the Pigalle. Sometimes when I watch him from the street, prostitutes walk by and ask me if I'm okay. I tell them I have a friend in the industry, and they laugh and offer me cigarettes. I'm friends with one prostitute in particular, her name is Sandrine and she says she is old enough to be my grandmother. She wears a shiny plastic skirt and very little on top. I can't stand in the doorway with her because it's bad for business. The skin on her legs is like leather, but she is very down-to-earth. She knows Michel and told me that he was once in love with one of the girls, but that nothing ever came of it. I tried to get the name of the girl when I was twelve, hoping that I could bring them together, but Sandrine took my head in her hands and very quietly told me that the girl was dead and that's the end.

I would like to know more about this girl because Michel has never had a girlfriend, so she must have been something special. Sandrine sometimes buys me a book and leaves it with one of the other girls if she's working. The last one she gave me was called *The Man Who Planted Hope and Grew Happiness*.

On this cloudy afternoon of my fifteenth birthday, I can see Michel sitting at the counter reading. If he knew I was here, he would be angry and express it by not talking to me for a day or so. It would put him in no mood to go out tonight, birthday or no birthday. I watch from within a crowd of shadows. Michel is reading. In Michel's books of Caproni's poetry, he has written his own little poems in the margins. Once, in a foolish moment, I opened one of his books and began to read one; he snatched the book from me and it ripped. We were both very upset.

He told me that his poems were not meant for me – that they were little flocks of birds intended to keep the other birds company. When I asked him who the poems were for, his eye pushed out a solitary tear that was rerouted by his scar.

He finishes work in four hours. He'll be expecting to find me at home watching TV ready to go out. He said I can go anywhere I want tonight, but times are hard. I think he has bought me new sneakers because I saw a Nike shoebox under his bed when I was vacuuming. I didn't open it. I like not knowing.

I know he's been saving for this night for the last two months. In the cupboard under the sink is a wine bottle full of money. When neighbors hear glass breaking in Michel's apartment they know someone is having a birthday. The neighbors like him, though it takes everyone a while to get used to his scar and the fact he's been in prison.

We live in the 11th arrondissement. The districts curl around Paris like a snail's shell. Sandrine is not in her doorway yet or perhaps she has already found some business. Michel serves the customers while balancing a cigarette between his lips. He rolls his own and tips back his head to exhale.

Walking home, I always like to pass the Pompidou Centre. If you've never seen it, you may think that it's under construction, but that's the way it was built, and you can see inside through giant glass walls. I like to watch tourists threading their way through its body like ants in a colony. Outside is a gold pot the size of a bread van. No one has ever planted anything in it, so it's probably just for show.

Michel has told me that today's my fifteenth birthday, but he doesn't know for sure. No one does. The story of how we met is an interesting one.

Michel says that before he found me, he was a very bad man, but that I changed all that. On the day he got out of prison, he says he was on the Metro, and I must have been about three – or that's what he says. He says everything happened in a split second. The doors of the train closed, and there I was, looking at him. He says my parents were standing on the platform banging on the glass of the door and screaming. He says I must have stepped onto the train by myself and then the doors closed before they could get to me. I often ask him what my parents look like, and he looks very sad. He says that they were the most elegant people he'd ever seen. He says my mother was an Asian princess and wore the finest furs with lipstick so red her lips seemed to be on fire.

Michel said that her long black hair curled about the edges of her face, as though it were too intimidated by her beauty to go near her features. He says my father was a tall American with one of the most expensive suits that had ever been made. Michel says he looked like a powerful man, but so handsome that his strength played second fiddle. He says they wept and pounded on the glass like children; he says that he had never seen people in so much anguish.

Michel says I began crying as soon as the train started moving and that he remained on the train until the final stop to see what would happen to me. He says he took me home and that I cried for a year about as often as it rained. He says the neighbors came over in one group to find out what was going on. When I was older I became angry with Michel for not finding my parents, and I imagined them living in a palace in New York, which they kept in darkness until they found me, their only child. Michel told me that he searched for them for a week without sleep or food but later discovered they'd been killed in a plane crash outside Buenos Aires. In my wallet I keep a map of Argentina that I ripped out of a library book. Sometimes I trace my finger across the city and wonder where their plane went down.

When I was nine, Michel gave me the option of going into an orphanage but explained how he had grown up in one and they were not pleasant.

I love to ride the Metro, even though gangs of Algerian boys sometimes spit at me. When the train pulls into the station where Michel found me, I often look around frantically. I can't help myself. Michel says they were the finest and gentlest people he had ever seen and that I would grow up to be just like them. One of Sandrine's prostitute friends once said I looked just like Annie Lee, and Sandrine slapped her, which shut her up. Maybe I'll ask Sandrine who Annie Lee was when I'm older.

Our apartment in the 11th is quite basic. All the windows open into a courtyard of other windows. With the lights out, I can see people's lives unfold. A person's life is a slow flash, and I watch my neighbors argue, make up, make love, and fry meat. I can tell that one of my neighbors is unhappy, because he sits by the telephone and sometimes picks it up to make sure he can hear a dial tone, but it never rings when he's at home. Michel says his wife left him, and if there's ever a time I can't think of anyone to pray for, I should pray for him.

I can hear Michel's key churning the lock.

"Happy Birthday, peanut!" are the first words out of his mouth. He kisses me on both cheeks and tells me to get ready. I switch off the television and look for my dirty sneakers behind the door. They're not there. Michel lights a cigarette with a chuckle.

"Go and look under my bed," he says.

I was right, and I shout something from the bedroom so he knows I've found them. He wants to know how they fit. I love the smell of new shoes.

I'm looking forward to having an American hamburger tonight – the same kind my father probably used to relish. Maybe we'll see an American movie. *Men in Black II* is playing all over Paris. As I press Play on my stereo and look at my face in the mirror, I hear a smash from the kitchen and a couple of the neighbors cheer through open windows.

Michel knocks and then pokes his head around the door.

"Prêt?" he says, and I say let's go then.

We walk arm in arm through twilight. Paris never gets too dark, because when natural light dissolves, you're never too far from a streetlamp – and they're often beautiful – set upon tall black stalks, each lamp a glowing pair of white balls in love with its very own length of street. Sometimes, they all flicker to life at the same time, as if together they can hold off darkness.

I can tell that Michel wants to hold my hand, but I'm much too old for that now, and instead he smokes and tells me that no matter where I go in life, I'll be thought highly of.

I wonder if Michel is a famous poet. My teacher at school told me that poets come from all walks of life and that their gift is God-given. I wonder if people will flock to Michel's grave at Père-Lachaise Cemetery a hundred years from now. I wonder if they'll leave their own poems at the foot of his tombstone and then talk to him and maybe thank him for his little birds, which sing to them in moments of darkness.

Michel pays for the movie tickets with change from the wine bottle. The girl doesn't seem to mind. Her left eye is off-center. She slides Michel the tickets without counting the coins. She studies his scar as we slip past her glass box. Michel hands the tickets to the usher. He rips them in two. Michel tells me to save the stubs, so I open my wallet and the map of Argentina falls out. Michel quickly picks it up and looks at it without unfolding it. I snatch it from him and shove it back into my wallet.

"Peanut's little birds." He laughs.

Then we find our seats in the darkness and disappear into the film.

The Reappearance of Strawberries

EIGHT STORIES ABOVE THE infamous rue de Vaugirard, the man in the ninth bed of the Bonnard Hospital ward had requested nothing but strawberries for several days. For most of that Tuesday afternoon all that could be heard were the tiny hands and feet of rain against the window.

While most of the patients disappeared into a medicated sleep, Pierre-Yves lay awake, aware that he was dying. Beside his bed was a bowl of strawberries that he was unable to reach out and touch. Whenever he imagined their sweetness, he remembered her and shuddered. They were piled up in a heavy yellow bowl.

Pierre-Yves breathed deeply in an attempt to bury the scent in his lungs, while outside on the street below he imagined taxis, filled with cigarette smoke, lunging between traffic lights. During his first night in the hospital, after falling over in a square populated by hundreds of pigeons, a memory brushed against him.

As light visits an attic through a crack in the roof, turning the dust to stars, she had appeared, not moments before her death as in dreams, but as he longed to remember her – staring across the river, quiet and charmingly obtuse. He could have taken her to America, he knew that now.

He observed how each raindrop united with its closest other and then, split open by its own weight, ran down the glass in one even corridor. Even after her family was killed, he did nothing – not one thing.

Without memory, he thought, man would be invincible.

As Pierre-Yves lifted himself into the past, he knew that he would not make it back to the present – to the rain and to the ward – but hoped he would make it as far as the garden, which wrapped itself around the cottage and trembled, as summer had trembled and pushed strawberries into the world.

As dusk began to drift through the hospital and unmoor the world with shadows, he remembered when she had told him of her uncle who taught her to ride a bicycle down steps and of the flowers she used to keep in a basket strapped to the handlebars. She had told him this one summer, the hottest either of them had ever known. They had escaped the sultry, slow pulsation of Paris to a small cottage owned by her grandmother. It was the sort of house that appeared to have risen from the earth. Ivy curled across the stone walls in thick vines, and roses sang their way as high as the upstairs window.

The Loire flowed coolly half a kilometer to the west and changed to a tongue of gold when the sun sank beneath randomly dotted haystacks in distant fields.

One afternoon, beside the velvet slowness of the Loire, they had found a meadow and spread a blanket between fists of wildflowers. Pierre-Yves remembered how she had talked a great deal about when she was a girl. She had explained how when she was very young, she believed that when she stepped in a puddle, a wish was granted. For the slow, lugubrious years after the war, Pierre-Yves never forgot this and would close his umbrella in a rainstorm so he could cry freely as he negotiated a path home.

At that moment, while the hospital ward was dipped in deepest night, he felt a duty to slip away from the meadow and again witness her final moments and the accompanying numbness. Though as the sound of soldiers' boots began to echo, and the smell of burning stung his eyes, he suddenly became aware of a sweet scent, a compelling bouquet hovering around him. The image of the infamous rue de Vaugirard, which was riddled with bullet holes back then, suddenly withdrew, and she was asleep within his sleep, in the garden behind the cottage – a fan of her hair upon his chest.

He watched the rise and fall, seduced by the mystery and delicacy of her weight against him. As the sky swelled and bruises drifted above the garden casting shadows, he picked a strawberry and held it below her nose. She opened her eyes and bit into it. He sensed something lingering and held her tightly.

As the flowers entered the mouth of the storm and began to shrivel, so did Pierre-Yves. And in the early hours of the morning, as he stopped breathing, a recently married nurse who had been watching him since dawn took a strawberry from the heavy yellow bowl and gently slipped it between his lips. In a dull office overlooking the Seine, the nurse's husband was thinking about her elbows, and how they make tiny hollows in the grass as she reads.

As Much Below as Up Above

I AM SITTING ON A beach, half on my bodyboard and half on the sand. I am surrounded by people who have made little camps with towels and rainbow-colored umbrellas.

It is quite hot, but a cool wind blows from the north. I am in my bathing suit, sitting on a foam bodyboard I bought at the concession stand in the parking lot. My fat hangs down as though it is trying to escape my body. I should exercise, if not to reduce the size of my belly, then for my heart.

The sea looks different in America, but I am still unable to brave the blind laugh of white foam.

All seas are one sea. Every ocean holds hands with another. Although I have a job in Brooklyn, and I even have a girlfriend called Mina, part of my soul is in Russia. If I can brave the sea one last time – just up to my chest – I know that I may be reunited with myself.

I came out to the beach alone today. Mina thinks I am at work. She only knows half the story of what happened so long ago. I suppose I only know half the story, too, as I am alive today and not in that metal case on the seabed. I can honestly tell you that I haven't had a solid night of sleep since the accident. I dream they are all still alive down there, and my brain begins to conjure fantastic ways of rescuing them.

A young couple sit down not far from where I am sitting. The young man is carrying a surfboard. He looks over and nods.

"A little cold with that wind, huh," he says – or asks, because my English is not perfect. I smile broadly and wave as a way of having nothing to say without offending his gesture. You have to do this with Americans because they are friendly, sometimes too much, but this is a noble failing in the culture. I love the summers here and am so white that people must look at me. Mina says I should apply a cream that protects you from the sun, from burning and from the cancer, but I cannot fear something that is not immediately danger-ous. Mina calls me a stubborn pig and sometimes she is right, but I am trying to adjust. Sometimes I think my dreams are real memories and my life with Mina must be heaven. Maybe I am in heaven and don't know it.

The young couple next to me have set out some chairs, and some of their friends have arrived. They all look different and are very kind to one another. They seem very happy to be here. A girl with the tattoo of a butterfly on her shoulder has just run down to the sea. She is diving into the waves, which wall up and then crash down upon her submerged body. Some of the young people have smiled at me and I have smiled back. I wonder if they think I am crazy, sitting on a foam bodyboard alone on such a beautiful day. I wonder if they are disgusted by how fat and white I am. I am glad they are close. They distract me from my friends' hands, which poke out from the waves – not calling me back, but waving me off.

If you can imagine bare mountains and a crisp blue sky, then you can see the view from the bedroom I was born in back in Russia. My father worked in a factory that made doors, and our house had the mountains to the back while the front overlooked the leaf-green sea, which was calm and deep. When my father and I used to row out to sea on bright summer mornings, after a mile or so, he would say, "There is as much below as there is above – so don't fall in, my little son."

The farther out we went, the darker the sea became. My father explained how the fish we hauled up from the deep broke the surface like lightning because they had never seen the light. Imagine living in total darkness, until one day you are torn from your world into a beautiful and cold landscape you never imagined existed.

Russia was different when I was a child, and I thought I would work in the same factory as my father. You may not believe me, but to a child, the factory was a beautiful place because there were always thousands of different kinds of doors sitting out in the sun, waiting for the trucks from Moscow.

I used to think when I was very young that each door led to a different village and to a different life. I wondered how many souls would pass through my father's doors in their lifetime, and later, as a teenager, I imagined couples closing the doors and then making love in moonlit rooms.

I was proud of my father's job because it was work for the good of the people. Once I had a dream that I was on an American beach not unlike the one I am on now. In the dream I fell asleep on the hot sand, and when I awoke, the people had all been replaced by my father's doors. Imagine that – a beach with no people, just a thousand doors, all freestanding in their frames.

When the government in Moscow changed, the factory closed, my father died, and I joined the Russian navy.

I think I'm going to ask my girlfriend Mina to marry me. She was born in Florida. She likes to hear the stories about my father, because her own was no good. I think she will say yes, but I shouldn't assume that, because I am gruff with her sometimes, and I find it hard to tell her my true feelings. Out of everyone in the whole world I believe she is the most important person.

The young men next to me are in the water, and the girls are watching. The onshore waves are as big as wardrobes, and I can see that some of the young men are frightened. The girls are frightened, too, but the scene still takes place.

During my first five years in the navy, I was taught how to fire missiles from a submarine. It was exciting because the submarine would shudder with each launch. It was quite an important job because everything had to be perfectly synchronized or the missile would not reach its intended target. On firing days, none of us dared sneak vodka into the launch room.

It wasn't a bad life. I remember having some very nice experiences with my friends in different ports. There were always girls who liked our uniforms more than they liked us. I was so young and nowhere near as fat as I am now. When my submarine was to be decommissioned we were all quite sad. It was our workplace, after all, and we had grown quite fond of it.

I met Mina at a Russian restaurant in Queens where I was a bartender. She was there with her friends for a birthday party. They seemed like very nice American girls, and I enjoyed having their laughter within earshot. I was fired from my job as a bartender at the restaurant on the night I met Mina. It was actually because of an incident with Mina's friend, but I didn't mind because Mina had written her telephone number on a piece of paper and then looked at me with eyes as big as teacups.

It is strange how some of the Russians I know don't like Americans but choose to live here. I think that their bitterness has more to do with themselves and that if they were back in Russia, they would find something there to complain about.

As Mina and her friends drank more and more wine, they became louder and even knocked a glass off the table. But they were such a jovial bunch that I didn't mind – it actually reminded me of the long nights with my comrades, when our K-159 submarine was the pride of the Russian navy.

When one of the Russian men at the bar began to talk about Mina's group, I tried not to listen. Mina's friends were not the only people in the restaurant drinking heavily that night. When the girls ordered coffee and chocolates, one of the drunken men at the bar began saying sexual things in Russian about Mina and her friends. I went into the back and washed glasses and tried to forget it because all men become pigs when they drink.

As the restaurant emptied I went back to my bar and started tidying up for the night. One of Mina's friends wanted one last drink, which I gave to her on the house, because I liked them and hoped they would come back.

As she turned around and started back to the table, the man at the bar who had been saying things took hold of her arm and she spilled the drink. He then began to say terrible sexual things in Russian, but in a smiling way so the woman thought he was being friendly. As she smiled and tolerated his drunkenness, I could not believe what he was saying to her. I poured two drinks and set them down on the bar loudly. I told the man in Russian that he should let her go. He looked at me stupidly, as though he wanted to say something but couldn't remember what.

He knocked back the drink, and then as the woman reached for hers, he grabbed it and tipped its contents down the front of her dress.

He was a grisly man, but remember – I had been in the Russian navy for over ten years, so I picked him up by his throat and dragged him outside. As I was doing it, I remember feeling intense pity for him, but when I went back into the restaurant and saw the woman crying, those feelings went away.

The man shouted things from the street, then went home. He was a friend of the owner, and within ten minutes, the owner himself telephoned and told me to take what I was owed from the till and to never come back. As he shouted through the telephone, about how I was a criminal and a disgrace, I lit a cigarette and watched the prettiest girl of the bunch approach my bar, say thank-you, and begin to write her telephone number on the top of a matchbook. I was reluctant to take it at first, because in the navy I had met many girls who were attracted to violence and they all turned out to be crazy. It was when she looked at me with those teacup eyes that I felt as though she would have given me her number anyway.

Two South American men worked at the restaurant as waiters, and I was friendly with them. They cleaned up the mess, patted me on the back, and said they would have done the same thing. The remaining men at the bar pretended to ignore everything and talked among themselves in hushed voices. They had laughed at the terrible things the man had said and were probably ashamed.

Despite all the fights and heroic acts I performed as a soldier in the Russian navy, I cannot bring myself to take this cheap foam bodyboard and step into the ocean. I am also very thirsty and have a headache. The young men are all back safely from the surf, and because of this I am trying my best not to start weeping – right here on the beach in front of everyone.

All the young men beside me are back safe, and the girls have wrapped them in towels.

A few months after our submarine was decommissioned, we were ordered to tow it out to a given location and then to sink it. By that time we had resigned ourselves to the loss and wanted to get it over with so we could move on to something else. The captain had told us that he was trying his best to keep us together as a unit wherever we were sent. Some of the other units had been sent to fight in the Chechnyan campaign. We had heard rumors of the horrors that were taking place on both sides, but our attitude remained positive: as long as we remained together, we were invincible. There were eight of us in total who drove and fired the submarine. About a hundred other sailors joined us for official cruising, but the eight of us were able to operate it without support. When we had to take the submarine for maintenance, each of us would bring whiskey or vodka down into the metal belly and we would drink a little en route. The captain turned a blind eye. We were one of the only units who could single-handedly operate a sub over short distances. The maintenance men used to call us "a skeleton crew."

I remember the morning of the accident very clearly, so clearly, in fact, it seems strange that I can't intervene and try and stop what happened. The sky was a cold, deep blue, and we could look out to sea for miles. It was freezing cold. We had fish for breakfast. Awaiting orders, we huddled together and smoked.

Dimitri – my best friend – had told us he wanted to get married, and we all thought he was crazy. Several men in yellow overalls waved to us from a tugboat moored a few hundred yards out to sea. They were going to tow us to the given location and, after the sub was sunk, bring us back on their boat. We were supposed to pilot the old sub while it was towed and then climb onto the tug before they detached the line. Even though it was strictly forbidden to drink while on duty, we had several bottles of vodka hidden in our packs so we'd be able to drink a toast to the old boat as it made its way to a watery grave.

As we lined up and were inspected by our superiors, the captain said, "We need a man on the tug to help with the lines." I remember this so clearly.

As I was on the end of the line, he pointed to me and said, "You – go down to the water – there is a boat that will take you to the tug."

I did as I was told, despite my bitter disappointment at being deprived of the last voyage and the farewell drinking.

The men on the tugboat were as tough as any of us. We shook hands and smoked, then watched my friends climb into the sub. It may seem strange, but as the hatch was closed, I felt a tingling at the bottom of my spine, the same feeling I felt as I watched my father – drunk as anything – row out to sea and never come back.

Four hours into our journey, the tugboat bolted ahead violently. I was standing at the front watching the bow cut through the icy black water. When the tug lurched forward, I fell back into some ropes, and although I didn't know it at the time, my arm snapped in two places. When I heard shouting from the stern of the boat, I rushed back, and as I looked out to sea, I saw the towline floating on the surface of the water. After a few minutes of chaos, the captain told us to sit down, that there was nothing we could do, that by now the K-159 was at least a mile deep and still sinking.

I shall never forget the faces of the men on the tug as we all smoked and waited for orders from our superiors. When they looked at me, it was with a softness I had never seen before in men, other than in my father's eyes when I'd wake up in the middle of the night to find him standing over my bed with a candle.

I shall never forget the terrible shame I felt sitting on the tug as my closest friends sank at a terrifying speed.

As if sensing my desire to fall into the sea, two of the tug men came over and placed themselves on either side of me. They gave me vodka and didn't say a word.

As we waited for orders, the captain tried to maintain radio contact, but something must have damaged the equipment, and he only picked up static. Sometimes, when I am driving alone in my car at night, I'll pull off the road into an empty parking lot and tune my car radio to static.

The newspapers claimed the tragedy was simple and nobody was to blame. The line by which the sub was attached had snapped, and the disabled sub had not the power to climb to the surface of the water.

The British sent help almost immediately, but a storm made any rescue attempt impossible. It's hard for anyone to say how long they survived. It would have been pitch-black and freezing cold. The worst thing is that they all would have known that a rescue was impossible.

I wonder what they thought about. I know they mentioned me and were glad I wasn't with them. I wonder if any of them secretly wished that they had been at the end of the line and picked to help on the tug. I bet that Dimitri, my best friend, thanked God for sparing my life. I know he kept a photograph of his girlfriend with him at all times, and I can bet he held it close as he perished.

I've often lain awake while Mina sleeps and prayed for Dimitri to give me a sign that he is okay; perhaps, like the fish my father and I used to yank up from the dark sea, he has found himself reborn in some bright place. I wonder if they drank the vodka – I suppose it would have helped to keep them warm. For Dimitri's funeral, his girlfriend and I, along with his parents, chose some of his personal effects and buried them along with photographs. His mother had watched me throughout the service, which included full naval honors. I know why she looked at me, because I still asked myself the same question.

After the funeral, I told Dimitri's girlfriend what he told us on the morning we set out – that he was going to ask her to marry him. She slapped me and has never spoken to me since. Whatever I did wrong, I hope I can be forgiven.

Mina knows that my best friend was killed back in Russia, but not the whole story. I will tell her one day, and if she holds me tight and thanks God, then I'll know I should definitely marry her and will probably ask her right then and there. I think we can have a nice life together in Queens or on Long Island.

I want to take my bodyboard into the water, not for myself, nor for my comrades, but for Mina. I want to surf along the lip of one of those waves; I want the sea to carry my unceasing love to their still bodies, I want the sea to tell them I've found someone I want to marry and that I have to say good-bye – but that I'll try and keep them going by remembering our good times together – at least for as long as I am alive.

Most of all, I want to believe that being picked to help on the tug was no accident. I want to feel it somehow happened like that because things happen for a reason. I want to believe this more than anything, because if it were just an accident, then God must have died before he could finish the world.

Not the Same Shoes

I T WAS PAST MIDNIGHT when he reached the old mine entrance. The rain had stopped. Puddles were silvered by moonlight. Water weighed down clumps of his hair, which sat upon his forehead like small black anchors.

The ground of Edmonson County had not been mined since Kentucky was divided by the Civil War. The structure around the entrance to the mine was a tangle of girders strangled by ivy. There were rotting coal wagons fused by rust to lengths of track.

The air was thick and humid. Plumes of his white breath rose into the darkness. Broken glass, like fallen stars, crunched beneath his shoes. His shoes – full of holes – were the shoes she had plucked from the shop shelf years ago.

"How handsome," she had said all those years ago at the store. He had stood at the mirror slightly bowlegged, his eyes askew as they both peered at the crooked body to which the shoes were attached.

"How handsome in those shoes," she had said as they bounced their way home in the truck, such a long time ago.

He bent his way past the old bunkers, farther into the night, past ghost miners gossiping over tin cups. He remembered the photographs she kept under her bed, the honey-colored portraits of ancestors. Welsh choirs, bearded men in tunics, and women's heads poking out from rings of white linen, coal-dusted cheeks against leaden skies, the first car in town, gas lamps in doorways.

He stepped over a collapsed wall. He continued walking until the rocks and broken glass beneath became a carpet of grass and then a meadow. The meadow sloped unevenly toward a river, as though slowly tipping its contents into the gushing tongue of water.

He stopped here and listened.

The low hissing of the river. His own breathing. Wind rushing between stems of wet grass.

They had just spent that afternoon together, soaking each other up after six years of not one word. No matter where he went, he had been unable to escape Edmonson County because it was her home and it haunted him; the fiddling of crickets; the smell of a hot night; a clear, cool pond – his senses had conspired to bring him back.

Now, on a sloping meadow hours into a fresh day, he found himself a desperate man, struggling to free himself from the shackles of a life he had not pursued. And her voice trickled through him, an icicle perpetually melting.

She was curiously delighted to see him that day when he showed up after six years. She was working at the same place. She did not act surprised, as if for all that time he had been hiding somewhere close by. They drove through town in her small truck. Roofs were being hammered, children kicked stones, she slipped off her shoes to drive.

In the country not far from her house, a heavy pink mist swallowed up the legs of cows and the trunks of trees. After miles along dusty narrow roads, they pulled into her driveway and parked next to a claw-foot bathtub filled with dry leaves. Several dogs scrambled off the porch tossing their limbs and barking. They ran in circles around the truck.

He watched her walk barefoot across the driveway and then followed her into the house. As he stepped onto the porch, a line of cats' heads appeared at the screen door and then disappeared when the thunder of dogs approached.

As he peeled open the screen door, he noticed small cats poised before him, watching his movements intently, as if he had inadvertently set foot upon the stage of a feline theater. The cats lounged on shelves, atop the refrigerator, and on stairs. Like strange mechanical toys, they raised their paws and swiveled their heads. The ones adrift on the floor were curled up and listened to their mistress in the kitchen as she skated a tall spoon around a glass of iced tea. The dogs bounded toward him again, salivating. Several of the cats were trodden on and hissed.

She stirred the iced tea and sang. Then he stirred it as she sat down and asked questions about his life. He stirred the tea until they were both silent – as though from its sugary bottom, something delicate had risen and usurped language.

Neither of them was married, and this gave the illusion that little had changed. With the glass of iced tea in his hand, he almost confessed everything.

Years ago, they were engaged to be married, but one day he left.

He forgot why he had left long before he realized that she could not be forgotten, that the boundary of their intimacy was impossible to cross.

Displayed on a lone shelf with English paperback novels was an old pickax with her granddaddy's initials, M.L. He contemplated that he was sitting on top of the him that had never left – a him that had not been away for six years, a him that was running over in his head how much money the tobacco crop might yield and how much help he would need hanging it.

In between talk were pockets of silence, in which he mused upon the confusing dichotomy before him. How easy, he thought, it would be to stay, to make this my chair. How accustomed I could become to the animals, why, after a day or so I would know their names and could call them for supper. He peered out to the porch and saw how it could be improved – making a mental note of tools for the job.

It was soon time to feed the dogs, and he offered to help – a way to continue the illusion of an everyday life. When the biggest dog rose from crusty folds of blankets, there lay a pair of shoes, a little chewed but intact. As he pulled them out, he remembered how she had chosen them in the shop.

She saw him holding them and turned away.

"They're not the same shoes," she said.

"They sure look the same – the ones you picked out."

"Not those, honey." The words shivered as they fell from her mouth. "They're not yours anymore."

After slipping the shoes onto his feet, replacing them with the ones he'd arrived in as a gesture of fairness, the light in the house dimmed and he followed her singing to the backyard. She was standing beside a tree from which two swings hung off the same branch.

"Swing," she said sadly, the hard blue of her eyes glistening. And so they swung for their lives, the end of the branch above like an old finger, cutting out a circle of dusk.

*   *   *

As morning flooded the meadow below with light and then shape, he pictured her back at the house asleep on the porch in a rocker, golden cords of her hair adrift on bare shoulders.

They are the same shoes, he thought, the ones she picked.

And he listened because wind was filling the old mine as though deep underground in silence and in darkness, the earth once more had grown rich and waited for the clumsy but devoted hands of men.

Where They Hide Is a Mystery

S INCE HIS MOTHER'S FUNERAL, Edgar had begun to walk alone through the park. When he was a baby, she pushed him along its many paths. In the afternoons she read books to him, and though he couldn't talk then, she knew he was listening, and he remembered her voice. When she died, his childhood split open beneath his feet.

His father, a handsome, stern man who smelled of smoke and cologne, had forbidden Edgar to leave the apartment without a grown-up, but his father generally stayed at the office until late into the night. Edgar knew he would not be missed.

Slipping out past Stan the doorman was not difficult. Stan liked a drink and would disappear every couple of hours for fifteen minutes, after which he'd sit in his room and try to appear as sober as possible, which made him look even more drunk.

Once Edgar crossed Fifth Avenue, he followed a path far into the woods. On entering the park, he often saw tourists having their portraits made, fire jugglers, slow games of chess, forlorn secretaries, and the homeless who gathered in groups to debate the weather in loud voices.

Nestled between a sycamore tree and a cluster of lilac bushes, there was a bench where his mother had told him secrets.

"Without you," she had once said, "the world would be incomplete."

The bench was not particularly ornate. It was small and wooden and in the rain would soften and grow dark.

Edgar had overheard his father say on the telephone that he would never get over his wife's death but that he would just learn to live with it. Stan the doorman had told Edgar that she was in a better place, but Edgar could not imagine anywhere better than the park, especially in spring when the lilacs – like tiny bombs – burst open and spill their fragrance upon a carpet of crabgrass.

Around the legs of the bench were clusters of tea-rose bushes, which his mother called Peter Pan roses, on account of their refusal to grow into the soft, many-layered cups of their cousins.

Not long after she was diagnosed, she would – despite the doctors' instructions – sneak out with Edgar, and they would stroll very slowly through the park. After three months, she could only walk with the help of a cane, and as she walked, she balanced upon it like a tired acrobat. When her wrists and ankles grew tiny and she could no longer leave the apartment, Edgar wrapped the cane in Christmas paper and put it under his bed. It had bent slightly by supporting her. It was crooked with the weight of her love.

A week after she died, Edgar was awakened by the sound of his father cleaning out her closet. Through a cracked bedroom door, he watched his father angrily scoop out her sweaters, skirts, underwear, and socks, and then put them into trash bags. On his walks through the park after school, Edgar would remember the sound clothes hangers had made sliding across the pole of her closet, and the breathlessness of his father – the agony of being left behind.

Edgar was angry with his father for disposing of his mother's clothes as if they were copies of old Sunday papers, but they never exchanged any words about it; in fact, they never spoke to one another except about school or work.

The morning after his father cleared everything out, Edgar had untied the string on one of the bags and rescued a sweater. It was under his bed with the cane and a birthday present he had been unable to open. A small card attached to the gift read: "I know you won't forget me."

On the wrapping paper were drawings of Peter Pan roses.

Edgar drifted farther away from his father. They communicated through silence that flowed between them like a river. In the months that followed her death, the river widened, until Edgar's father was a motionless speck in a wrinkled suit watching him, arms akimbo, from the opposite bank.

Sneaking out past Stan the doorman, and then sinking into the lush green of the park was the only activity that bore any significance for Edgar. He ate to keep himself from feeling dizzy, and he slept so that he would not fall asleep during the lugubrious activities of daily life.

School was an ordered dream. He paid attention in class and he ate lunch with the other children, but their laughter only reminded him of how unlucky his mother had been. When invited over to play at other boys' houses, he quietly declined.

Edgar had taken on the life of a shadow, while his true self – like a stone figure of Narnia – remained at the bedside of his shrinking mother.

Christmas came and went. Stan the doorman brought in a tree and helped Edgar's father string lights through its branches. Presents arrived and were opened. A turkey was carved, but joy had regressed into the trunks of the trees, and into the sleeping bombs of the lilacs.

Edgar's father acquired a dog, which Stan offered to walk but seldom did. Like a piano bought for the purpose of decoration, the dog somehow knew that no true pleasure was taken from its presence and it spent most of the day and night in its bed, and then one day it disappeared and nobody noticed.

Edgar's father began to work every other Saturday, and then every Saturday. The apartment fell asleep under dust. Life became quiet and drawn out like a wet Sunday afternoon. By the time winter passed and the earth began to soften, the river of silence between Edgar and his father had become a sea – but it was not rough, nor did the tides bring news of change. Beneath the surface swam unsaid things.

On the one-year anniversary of her death, Edgar's father left the apartment before Edgar woke up. One hour before the car arrived to take Edgar to school, he made himself some cereal and then pulled her sweater from under the bed. He folded it, and by removing his homework and a history book, he found a space for it in his backpack. The scent of her sweater almost drove him mad, and during recess, he found an empty cubicle in the bathroom, opened his bag, and inhaled what little of her life it had absorbed.

After school as usual, he crossed Fifth Avenue and headed for the bench. Along the main path, a tourist laughed uncontrollably as he posed for a portrait. His girlfriend laughed, too; they kissed. At first, Edgar had thought tourists were foolish to want pictures for themselves and their loved ones, but after his mother died, he realized that memory needs all the help it can get, and things are sometimes like keys.

When Edgar arrived at the end of the grove that hid the bench, the scent of lilacs picked him up and carried him forward, but then he stopped because there was a man on the bench with his eyes closed.

The man was Indian and had a turban tied around his head. He wore a brown suit and a stiff raincoat stained with water marks.

The turban was almost the same color as his suit, and bits of thread dangled from it like the beads that sometimes hang from lampshades.

As Edgar approached, the man opened his eyes and peered up at him.

"I'm sorry," Edgar commanded, "but you can't sit here."

The man adjusted the turban slightly. One of his eyes began to wander to the side of its socket, as though it yearned for a life of its own.

"I can't sit here?" he said.

"I didn't know anyone knew about this place," Edgar said, looking back upon the path.

"Oh, I think it would be very popular," said the man. "It's lovely."

Edgar sensed that the man had no intention of leaving and so climbed up onto the bench beside him.

"How do you know about this place then, if it is such a very big secret?" The man leaned into a purple nose of lilacs and sniffed.

"My mother used to bring me here," Edgar said.

"Oh?" he said, though this time, he seemed surprised. "She's not here today?"

"She's dead," Edgar said.

The man began to laugh and then jumped off the bench.

"You must be crazy!" he said, adjusting the turban on his head. "People don't die!" He laughed again, though not mockingly, but with utter incredulity.

The man's loose eye drifted in its socket, while the obedient one remained fixed on Edgar.

"You must be crazy," the man said again, sitting back down on the bench. Edgar shrank back and looked up at a small opening in the trees. It had clouded over, but the vegetation around him swelled.

"You're not scared of me, are you?" the man asked.

"No," Edgar replied. He was not scared because he felt that life had already done its worst.

"Well, don't worry about my terrible eye." The man pointed. "It sees everything quite clearly when it wants to."

"But I was with her when she died," Edgar said.

"Stop talking crazy," the man insisted, which made Edgar cry.

The sky darkened suddenly, and a soft wind shook the bloated ends of the lilac trees.

"Could it be that your mother is actually here? With us now?" the man asked softly. "Your tears are falling upon her small hands," he said, kneeling down at Edgar's feet. He cradled a wet tea-rose leaf in his hand. "See?"

Edgar looked down and imagined the fragrant cups of roses, which in summer would pop open around the bench. He remembered his mother's fascination for small things.

"It's just a Peter Pan rose," Edgar said.

The man laughed, and his eye slipped from its moorings. "And I suppose that the wind is just air? And not laughter's laughter?"

"I wish I could believe you," Edgar said.

"Terrible." The Indian man shook his head.

"I don't understand how she could leave us," Edgar said.

"I know, it's awful."

"Why did it have to happen?" Edgar asked.

"She's just changed clothes."

Edgar imagined repeating all this to his father – the ensuing sigh, and then the click of the door as his body made a quiet exit.

"If you think she has gone for good, then you're cutting yourself short, my friend," the man said. He pulled an orange from his pocket and began to peel away its skin with his nail.

"My own wife," the man said with a mouthful of orange, "is the blend of light in late summer that pushes through the smoky trees to the soft fists of windfallen apples. Would you like some orange?"

"No thanks."

"Oh, you really should, it's rare you find such a sweet one," the man said. "And I can tell that you haven't been eating."

Edgar shuffled in his seat.

"What would your mother say?" He held out a segment of orange. Clouds above them broke apart and trees echoed with birdsong.

Edgar and the man chewed silently.

"I'm very sorry," the man said when they had finished the orange.

"My father threw away all her clothes."

"That's not uncommon."

"Why?" Edgar asked.

The man turned to Edgar. "He probably hasn't said much to you either, has he?"

"No, he just works, and then when he does come home before I go to bed we have dinner, and then I go to my room while he reads the newspaper."

"And I suppose you think that he doesn't love you?"

Edgar nodded.

"Big problem," the man said to himself.

"What is?" Edgar asked.

"Well, he loves you both so much that it consumes him." The man's loose eye began to revolve. "When somebody leaves this plane – or, if you like, goes into another room – those left behind sometimes try and stop loving – but this is a mistake, because even if you have loved only once in your life, you're ruined."

Edgar imagined the sad, bent figure of his father.

"Before I met with my wife, I loved her very much. I didn't know who she was, but I had this fire inside me for someone I knew existed. Now that she hangs out stars, I still love her, though we speak another language altogether."

"Is she dead, too?" Edgar asked.

"Are you listening to a word I'm saying?"

"Sorry."

"Okay, you're forgiven, but no more of this silliness."

A bird dipped between the trees and came to rest on a branch.

"You have to help your father."

Edgar imagined his father at the office, the dark rings beneath his eyes. The beauty of his slowness.

In the early stages of his mother's illness, Edgar had secretly watched his father get down on his knees and gather up the clumps of her hair from the shower drain. Before anyone truly believed what would happen, Edgar's father had tried to save everything, and he kept the hair in a pillowcase.

"Come," the man said. "This is a very pleasant seat, but let's go for a walk."

Edgar didn't move.

"Show me all the places she took you. Let's ride on the subway and sing her favorite song."

Edgar couldn't think of anything to say. His mother had told him never to talk to strangers.

"I know that you might be afraid – what I'm saying is hard to believe, but it's possible to continue loving, if you know how."

Edgar felt for the sweater in his bag.

"You are hungry and so am I," the man said, rubbing his chin, as though it had suddenly appeared on his face. Adjusting his turban, he said, "Okay, I have a very nice suggestion. You are going to tell me the favorite eating place of your mother, and then I am going to go to the favorite eating place of your mother, and if you like, you can join me there."

Edgar told him about a Chinese restaurant on the Lower East Side, and then the man walked to the end of the grove and was gone.

One whole year – 365 days ago, her eyes had closed and her hand (which had shrunk until it was almost the same size as Edgar's) released her son's hand. Her soul, like a spring coiled between two doors, was vaulted into the unknowable as one door opened.

A boy at school had told him there was no such thing as a soul, that people were just machines. And even though the boy had meant no harm and everything he said made sense, Edgar felt as though there was some information that had been withheld, not only from the boy, but from everyone.

Moments before his mother died, Edgar remembered a sudden energy had filled her. For several minutes, her eyes opened very wide. She even tried to sit up. She looked around the room and then at Edgar's father, who sat – frozen with disbelief – at the end of her bed.

Anniversaries are sad and beautiful. Snow momentarily turns to rain.

Edgar pushed open the door of the Chinese restaurant – advertisements flapped upon its door like wings.

He slid into the booth opposite the man, whose loose eye was following the waiter back to the kitchen.

When Edgar sat down, a Chinese woman appeared through a bead curtain.

"Long time since you come, Edgar."

"Yes," Edgar said, and felt his mother warm his insides.

The Indian man cupped his hand on Edgar's shoulder.

Edgar ordered all the dishes his mother had loved. Moo shu pork, pork-fried rice, hot and sour soup, won ton crispy duck, and General Tso's chicken.

There was a fish tank opposite their booth, and Edgar wondered if the fish remembered them.

It was a strange thing to taste all her favorite foods. The smell of the duck and the thick smoothness of the soup all conjured her.

He could see her long fingers on the table, occasionally scooping steaming food onto his plate. She pushed her strawberry blonde hair behind her ears, and her eyes widened with each mouthful. They discussed school, the importance of nutrition, and where they would go for a vacation in August when New York was unbearably sticky.

The strange man opposite Edgar ate in silence.

After the meal, the Indian man scooped out handfuls of quarters from his pocket. The Chinese woman counted them on the bar loudly.

Edgar opened his fortune cookie. He broke the stale biscuit and read it to himself. It said:

"Long Roots Moor Love to Our Side"

Next, they went to a Laundromat in Chelsea and sat in orange, molded chairs beside churning washers. It was late, but Edgar knew that his father would not be home yet.

"Even though we always had a laundry service," Edgar said, "Mommy used to bring me here for fun."

The Indian man nodded. Several Polish women folded towels next to them.

"Grandma used to bring Mommy here when she was my age, and they had long talks."

"Did you have nice talks with your mother here?" the Indian man asked.

"Oh, yes," Edgar said. "She taught me all the different names for clouds and how to predict the weather before it happens."

They both laughed because outside a cloud opened with such violence that the street was suddenly filled with laughter and the excited screams of people running as if they were children.

"It's like we are in a machine being washed together," the Indian man noted.

Edgar nodded. "We used to sit where those women are," Edgar said, pointing to the women with the towels. "Mommy used to have candy in her purse, and we would buy a soda from the machine and have a sugar picnic." Edgar couldn't help but laugh as he remembered. "She told me not to tell Daddy, but one day her purse fell off the table at supper, and candy went all over the floor, and Daddy just looked at her in surprise, because there was more candy than he had probably ever seen."

The Indian man laughed, too, and then bought Edgar a soda and some candy from the machines with some of the quarters left over from lunch.

Edgar laughed so much that pieces of candy fell from his mouth, but the Indian man didn't seem to mind at all.

In the hot Laundromat, Edgar could almost smell his mother's perfumed wrists. The powder machine, with its very small but brightly colored boxes of washing powder, reminded Edgar of the small box of Joy that was on the shelf above his bed. When his mother gave him the two quarters to buy it, she had said:

"I will always give you joy"

As they left the Laundromat and walked toward the subway on Fourteenth Street, they both stopped, because there was a homeless man sleeping on a vent.

"He was once a little boy," the Indian man said sadly.

The man was covered with several blankets and lay on wet cardboard boxes. His hair was thin and ragged. His skin was coated in dirt. His shoes were three sizes too big and had no laces.

"He still is a little boy waiting for someone to love him," Edgar said.

Edgar pulled his mother's sweater from his backpack.

"What are you doing?" the Indian man asked.

"Finding a new way to love Mommy," Edgar replied.

He laid the sweater next to the man's hands, and as he did so, the cold, dirty fingers sensed the sweater's softness and reached out for it. At his feet was a badly written sign that read:

sometimes we all need help

"That was nice, what you did," the Indian man said.

"It was nothing, really," said Edgar.

"It was nothing and it was everything," said the Indian man.

"What do you mean?" asked Edgar.

"You'll see one day," he said.

A cool wind blew across the subway platform, and Edgar tried to remember what the Indian man had said, not wind, but laughter's laughter.

When the train squealed to a stop, Edgar reached for the Indian man's hand and they boarded, sitting next to a boy and his mother.

The mother was peeling the shells from pistachio nuts and putting the nuts into a bag. The boy watched her, a basketball balanced on his knees.

The boy's mother was pregnant.

"All the secrets are in there," the Indian man said, pointing to her abdomen. Edgar looked at her bulging body. He had once been inside that warm house.

When they reached their stop and left the station, it was dark, and for a moment both Edgar and the Indian man were transfixed by the night sky.

"We leave one womb for another." The Indian man laughed.

Although the stars appeared to be close, they were millions of miles away.

"The light from the stars takes so long to reach us that sometimes a star will have expired by the time we can see it," the Indian man said.

"Some of these stars are dead?"

"Nothing dies in the way that we think, Edgar," the Indian man said. "Perhaps what really matters is that they are so beautiful, whether they are still awake or not."

They walked through the park, but it was so dark that even though surrounded by trees and bushes they could not see any of them. They felt only each other's presence.

As they neared Fifth Avenue, the moon crisped the tops of trees, and Edgar knew that his father was home. As they stood on the edge of Fifth Avenue, the Indian man's eyes seemed to glow and their light touched Edgar's face.

Without saying a word he adjusted his turban, turned around, and walked back into the park without once looking back. Edgar watched. The Indian man's painful amble suddenly took on a strange majesty. He seemed to grow as tall as the trees. Then his form grew bright.

Edgar looked past the avenue, past the buildings, through the clouds and into the universe.

No solid object separated him from infinity.

The sea between Edgar and his father began to drain, and in the distance burned the fire of a man waiting to be rescued by a small boy he once knew.

The World Laughs in Flowers

A FEW HOURS AGO I boarded a plane at Los Angeles International Airport wearing no socks. By dawn tomorrow I shall be walking beneath the fruit trees of Athens.

Last week I received a letter from Samantha in Greece. She informed me of her forthcoming marriage to her childhood friend. We had spent only a few weeks together, five years ago, but when you finally meet the person who in daydreams you had sculpted without words, the transparency of time becomes the color of hair, and shapeless years become the shape of lips.

Perhaps we are each allotted only a certain amount of love – enough only for an initial meeting – a serendipitous clumsiness. When it leaves to find others, the difficulty begins because we are faced with our humanness, our past, our very being.

The conditions under which I left Samantha were complicated by my drinking.

I had been drinking so much back then that my skin was beginning to change color. I remember watching Samantha for the last time through the shutters as she skipped up the front steps of my apartment building, her bag swinging. I had thought I would live in Greece with her forever. But sometimes, when confronted by something of unfathomable beauty, the bars of the cage around us begin to tremble. So I ran away to protect myself and remained a prisoner.

I am somewhere above the Atlantic Ocean. I look down into the darkness and imagine a scatter of uninhabited islands. For the years Samantha and I have been apart, I have been marooned. And as if I have been stranded on one of the imaginary islands below, I am now finally drifting away on a raft tied together with thick grasses of fear and relief.

A few days after receiving Samantha's letter, I couldn't sleep and got up. I decided to go for a walk along Sunset Boulevard. It was quiet. Dawn swept through the streets. I saw a woman in a wedding dress waiting for a bus. She was slumped on a wooden bench. Her dress swam around her and across the bench, obscuring an advertisement in Spanish. Her feet hung an inch off the curb.

A veil covered her eyes. Her mouth quivered. Her lipstick looked smeared. I realized that since leaving Samantha, there was a part of me that had never stopped grieving. And all this time, it was not Samantha for whom I had often woken up sobbing, but for my self, for the plague of indifference that had kept me from her all these years. Like a ship, I had dropped anchor in the middle of the sea. I had chosen to quietly rot.

There was a man in jeans bent over beside the woman in the wedding dress. He was sifting for cans in the trash. I remember the concentration on his face. He was the street's unofficial archaeologist. I thought how simple it would be for us to change places.

When suddenly I realized that I knew the woman in the wedding dress, I decided to buy a seat on the next flight to Greece. I went home, found my passport, and hailed a taxi for the airport.

I wonder how happy Samantha is and how many photographs have already been taken of her and her childhood friend.

I imagine her voice.

I can see her family house, perched high above the city, its white stone walls erupting out of scorched earth, emptying coolness into a blue shell of sky. Her father is playing backgammon on the veranda. His mustache is twitching. There is soccer on the television.

As the homeless man rummaged deeper into the trash for cans, the woman in the wedding dress began to cry, and I saw through the veil a face from long ago. But instead of rushing over and calling out her name, I just stood there.

The woman in the wedding dress waiting for the bus is called Diane, and we lived in the same apartment building years ago. She was training to be a nurse, and I was in my final year of a PhD in ancient history. She lived across the hall, and we would drink chamomile tea together. Sometimes she would discuss her knowledge of hospital procedures. Other times, I would clumsily fight my way through a passage of ancient Greek or explain the significance of ancient bartering.

Sometimes we would hold hands for no reason or pet her cat at the same time. I had planned to fly to Athens and write my thesis, so the night before I moved out, we had a farewell dinner. After a long meal with wine and the retelling of old stories, we made a promise. With my elbows on the kitchen table, and her fingers skating across the vinyl, we agreed that if we were not married by the time we were forty, we would marry each other. Then we made love. I always wondered what happened to her. Los Angeles is a place of nightmares and fantasies.

Everyone on the airplane seems to be asleep. There are hundreds of dreams taking place around me.

I was nearing the end of my stay in Athens when I met Samantha. I had divided my time between drinking and researching the mysteries of ancient dialect for my thesis. We first kissed on the rooftop of my apartment building amid the clanking of air conditioners, below an orange sky sprayed lightly with stars. Love reveals the beauty of seemingly trivial things – a pair of shoes, an empty wine glass, an open drawer, cracks on the avenue.

I stopped drinking soon after I returned from Greece.

I stopped drinking not to prolong my life, but because abstinence allowed me to continue loving her, as though by not drinking I proved myself worthy of her companionship.

My memories are arranged like puddles – they are littered throughout the present moment. It seems arbitrary, that which the mind remembers, but I know it is not.

During the years after I left Samantha in Athens, I would often stay awake all night – not only because we were lost from one another, but because when we kissed, I had only tasted alcohol. Her childhood friend, her husband-to-be, knows how she tastes now. This is his privilege.

When the woman in the wedding dress began to cry, the homeless man who was searching for cans in the trash stood up straight and put his hand on her shoulder. Between them sat a plastic bag stuffed with crushed cans. There must have been at least two hundred. Each can had touched someone's lips.

As an archaeologist, I've often wondered how we as a race keep going through all the misery. The answer is revealed: the potential for closeness with strangers.

Floating above the mountains of the Peloponnesos, slowly descending toward Athens International Airport, saltwater caresses and soaks into the land. As passengers begin to stir, I imagine old women hanging out sheets and slicing lemons. Samantha will still be sleeping.

Outside the airport, there is a billboard advertising perfume. It shows a young, beautiful couple with the slogan: *How Does She Smell to You?*

Sleepily, I imagine the two people on the billboard are Samantha and me, and instead of taking a bus directly to Samantha's house, where her courtyard will be bursting with irises, I take a taxi in the opposite direction to the port of Piraeus. After drinking a glass of water in a café, I find the owner of a boat and pay him to take me to a small uninhabited island thirty kilometers southwest of the mainland. As we make our way out to sea, he offers me a slice of spanakopita – spinach and feta cheese pie. When Samantha made this, years ago, flour would collect on her cheeks and forehead.

As we near the island, there is a wind blowing up from the south, so I ask the captain if he can dock on a northern beach. He seems perplexed but shrugs his shoulders. When I request that he wait three hours for me, he shrugs his shoulders again and lights a cigarette. From his old radio I hear a song with the words *agapi-mou* – my love.

Slowly, I make my way to the highest point of the island. I can feel the skin on the back of my neck start to burn. I am thirsty, and sweat runs down the ridge of my back in salty corridors. I have traversed this island before. I have sipped wine amid its flowers.

I wade through purple sea daffodils and poppies. There are clusters of cyclamen, nodding – urging me to the highest point of land. I once told Samantha how the ancient Greeks referred to cyclamen as *chelonion*, because their tubers are shaped like turtles. She had kissed me and said, "The world laughs in flowers."

As I reach the pinnacle, the skin on my neck and arms begins to blister. I am as close to the sun as the island will allow, and flowers give way to dry and hollow stems of yellow. The soil has turned to bloodred dust.

As I buckle to my knees and then lie on my stomach with my chin embedded in the crimson earth, I can see a carpet of flowers lining the hillside, a gradual descent in color.

And then, as I close my eyes, the wind – after skimming along the sea, peeling its salty freshness – races up between the wildflowers, slowing as it gathers the weight of their bouquet. When the wind finally comes upon me and inhabits my shirt like ice, I inhale the memory of Samantha.

If I were to fly home without seeing Samantha, by the time my plane arrived in Los Angeles she would be married. Diane, in the wedding dress, would have boarded her bus, and the homeless man would have sold his cans.

Up here on this forgotten elbow of land, I have nothing to lose, and though I am more afraid now than I have ever been, I am relieved, I am unburdened, I am ascending.

Some Bloom in Darkness

for Eugène Atget and Erik Satie

S INCE WITNESSING A VIOLENT incident at the railway station
some months earlier, Saboné had not sketched a thing. He
had not sketched the pigeons that dripped from the ledges of the
Museum, nor had he shuffled through the Museum, where he liked
to sit and watch people rather than paintings. Since bearing witness
to the violent incident some months earlier, Saboné often became
breathless with anxiety, as though he were the perpetrator of a terrible crime that he could not recall.

Saboné found a genuine pleasure in small things. He had lived
with his mother in an unpretentious suburb of Paris until one day
she died, and Saboné thought it best to move and make a fresh start.
Since then, he had regressed into a shadow existence of adult life
that seemed without beginning or end.

Over the years, he had become quite skilled at sketching things.
And as he aged, Saboné realized that he was like his sketches – that
it was possible to be alive and not exist at the very same moment.

The small apartment Saboné found after his mother's death
overlooked a fountain. Water bubbled through the mouth of a child.
Saboné's evenings were quiet, but for the crackle of a fire in winter
and the sound of his fingers turning the pages of books. However,

not long after his mother died, a wild and ungovernable desire grew inside him.

He hoped that by accident – perhaps on one of his long walks – he might meet a young lady of similar circumstance with whom he could spend Sunday afternoons and meet after work for large cold-platter suppers on the noisy rue du Docteur Blanche.

But this desire to meet a young lady – this sentiment, which drew him out to the cafés on the avenues – was accompanied by such an equally powerful feeling of utter insincerity that these desires, which brought welcome respite from his shadow existence, slowly migrated like a flock of rare birds.

His life went back to normal until one day after almost ten years he witnessed a violent incident at the railway station where he worked as a simple clerk. Those desires suddenly returned, and soon enough, Saboné's eyes burned for the girl who stood in a shopwindow on his walk to work. She was very pretty, and Saboné assumed he had passed her many times before on his early morning walk to the railway station, but for some reason, he had never noticed her.

In addition to this new passion for a girl, Saboné caught himself doing odd things, like talking to birds and removing his hat whenever he passed statues in the gardens.

For days, he held the image of this shopgirl in his mind, carrying it around like an egg until he could get home and escape into sleep where it hatched into a fantasy.

Without constant vigilance, Saboné slipped into daydreams. After his mother died, his daydreams began to include voices, which Saboné concluded were just overheard conversations being replayed by a decadent subconscious.

Some daydreams seemed to want to swallow him up for good. Like wild horses, they would follow him in the day and then wander the plains of his dream life, but always upon him – until he would barely remember his own name.

In his top dresser drawer, Saboné kept the sketches he thought were acceptable. He possessed two in total: one of a door with elaborate rusting hinges, and the other of a cat he had once seen peering up into the street from under a drain.

Every Friday, the girl in the shopwindow would have a new outfit and be standing in a different way.

Saboné often daydreamed while perched in his ticket box at the railway station.

"Monsieur!" the customers would cry, and Saboné would suddenly realize that it was a rainy afternoon and that he was not an Egyptian king, nor had he been sold into slavery by mistake.

The girl in the shopwindow who so preoccupied Saboné's thoughts was not really a girl because she lacked a human heart. She was made of wood. From a distance, however, she may well have been mistaken for one. And from the way she peered into the street through her glass eyes, Saboné decided that she might as well be a girl, because he believed that girls peered longingly and had secrets.

Saboné's small apartment room, where he would return each night after dispensing tickets at the station, was not big enough for two, but if she were able to come home with him, he supposed that there was certainly enough room for her to sit down quietly (if she wished to).

Saboné's face was a gray tower with a child peering from the two black windows for eyes. His was the sort of man who would suddenly stop walking and poke objects with his walking stick.

Before he began to notice the girl in the shopwindow, Saboné experienced a violent incident at the station. He had been up all night dreaming and had awakened exhausted.

All morning, through the cold glass of his ticket window at the station, Saboné was so drowsy that he had barely been able to read the schedule, to which several minor adjustments were to be made owing to expected bad weather. Instead, with dreamy irreverence, the overtired Saboné began to sketch a woman who since buying her ticket had been sitting still not very far from his booth.

Saboné's hand glided across the paper, making the tiniest lines. Soon, they began to resemble a person, and with only a few strokes more the image began to tremble before him, as though he had tricked some part of her soul into inhabiting the picture. He admired it and then folded it several times before dropping it into the wastepaper basket as if it were the wax wrapper from some tasteless baguette.

When an arm of sunlight stretched through the glass roof of the station and engulfed her, Saboné smiled, but his mouth showed no trace of it.

At several minutes to twelve, a short, well-dressed man approached the woman, but he did not sit down. They began to chat, and Saboné wondered what the man wanted, or whether he was an old acquaintance relaying some story that had filled the void between their last meeting.

In the same way a sudden noise outside his room would release Saboné momentarily from his dreams, the short man clenched a fist and struck the woman squarely on the nose. He straightened his tie and looked as though he wanted to say something, but people were suddenly standing up, so he walked away quickly and quietly. The woman did not make a sound, but fought to control the stream of blood with a lacy handkerchief, which was soon crimson. People stared. An old man called for a gendarme.

Saboné began to shake. If he left the ticket office, the door was fixed so that he would not be able to get back in. If he asked her into the ticket box, there was a danger that someone would see and he would be dismissed – and Saboné had never been dismissed from anything, nor had he ever spoken in anger or raised his voice.

When the bleeding stopped, her eyes were swollen from crying and her nose was the color of a plum.

At fifteen minutes to one, with the handkerchief still pressed to her face, she stood up and left the station. Saboné strained to catch every last glimpse of her before she turned a corner and was gone. From the bundle she carried, she appeared to be a common girl, and Saboné wondered if she were even able to read.

Despite the demands of an old woman with an ear trumpet who wanted to know if she could leave Paris for a month but come back at the same time, Saboné reached under his desk and fished the sketch of the woman from the wastepaper basket. Without any flicker of emotion, he slipped it into his pocket as though it were evidence of the crime he had committed but had no memory of.

He explained to the old woman that she could leave on a train that departed Paris at eight minutes to two, but that it was impossible to return at the same time.

"Impossible!" she affirmed to the queue of people behind her, as though she had always suspected it.

By the time the girl in the shopwindow occupied a place in most of Saboné's daydreams, it had been two weeks since the violent incident, and the memory of it was like the memory of a dream – but it was heavier than a dream and had somehow anchored itself to Saboné. He would often think he saw her at the station. Perhaps by drawing her he had bound their shadows together – like two nights without a day between them.

When passing the girl in the shopwindow on the rue du Docteur Blanche became something Saboné looked forward to – even more so than sketching pigeons or eating supper beside the fountain – he grew afraid and found an alternative walk to the station through the city gardens. He didn't want to lose himself completely. Without her staring down at him from the window every morning and night, he could get some time to decide what to do. But Saboné began to wake at irregular hours of the night and think of her, like certain flowers in the park, flowers that will only bloom in darkness.

Saboné had one friend – a man who lived in the apartment below. His name was Oncle, and he was so large that he barely fit through the double doors of his own apartment. Saboné had never seen him venture beyond the fountain. Oncle would sob bitterly in the night as though his girth hid a swirling ocean of shame.

Saboné and Oncle exchanged cards at Christmas and often left notes for one another to acknowledge changes in the weather.

Oncle wore loose, shiny gowns and velvet carpet slippers with a gold "O" stitched on to each one. His only request in the friendship was that Saboné bring home any spare or used train tickets, which Oncle liked to arrange very prettily in cloth-covered books.

Oncle knew the train timetables by heart, and it often occurred to Saboné that Oncle would have been a far superior ticket dispenser than he if his friend were able to leave the apartment.

One wet Sunday afternoon, after a lunch of cold meat and beer, Oncle puffed on a cigar and mulled over Saboné's predicament regarding the girl in the shop. Finally, with rain upon the window like a thousand eyes, Oncle said sensibly, "Go into the shop, Saboné, and politely enquire."

The thought of entering the shop filled Saboné with such fear that, following lunch with Oncle, he immediately went to bed and was carried away by dreams, like a leaf falling from a branch into a slow river.

He awoke in the early hours of the morning, and although it was still dark, his room glowed with the soul of the snow that lay outside upon the streets and smoky roofs.

Saboné slid into his robe and crept to the window.

The courtyard and the fountain below were in a deep sleep. Saboné imagined bringing her back to his apartment. He imagined carrying her across the wedding cake snow of Paris and then her face when she saw the fountain.

The gray city was completely smothered by snow the next morning. The shop bell rang loudly as Saboné entered, kicking snow off his shoes as he went.

There were racks of dresses. There were feathered hats upon the walls like exotic birds. Inside the shop, there was no sound.

As Saboné made his way over to the window to see the girl, something appeared from between a dark rack of furs.

Saboné was not sure if it was a woman or a painted doll, but a small trembling creature suddenly appeared before him. The woman's lips were bloodred, and her skin was very white.

"Yes," the woman stated as though answering a question. She raised her cane at Saboné. "You have come to see the furs, have you?"

Coffee was brewing in the back of the shop.

"Well," she said, "do you see anything that pleases you?"

A thick paste of makeup moved when her mouth did.

"I've been noticing the girl in the window on my way to work every morning, Madame," Saboné remarked.

"I'll bet you have," the woman barked, "and you're not the first young man to politely enquire." Then breathlessly, "Reminds you of someone, does she?"

The floor of his soul creaked, as though in the silence that followed Saboné's quivering lips imparted the secrets of his loneliness, which even he did not understand.

"Who, the girl?" he said in a high-pitched voice.

They both turned to the window and watched the snow as it soundlessly found its place upon the earth.

"What is one to do?" the woman remarked. "The city gardens are quite impassable at this time of year."

"Did you know there are flowers there that bloom in darkness?" Saboné asked.

"But who goes to the gardens at night?" She snorted.

Saboné felt anger spread through his body like fire but said quietly, "I don't suppose anyone does."

As he stepped into the street, he lost his footing and jarred his head against the ledge of the shopwindow. A few spots of blood appeared in the snow. Saboné bent down in awe. His very own blood lay before him. It had been inside him for almost four decades. It had passed through his body and lubricated his dreams. The object of his desires peered coldly from the window at the few drops. He knelt down as more drops collected in the snow, and then he fingered the soft gash in his head. His forehead turned numb from the pain, and every few steps Saboné looked back at the red dots – at the eyes of his soul in the snow of the street.

When he arrived at the ticket office – late for the first time in thirteen years – the head ticket dispenser inspected him from above his spectacles. Saboné felt a line of blood warm his cheek.

"My dear boy – you've had a spill."

By evening, the station was almost deserted, and nearing suppertime a man approached Saboné's window and asked for a ticket to "anywhere."

"Where is that exactly?" Saboné asked.

"I can't say," the man said, without any flicker of emotion.

Saboné thought of it that night in bed.

At approximately four o'clock in the morning, Saboné sat up and went to the window. The moon was bright but expressionless. He dressed and went outside. Then he walked to the city gardens.

In moonlight, the statues moved their eyes and glowed. Saboné was not fully convinced that he was awake but wondered why he had never before swum through snow and moonlight – and why, after so many years of awkwardness, he suddenly felt as though he had found his home – and that perhaps he was a character in the dream of Paris.

Most of the plants in the garden balanced tiny burdens of snow on their tops. Although Saboné knew that it was winter and he would not see any in bloom, he realized that he had been mistaken, that it was not in darkness in which some flowers bloomed, but in moonlight.

He scooped up some of the unbroken snow and chewed it. Then he laughed. How silly he had been to fall in love with a mannequin. Silly, he thought, but understandable, considering his circumstances.

As the path widened, Saboné noticed someone sitting on a bench, and he stopped walking.

Then he recognized her and recalled the image of her bloodied handkerchief, and the spots of blood that followed her across the station to the platform – the eyes of her soul.

Her presence convinced Saboné that he must be dreaming, because she was so very white. When he got close, her eyes, which were wide open, did not follow his movement.

At last he reached out for her, but she did not move. He stroked her face with his fingers, including the nose, which, although white and free from any storm beneath, was completely frozen. Crumbs of snow that had collected in her hair were still intact.

He knelt down in the snow at her feet and remembered the sight of his very own blood outside of the shop.

He pulled himself up onto the bench. He reached around her with his arm and moved her closer. He squeezed her until he felt the bones beneath. Then he settled down and became quite still. He found the drawing of her in his jacket pocket and unfolded it. Then he put his arm around her again and wished that everyone he had ever met was somehow able to see him. It was some time before they were moved.

Distant Ships

I THINK OF LEO VERY often these days. I think of him tonight as I sort packages for a truck that's headed for London. It is so cold in the warehouse that we wear our breath like beards. The office sent down a box of gloves last week, but I enjoy the feel of cardboard against my old cracked hands. I have worked for the Royal Mail for almost three decades now. I thought they would let me go when I stopped speaking twenty years ago, but they've been good to me, and when I retire in ten years I'll be given a state pension and a humble send-off. I enjoy my work. It's the only reason I leave the house, except for my walks on the beach.

Each package has somewhere to go and the contents remain a mystery. Occasionally I'll find a box where the address has been written by a child. I used to put these boxes to the side until the end of my shift so I could study the penmanship and compare it to Leo's. In a child's handwriting, language is exposed as the pained and crooked medium it really is. Since losing Leo, these packages are like shards of glass.

The warehouse is divided into sections. There are no windows, and sometimes I imagine the factory is in Oslo, Mumbai, or Rotterdam. Outside, the sopping Welsh hillsides roll away in one direction like old giants under blankets of moss. In the other direction, the land suddenly stops as though woken up. Where the land stops, something else begins, and the sea stretches north until it starts to freeze, and then it clings to the earth like a child to its mother.

Small muddy vans roll in from villages in the valleys. These vans are unloaded and the packages sorted by nearest city. Every two days, hulking lorries chug from the warehouse to Glasgow, Manchester, London, and Penzance.

As I walk home each morning in the dark, I picture headlights carving through night's flesh. I love the names of the towns on the packages the same way I love the different species of weeds that blindly push through the shell of earth around the forked gate of my house.

Hundreds of years ago, the village relied solely on fishing. I have a book of paintings in my sitting room at home. One of the paintings has young women in aprons standing on cliffs watching a ship get smashed against the rocks. In the foreground is an arm of sunlight reaching down to the surface of the sea. I couldn't tell you who painted the picture, but I understand the inclusion of that long beam of light, I understand the grief that makes such details necessary. There is little fishing work in this town now.

Although the warehouse provides more of a steady income than fishing, all the boys in the village dream of going to sea. They dream with their windows open of ancestors on the sorts of ships you only see in bottles now.

Sometimes I walk along the rocky beach beneath the village. The dark green water sweeps in, and I scream with the roar of dragging rocks. I spend hours peering into rock pools at fish and crabs. I wonder if they know they've been cut off. I like to sit on the cold pebbles until the tide sloshes over my shoes and water soaks through my socks and pulls at my toes like some hysterical being.

When early morning comes and my shift ends, I write down the number of vans that I unloaded. After thirty years, I've never made a mistake, because for me, each truck is like a person. As a boy I always felt that vehicles had faces.

I clock out and find my coat in the break room. There is a half-eaten sandwich on the table. A calendar of topless women hangs from one of the lockers. The women look cold. They wear large smiles. Perhaps photographs can fake happiness, but never grief.

The warehouse is half an hour's walk from the village, first through a narrow country lane and then up a hill into town past hedgerows thick with birds peering out from their nests. In summer, wild berries replace the black eyes of the birds.

In a few hours dawn will flood the world. I stop walking and lean against a lamppost. My left leg always hurts, and it's worse in winter. Everything is worse around Christmas.

The light from the streetlamp falls upon my hands. They are the color of stained glass. In the village church there is a magnificent stained-glass window. Sometimes I kneel beneath it and drown in color. When the pain in my leg is back to a dull throbbing I continue walking. Stones caught in the tracks of my boots scrape the concrete. I miss autumn – the season when summer takes on the memory of its own mortality. And then winter. And then the miracle season, when everything begins again fearlessly.

The walk home is always slow, and rows of slate houses glisten. Their black foreheads are white with tomorrow's breath. Curtains are pulled across the eyes from within.

A bird hops around a lamppost. There is a plump worm in its beak. It flies away as I approach.

I pass the corner pub. Even though it's against the law, pubs in the village are open all the time on account of the few remaining fishermen who return an hour or so before dawn, with a thirst built up from being on the water without being able to drink any of it. The light spills out into the street with the sound of laughing. I smell beer, and a dull thud from the jukebox reminds me of my leg, which reminds me of Leo.

A mist wraps around the town. Its white arms spread through the streets. Dogs bark at kitchen doors.

I used to go into the pub for a pint or two. But I haven't been in for about six years. It's all so useless.

After Jeanne took Leo's things to America twenty years ago, I felt a sense of relief. The house was quiet, and for some reason I began to think about my mother, who died when she was sixty-eight. The same year Jeanne and I were married. My mother slipped on some ice and broke her hip, then without any warning she died in the hospital. It was like the closing of a book I never thought could end.

I spent last Sunday watching the fishing boats chug home, their hulls thick with silver pellets of fish.

I haven't said a word in twenty years, but there was a time when you wouldn't have been able to shut me up. I've lived so long without the pain of language. My life is a letter with no address.

If you were to watch me for an afternoon, you'd notice that my hands are always moving. Like blind siblings they are always touching one another.

I like watching the fishing boats. Each boat's arrival is celebrated by a spray of birds. Seagulls from a distance look like eyes drifting over the waves. Last week one of the young captains asked if I needed work. I shook my head. He was a handsome boy, probably about the age Leo could have been. I wonder who has inherited the life Leo left behind.

I live in the house I grew up in. My parents' room is the same. It is the guest room, but the only guests are ghosts who drift in through the doorways in dreams.

Everybody in the village knows my life story. But I'm too old to think my sadness is special.

Jeanne is my age, but lives a different life. In this village with its damp shoes and Sunday hymns, you are old the moment someone you love dies. And then Sundays are spent watching light move across the garden from small hot rooms that smell like ironing.

Jeanne lives in Los Angeles. We're still married, though we haven't spoken since Leo. I think they make pictures in Los Angeles. Perhaps her life is a long fantasy.

Sometimes I linger outside the junior school at the bottom of the hill. At this time of year, Christmas decorations hang in the windows. Beyond the school are mountains dotted with sheep and the odd light of a tractor grinding its way home. Sometimes I time my walks to coincide with the three o'clock school bell. Children gush into the playground like hot water and into the arms of their parents. I would give everything, even memory – especially memory – if I could hold Leo again. The weight of his absence is the weight of the entire world.

I stopped speaking soon after the accident in the hope I'd retain the memory of his soft, lispy voice. Sometimes I cup one of Leo's words in my hands like a trembling bird. After the accident, the doctors said I had only a few months to live. Jeanne went back to America, and I waited for that journey home. I felt like packing a suitcase but didn't know what to put in it. That was twenty years ago. I have stopped going to doctors. They only believe what they think they know. They are like priests – blinded from spirituality by religion.

Jeanne would be shocked if she could see how bleak everything is, though the village hasn't really changed, except for cars being allowed in the marketplace and a link road through the mountains for lorries. When I thought I was going to die after the accident, I started writing a book, and then never stopped writing. It is called *Dreams Are Lost Cities of Childhood*.

I have worked on it every day for twenty years. I will not be finished until I'm dead. The book I'm writing is the book to end all books. My death will be the concluding chapter. I have drawn all the pictures, too. The book is about my life with Leo and Jeanne. I cannot draw myself, so I mark my body in the pictures with an X. Sometimes when I read old chapters, I am suddenly in the midst of how things were – it's like being on a theater set that someone has built of your life. Memory is like life but with actors.

Jeanne wakes up to sunshine. She drinks orange juice. Los Angeles is warm, even at this time of year. Leo would be a man now. Some people have Christmas at the beach in America. They do in Australia, too. I wake to rain tapping on the window like a hundred Welsh mothers. Each drop is a note on the minor scale.

Jeanne came here to study the climate. There is a university in Bangor. Students come from across the world to watch clouds. I remember watching her marvel at the slow, swirling explosions of white. I offered her a paper cup of cockles. That was when you could buy them from a cart, but it's long since gone. It was where old people met and talked about the war. Jeanne's accent was smooth and rich. I used to wish that my ancestors had gone to America. Perhaps then things would have been different. Perhaps we could have met at the cinema, a drive-in. Perhaps Leo and I would have worked on an old car together – the sort people build in their garages.

Twenty years ago, I drove off the side of a cliff. I was trying to make Leo laugh by turning around to make faces. It's as simple as that.

Leo's body was recovered half a mile from the wreckage. He looked as though he were asleep, but his insides were liquid. I like to think he was carried from the car by the same angels that drift in and out of the stories I've grown fond of reading by Milton and Blake. They wrote beneath the same moon that's above the village. Everything that's ever happened, the moon saw.

They tell me I survived the accident.

It's Wednesday morning. Darkness at this hour is seldom remembered. Most people are about to wake up. I stand lopsided outside my front door. It is not really a door, but another gateway to sadness. It begins to drizzle. The fog rolls away and creeps up the black hillside. Fires are being lit. Mornings in Wales reek of frying eggs and wood smoke. Children are stirring in warm beds. Soon they will be released from the arms of dreams. All arms are envoys of God. It is night here, but day somewhere else, and somehow it keeps going and going whether we're a part of it or not.

Suddenly the sky is full of rain; drops the size of thumbs. It will soon be Christmas. The children at school are putting on a play. They make their own costumes. Night is a tattered veil suspended. The moon is full and absent all at once. Leo's face waits for me in every mirror. Dreams are the unfinished wings of our souls.

No Greater Gift

WAY ABOVE THE PARK, traffic has stopped. A fat woman in tight clothes pushes twins in a stroller. The eyeballs of the twins slide up to the elevated train. The train grieves into the station.

Gabriel watches the twins and then looks into the space they are being pushed. Gabriel looks down at his watch and shuffles into an alley behind a bakery. His package should be ready.

A steel door opens separating a word sprayed in white. Two trembling hands emerge holding a box tied with string. There is a bird tattooed on one of the hands. Gabriel places his hands on the top and bottom and only when the other hands feel the responsibility of weight transfer do they release and disappear back behind the steel door. Gabriel taps twice and looks around.

As Gabriel makes his way through the alley toward the subway, he pauses beside a motorcycle lying on its side. He is tempted to open the box for a quick peek at what's inside.

Two men waiting for the train look Gabriel over. Their pants are baggy and remind Gabriel of sails. Their eyes want to know what he is carrying and why he is handling it with such care. They look at the hole in Gabriel's sneakers. They look at Gabriel's scar. He was in a fire. There were several deaths. It crosses his cheek and disappears under his ear. People notice it because it is a lighter shade of brown than the rest of his face. His mouth hangs open, a habit that makes him look absent but that his wife loves.

As he stares down the track into the light of an approaching train, he considers what he is doing and thinks about his mother. The train brings with it a cold wind that makes the two men on the platform forget about Gabriel.

The silver doors slide open. An intercom spits out a muffled message. The subway car is full of short Mexican men with paint on their sneakers. They are huddled together but don't talk. One of them is reading a tattered children's book to improve his English. Gabriel notices a boy and a girl, perhaps seven or eight years old. Their grandfather – a mustache curling down each side of his chin – is asleep with his mouth open. The boy is amused by this. The Mexican man reading the children's book is concentrating so hard that he doesn't notice the girl lean and mouth the words as he thinks them.

The train crosses an unmarked boundary into Brooklyn. Gabriel looks at the other passengers, but only an old woman in black is watching him. As he looks at her, her eyes fall on to the box and then she turns her body away from Gabriel toward the glass of the door. Gabriel's mother once told him that if you keep thinking of someone dead, you summon them.

As the train rushes into light and slows, Gabriel is able to see the people who might step into his car. He notices a transit cop. The transit cop doesn't move from the platform, then is lost behind the rush of men in suits and women in long coats with long hair. He moves the box onto his lap and rests it on his thighs. As he pulls the bottom of his coat over it, he realizes how dirty he must look, because his sneaker has a hole in it and his coat is stained black in places. He looks at how clean the new passengers are and remembers the smell of freshly ironed shirts on Sunday nights. He hasn't worn a shirt like that since his wedding. His mother was still alive then and made paper butterflies to put in his bride's hair.

The people standing around Gabriel do so uncomfortably. He is hiding something, and they know it. He wants to stand and offer his seat, but the package must be delivered intact. When Gabriel coughs, people bury their heads. His wife wants him to see a doctor, but doctors cost money, he tells her.

A woman with short black hair in a pink raincoat is laughing to herself. The woman reminds Gabriel of his sister who lives in a suburb of Havana. She is always depressed because the man she loves is a drunk.

Gabriel is being watched by tourists. He knows they are not from the city because they are each holding a map and the women have hair that is neither fashionably styled nor untidy. They are huddled together like the Mexican men next to them. The women chatter and the men stare coldly at the floor and at the bulge under Gabriel's coat.

The car is continually full, because when people alight, others are there to take their place. Gabriel wonders how many people occupy one seat in a day, and if the seat could record the thoughts of the occupants, what it would say about human beings.

Another stop and a young blind man is helped onto the train by a girl with bleached hair. She tenderly applies pressure to his elbow. A suit immediately rises and the young blind man sits, nodding gratefully for each gesture. Everybody looks at the blind man because he cannot look back at them. He knows people are watching him and sits very still, only once adjusting his white stick so it's propped against his thigh.

Gabriel closes his eyes and imagines being blind. He feels the box below him in the darkness and grips it tightly, making sure it is still only a bulge under his coat. When he opens his eyes the train is not moving and the blind man has vanished. The doors are open. It is his stop. Gabriel rushes between the bodies stepping into the car. He repositions the box under his coat and then walks toward a stairway at the end of the platform.

Leaning against a steel girder, Gabriel peers down at the tracks. Only last week someone jumped.

There is a Chinese woman playing a bamboo flute. It is cold but she is barefoot. Tied around her neck is a pink scarf. Gabriel listens to each note. It is a very slow song, which Gabriel thinks is somehow related to the pink scarf. She has no box or hat to collect money. He lays a quarter next to her foot.

Gabriel steps into the empty car of a new train and sits below an advertisement for laser eye-surgery. He carefully raises the box to his nose and sniffs. From the smell, he tries to conjure a picture of what could be inside and what his wife will think.

Gabriel stands up and looks into a neighboring car. He can see a homeless woman with her head slumped over. She is holding a shoe and crying. Gabriel cannot make out her features because the glass in the door has been written on.

Gabriel thinks about the photograph of his sister from Havana taken at Coney Island when she came to visit. She has her arm around Gabriel's wife. It is Gabriel's favorite photograph because it is how he dreamed life would be when he was a child.

He remembers how they had laughed and eaten hot dogs with ketchup dripping off the ends.

Gabriel alights and then waits for the train to disappear into darkness before making his way aboveground. On the yellow strip that separates the platform and the track there are broken crack vials. Gabriel tries to conceal the box with even greater effort.

His footsteps echo as he makes his way on to the cold street. As he passes a gas station, he can see two fat men watching soccer on TV and smoking. Farther along he passes a man yelling into a pay phone and notices that the receiver is not connected.

The houses here have white bars dividing the glass and the street, but through the bars Gabriel can see people eating, watching TV, and arguing. In one apartment there is a boy sitting alone eating an orange.

Gabriel turns down a street, which used to be a row of crack houses. But they've been bought and will soon be demolished. He comes upon an old factory building. With trembling fingers he pulls out a key from his pocket and pushes it into a thick steel door. He steps over an empty suitcase and begins the climb to the top floor.

His hands are shaking so much that he is worried about damaging the contents of the box. He reassures himself that it will be soon be out of his hands. When he reaches the top, he stares out through a glassless window at Manhattan. The Empire State Building is shrouded in mist. Perhaps one day it will be on display as an ancient obelisk. From below the window a woman screams once.

Gabriel knocks seven times on the door and then slides keys into several locks. He pushes on the door and slips inside. At one end of the room is the faint glow of a television. Beside a sunken couch is a bed covered in mostly broken toys.

Asleep on the couch is a boy just turned three. Gabriel kneels before him as his wife emerges from behind a curtain.

"José sneak it out the back like he say?" his wife asks. Gabriel nods.

The light from the TV flickers across the boy's face. Gabriel touches the boy's knee and then shakily unties the string of the box. As the boy rubs his eyes and sits up, Gabriel presents the box to the boy and opens the lid.

* * *

"Surprise!" Gabriel and his wife say.

The boy stares at the cake – the skillfully written number three – the thick icing that rounds the cake like a crown and the cream that lazes from the middle. The boy doesn't touch the cake but covers his face with his hands and peeks at it from behind his small fingers.

Snow Falls and then Disappears

MY WIFE IS DEAF. Once she asked me if snow made a sound
when it fell and I lied. We have been married twelve years
today, and I am leaving her.

She is in the bakery on the corner where it is warm and they know
her. She will return within an hour to our apartment with a box full
of little cakes ordered especially for this day. She will return home
and toss her keys into the ceramic ashtray. She will place the cakes
in the fridge, where she likes to keep canned goods. She will curse
my tardiness. After several hours of my absence she will develop a
further deafness.

There is a very small tear in the couch I never noticed until now;
a piece of leather hangs off like a tongue. It is a small rip but has
ruined the entire couch and thrown the apartment into disarray.
The ashtray is empty and tempts me to smoke again. My lungs are
hollow and long for the return of weight.

She plays the violin every day, and I am taking it with me. It
was made in 1783 in Prague. My bag and the violin sit on the bed,
poised for exile. The violin goes out of tune whenever it enters a new
environment, as though it loses confidence before a performance.
She told me that in the darkness of its body, swimming between the
maple ridges, there is a piece of her living secretly, fed by scherzo

and allegro. I am taking the violin for this reason. The violin leans against my bag on the bed. Inside, quiet as dust, a part of my wife awaits resurrection.

I have a habit of lying awake between dreams, when there is no traffic and it is very cold outside, so cold that a rough white skin forms across houses and cars. I lie next to her and imagine the vibration of pumping blood reverberating through her ears; a countdown to irremediable deafness.

She is watching the fat baker squeeze icing in the shape of our proverbial hearts onto little cakes that we are supposed to share with our shallow friends tomorrow night. She is not shallow, but deaf and ungovernable. She once told me that she loved me because I was the only thing she could hear. She can feel the vibration of the strings through the carved vessel of her instrument, but I am inside her. I am a song soaked into each bone of her secret body where the world has not been able to wander.

The baker is packing up the cakes into a pink box that he will tie with a pink ribbon. The baker knows her by name and has a tight pad of paper and a pen to write down the cost of her bundle and express his gratitude. I want to leave before she leaves the bakery, otherwise I will be caught and have to wait another year. I have to be on my way to the airport with her violin and my clothes before her keys leave her hand for the ceramic ashtray.

I have already burned all the photographs; they made a crackle and set off the smoke detector, which I promptly smashed. She won't need it because she is deaf and it gives off only a minute vibration.

I am taking one of her favorite dresses, which I know is a mistake. I remember falling asleep as she laid it out among the tendrils of tomorrow. The dress was a bridge between today and tomorrow.

And then together we drifted helplessly into sleep – ice melting through cracks in the floor.

I have written down all the reasons why I am leaving, though I am overcome with a sad strength for the world because I have not spoken to anyone all day. My resignation to being alone is a sea under which I can breathe.

We met in Minnesota, in the lobby of a Days Inn right off the highway. I sat opposite her. When a waiter brought her a tray of coffee, I realized she was deaf and could not hear the cups singing. Their song made me think of my mother, wheeling herself around the kitchen, gliding through steam from the pots and pans on the stove. Many years later when she passed on and I sold her house I noticed the grooves of her chair in the linoleum floor; it was a Braille only I understood – a mother's geometry.

I am booked on an airplane to Minnesota, where I will rent a car and arrive at the hotel where we first met. There I will sit in the same seat and read the same passage in the same book. There I will wait for her to find me again, so we can step into the direction we left behind and forgot about. It is a canvas unpainted by memory.

My mother was disabled because she was shot in the legs by a Nazi officer in Berlin. In reaction to the linoleum floor forty years later, I wrote a book about her and by accident found a picture of the officer who shot her. His name was Hans.

I have recently hung a blanket across the bathroom window and unscrewed the lightbulb. This was a strange operation induced by the sight of my wife's toothbrush, which sat bolt upright in a chrome stand. Whenever I washed my hands or bathed, the toothbrush would stare silently at me, challenging my faltering courage.

★　★　★

When a person disappears one day on her walk home from a bakery, the toothbrush becomes a symbol of hope.

I would wake in the night to feel its bristles, to check for wetness. If I am able to see its yellow spine, I'll have to wait another year. I picture the bakery and the cakes; I can smell the butter and taste each hot mouthful.

The Nazi soldier who disabled my mother was called Hans, he was my father, and they were lovers. That is why she lived and made it to America, because I was inside her. I was her protector, a tiny forbidden inception. I have a picture of him, which I never showed my wife, because she might not have understood why I am proud. I have inherited his stoicism. I have inherited his ability to love. We are united through loss.

The square clapped and crackled with gunfire. Heads fell against wet cobbles. People were separated from their shoes.

My father. His eyes shut. Dispatching round after round into men, women, and children. And then reason suddenly gripping him. He opens his eyes quickly enough to lower his gun.

Although my father snapped the bullets into my mother, I like to think it was his love for her that instinctively deflected them away from her heart.

As people became bodies, indistinguishable from one another, my father scooped up my mother. He took her to the Jewish ghetto and found a doctor whose family was starving. The doctor stopped the bleeding and removed the bullets of my father's pistol without asking for so much as an apple. Before I imagined deafness, I would lie awake thinking of my mother on the train hurtling across frozen Germany – the mountains dotted with soldiers in heavy coats, smoking and thinking of their wives. I could picture the border guards perusing her papers and wheeling her onto a cold platform, where freight trains stuffed with meat and fruit and wine would trundle lugubriously before people whose stomachs were paralyzed with hunger. My mother had a photo of her mother's flower garden tucked down her dress that separated me from a torn continent.

It snowed the morning she left Liverpool for New York. That's how I knew that I would marry the woman drinking coffee – when she asked me if snow made a sound when it fell. She wrote this question on the palm of her hand.

There are some lies that, under the right circumstances, are the only truth.

We slept naked that night in the hotel, a bundle of limbs, an arrangement of muscle and bone held together by fear and newness. Although I knew she would have invited the waiter up to her room had he been sitting where I was and looking at her as I was, I didn't care. I wanted to stretch into the ridge of her spine and complete her back, as water freezes in the crevice of a rock. The next morning it was snowing, and she asked me. I thought of my mother and said, "Yes." I wanted to carry her deafness away from the restaurant and lay its marvel in the snow. That night I went to her performance. She played Bach's Concertos in A Minor and E Major for Violin, and I pictured my mother changing her name at Ellis Island and then making her way to my birthplace.

I learned my wife's sign language. "Ballet for Fingers" we called it. We never spent one day apart until she disappeared walking home with a box of cakes. I wonder what happened to the cakes, were they ever eaten? By whom? The cakes torture me. And now the bakery is open again, its lights spilling out on to the cold street below the windows of children's bedrooms.

My father was killed by a seventeen-year-old Polish partisan in the fall of 1943. He was younger than I am now. My mother never spoke much of Europe, though I could picture it through her stories of her father, who sold bicycles until his shop was closed down. Once, I brought a friend home from school. He was born in Switzerland and spoke fluent German. I remember presenting him to her, and as his mouth pressed into the language, my mother began to cry and the boy stopped what he had only just begun.

Sometimes, language is the sound of longing. The small Boeing will be my ship from Liverpool. The violin will be my exit papers.

As the elevator slows to the level of the lobby, the doors separate to reveal a frail Russian named Eda who has lived in the building for sixty years. She puts her hand on my sleeve and looks concerned. She wants to know how I've been coping and where I am going with the violin. She wants to know if, after so long, there has been some news. I tell her that my wife is in the bakery buying cakes iced with proverbial hearts, and I have to be in the car heading for the airport before she returns. I tell her it is our anniversary and I am leaving her. This makes her cry and she lets me go, giving me strength – the strength of my father as he carried my mother through the freezing rain, along cobbled streets, between tall dank houses scarred with lines of bullet holes, pushing his way through the nightmare, his face streaked with blood, his heart burning with disgrace. I can picture them clinging to one another, though lost from each other forever. I can see his face as the Jewish doctor feverishly looks for the bullets. I can imagine the night she left and the emptiness that followed him. I imagine his memory of my mother, her falling torso, the smell of her wet hair, the trail of blood through the ghetto, the falling of snow.

The Shepherd on the Rock

I HAVE ALWAYS BEEN ATTRACTED to the idea of heaven, and that's why John F. Kennedy International Airport seemed like a good place to live out the last of my life.

You can tell who travels often because they have a convenient pocket or special wallet for their passport. The less-traveled forage for their documents, then drag their luggage into the rectangle made up of lines. Every time the line moves, another person joins.

I imagine I am watching the dead ready themselves for ascension into His kingdom, and though I no longer believe in God, the idea of a heaven and hell seems to me quite useful ways of rewarding the good and punishing the bad while they're still alive.

I'm homeless because I suffer from a madness I am too ashamed to bear responsibly. When I am momentarily free from these terrible feelings, I spend whole days and nights at the airport, sometimes sitting in a plastic chair for several hours and at other times ambling around the food court. When the terrible feelings return and from the base of my spine they stretch through my body like ghosts, I slip away from the terminal and find refuge in a shipping yard where floodlights ensure that day never completely ends.

When the madness comes I wrap myself in blankets and squeeze into this small space under one of the giant rusting containers where

I know I'll be safe. Underneath, I watch the rust spread across the metal like a slow tide of autumn.

An attack begins with amnesia. I suddenly forget things, such as what I've eaten for breakfast (if anything) or when I last smoked a cigarette. Then my limbs begin to tremble slightly and my teeth knock (imagine the chattering of plates in a kitchen cabinet moments before an earthquake).

The violent shaking often lasts for several hours, but that's not the worst of it, because the ghosts trapped in my body have found a small door that leads into my memories, and so for two days and nights, I am taken blindfolded down a path into myself and forced to relive random scenes from my life. Imagine that, forced into your self.

On the morning of the first day of madness, I may be swimming with my father in a cold pond as my mother looks on breathlessly, her apron flapping in the wind like a white wing; then by afternoon I am back at the seminary in Dublin being handed my degree as my hand is shaken vigorously by the cardinal.

I hide myself now so as not to hurt anyone. When the madness passes like a child's night of terror, I wake up and can barely walk from thirst – I also defecate in my clothes, which is unpleasant, but there's a homeless shelter two hours' walk from the container yard, and so I'm able to wash my clothes and take a hot shower. A young woman from Puerto Rico who works at the shelter always gives me a little money and a good meal. She sits down with me sometimes and says, "Whenever you're ready for a change, Paddy – just tell us." She calls me Paddy because I'm Irish and she doesn't know my real name. She often tells me about her life, without asking anything about mine. I like it like that because I wouldn't want to tell her that I used to be a priest because she wears a gold crucifix – faith is a balancing act.

If there really is a God (I'm not saying there isn't – I'm just saying that I don't believe in Him, like a mother who's given up on her son's delinquent ways), I hope He helps her find the love of her life as she's a decent girl and deserves more than a string of no-good boyfriends. I've seen a few young men at the airport who I thought might be good for her, but you never know if they're coming back. Anyway, I pray for her as I walk briskly back to the airport all fresh and without that terrible stench coming from down below. I can sometimes go two full weeks without an attack, but I exist utterly in its shadow.

It was my mother's idea that I become a priest, but it was my love for people that convinced me she was right. My seminary friends and I never spent evenings at the pub or courting girls on benches by the river Liffey like other students in Dublin at the time. We'd sit around listening to the wireless with tea and toast, or on nights when a heavy rain or the quiet drama of snowfall caused a stir, we'd talk about a love for God and the many incomprehensible sides of His character.

I was a great reader and listener of music. I remember having great admiration for Voltaire, whose belief in God seemed quite secondary to his compassion. He said, "If God did not exist, it would be necessary to invent him." I agree completely. A short time after leaving the priesthood I was feeding pigeons in the park when I met the woman who would become my wife.

That was long ago. I now live at the airport. I know all the different terminals and have spent so much time staring at the Arrival and Departure boards that I could tell you when the next plane is leaving for anywhere.

It's always nice to know an airplane has been somewhere and is back safe – you can tell this by the flight numbers. When I watch people line up at the check-in desks, I sometimes try and make eye contact with children so when I pray to allay their fears, I can see the pools of their eyes and then drop my prayers into them like coins being dropped into a well.

You might say that praying is useless if I don't believe in God anymore, but let me tell you my opinion: praying for someone is a way to love them without ever having to know them.

I pity anyone who knows me, because after the trembling – when the ghosts howl at my blood and twist their ethereal limbs about my bone – I'm not myself. I once killed a dog. It was a terrible mess, and I cried for days about the dog's soul.

The ghosts always find out where I'm hiding and escort me onto the stage of my childhood. The ghosts wait in the wings as characters from my past begin to appear upon the stage. My lines are already written and cannot change; my role is the same and the only member of the audience is my self.

I try not to talk to anyone at the airport (because they'll want to know about me, and keeping things from people is a form of deception), but I'm a chatterbox at heart and sometimes get roped into a discussion with a passenger as he or she waits to be called to ascension; this is one thing we have in common.

I remember a nice story that a young pregnant lady told me about how she met her husband. I don't remember much of what she said, but I remember thinking that inside her belly was the complete soul of an unknown in a vessel the size of a bread loaf. I've often wondered at what moment the soul inhabits the cells. I suppose it's like a light that gets switched on when everything is in place. But don't ask me who switches it on, because I wouldn't like to say.

I do enjoy watching people disappear through the doors into a sun-drenched corridor.

On the door it says: TICKETED PASSENGERS ONLY.

Imagine there were a heaven and getting to it were this easy. You just received your tickets in the mail, and then after several identity checks and a few extra charges, you were on your way.

The damned would have to remain on earth in perpetual doubt.

Once an airplane swings up into the clouds, it may as well be on its way to some celestial paradise. It's hard for people to say good-bye to their loved ones. I remember an Indian man who went through the doors with several plastic bags of clothes. His children wouldn't stop crying, and once he'd gone, those he'd left behind strained to see through tiny windows for one last glimpse. This happens often, and on one occasion there were so many people trying to catch glimpses of their loved ones, an airport employee had to intervene.

You may wonder why I haven't killed myself because living with madness or watching it flood the heart of someone we love is unbearable. Don't think I haven't considered it. If I were to do it, it would be when the amnesia starts, before the trembling. I would go to the shipping yard, climb up the side of an oil drum, and toss my body from it. I wouldn't mind a nice burial – with a service, so I'd probably try and find a dog dollar and then the powers that be might feel compelled to do the honors – how would they know I'd lost my faith?

Back in Dublin as a young man, I was obsessed with a song by Franz Schubert called "The Shepherd on the Rock" – you may have heard of it. I would lie down on the covers of my bed and, half asleep, put the record on, then watch the last of the day drain from my room. The song is about a shepherd who lives in the mountains with his flock. Apart from his sheep, he is completely alone. He dreams of a love far away (I always imagined a distant, flickering village), and then he starts to feel terribly depressed. Just when it seems as if he can't go on, something happens in the song – a slow unraveling of hope and beauty spreads throughout his rocky province and he is suddenly filled with inexplicable joy. I've planned my death so many times, but then, as I'm drifting through an empty terminal like wind, or reading a forgotten magazine in the restroom, I feel a strange sensation, a sense of happiness, and I remember my son and wife.

If only the terrible ghosts would take me to the park on Sunday so I could kick a ball around with my boy like I used to, or sit me back in the hot kitchen with a towel around my shoulders, as my wife set about giving me a haircut.

If there is a heaven, I wonder whether I'll see them there and whether my madness will remain on earth, like clothes shed before a swim.

A family once sat beside me in the terminal. I shall never forget it. They were en route to London from Minnesota. Only the father had left the country before. There were three of them in total: a father, a mother, and a son.

The boy was in his thirties and wore a special padded head restraint. His face was contorted with an expression of pain, and his clawlike hands were pressed tightly to his chest. His eyes were neither jittery nor vicious, but slow, soft green hillsides upon which he had been trapped for decades.

We couldn't stop looking at one another, and when his bony limbs erupted in spasms, his mother said, "He has something to tell you – there's something he's trying to say to you."

Like the shepherd from his rock, I thought.

I wonder if in heaven his fingers will uncoil and reach out for his mother's soft curls. I wonder if he'll take his father for walks through clouds with pocketfuls of words. I still think about that man and sometimes dream of him naked and beautiful beneath the earth in a dark, slippery cave trying to feel his way into the light.

Two Sundays ago I passed a church that looked like the one where I used to give Mass, and I had something of an epiphany. I realized that it wasn't God, the Devil, or death that terrified me – but the fact that everything continues on after, as though we'd never existed. I sat on the steps and listened to the singing inside, to the strength of many voices singing as one. Birds swooped down to snatch scraps of food off the roadside.

Last night, I spent the evening watching snow fall onto the runway from a quiet corner of the terminal.

Different-sized trucks were deployed, and they circled the tarmac like characters in a mechanical ballet. As the flakes thickened and lay still, I wondered if my wife could see me from beyond and how ashamed I would be if she could.

And if the snow were never cleared off the runway, it wouldn't matter, because it would one day disappear of its own accord; then one day return, perhaps accompanied by wind, or by stillness, or by the sound of breathless children pulling sleds.

Everything Is a Beautiful Trick

I AM STANDING ALONG MY road. It is early evening, and each house is tucked back into a pocket of vegetation. The only cars are stationary and barely visible through low branches, which hover over the houses and cars like hands.

My wife naps back at our old wooden house – a house so tired its limbs creak as though it is speaking back to the weight of our random movements.

I cannot walk farther because something sweeps through me – something so sad it renders the world broken and perfect all in the same feeling. I can tell that someone very close to me has died – that Magda has been taken away.

My wife was jealous of Magda for many years, even though they had never met.

I have stopped walking beside a house several houses down from my own. There is an old car in the front yard, its doors heavy and tires flat. A skin of pollen has gathered across the windows. The vinyl roof has peeled and flaps in the wind; the promise of a storm.

The windshield wipers are frozen in place halfway across the glass. Coated in pollen, they resemble two arms reaching out from under the hood. Ghosts kiss in the backseat. Memories spill out through a cracked window, melt into the ground between tall grass, and are pushed back up as wildflowers. Somewhere along the street a screen door yawns.

The feeling that Magda is lost fills me, swelling the skin of memory like a balloon being inflated.

Above the car there is a grocery bag caught on a branch stealing mouthfuls of wind.

My father adopted Magda from Poland, from Kraków when I was seven. My mother had left by then. Magda didn't know her at all. Magda was a long girl with short, unevenly chopped hair. Her left arm was missing at the elbow.

We shared the attic at our small house in Cornwall. We would wake early on Sunday mornings and make breakfast for my father, who would be out surfing. Even in winter, he would paddle through the freezing fog into deeper water.

Some mornings, the sky was so dark and the wind so fierce we would light candles and pretend we lived in a cave.

My father began surfing in storms after my mother decided one day that she wanted to live in Australia with her boss and his children. I was two. I barely remember her, but I am still in love with her ghost.

After setting out a brick of bread and a nest of boiled eggs, Magda and I would keep watch from the staircase, and when we saw the lights of his old Land Rover bouncing up the muddy driveway, we would skip down and open the door. This became a weekend ritual. When he stepped into the warm kitchen, he would laugh at the candles and rub my head with his salty hand. He would give Magda his wet suit, and she would drag it into the bathroom with her only hand, leaving a trail of sand and seawater on the carpet.

Over breakfast he would tell us about the sea and if anything had been washed up. Once, an American airplane from World War II tumbled onto the rocky beach after a terrific storm. My father took us to see it after breakfast. The rain was so fierce that Magda and I shared a garbage bag with holes cut for our heads. We were amazed by the fuselage of the airplane, which lay on its side. Two barrels of a machine gun poked out of a glassed dome. My father said its wings probably broke off when it hit the water. He said they'd probably not be long in coming if the tide was right. Magda and I wanted to go inside, but my father said no in a voice that meant no bargaining. Magda suggested we say a prayer to the sea, and my father said he couldn't have hoped for a more sensitive daughter. That was one of the best mornings of my life.

As my father told us stories over hot bread and eggs, seawater would sometimes drip from his nose.

When Magda first arrived from Poland and could only communicate with her eyes, we would take long walks together through the village and always stop at the same place to sit and watch old people lawn bowl. Later, when she could speak English, she told me her name for the bench beside the bowling green – *niebo*. Heaven.

On summer nights when the lingering light blushed and then disappeared, I often mused on how objects kept up with us. How lucky, what magical synchronicity, that soulless things should not only occupy the instant, but travel through time with us at the same speed, as though everything were perched high on the crest of a wave surging forward into the unwritten.

Later, on that same bench before the bowling green, when we were both eighteen years old, I told Magda about the mystery of soulless things keeping up with us, moving through time at the same speed. She laughed intelligently and told me that sometimes it is we who get left behind, anchored to memory. That is why she said she liked watching the old people in white play bowls, because they had slipped from time and hovered above the past.

We were on the verge of separation.

As we sat on the bench, as we often had for twelve years, I knew something was being taken from us. We were on the boundary of adulthood: I was leaving for America – a surfing scholarship to a college in California – and she to a prestigious university in Warsaw.

I still imagine Poland through descriptions in her letters she wrote from her university – storks nestling on rooftops, the grassy, minty dullness of marjoram, and the heavy pungency of caraway blowing through the Carpathian Mountains.

It was in silence on the bench beside the bowling green that I knew I would never see Magda again, or that if I did, we would have evolved beyond reconciliation. Without words, we mutually allowed experience to swallow us whole. It was the only way forward. But her absence would haunt me in the same way my mother's absence haunted my father, and the missing part of Magda's arm haunted her.

Now that I'm married and living in California with my wife, I think living with the absence of someone we love is like living in front of a mountain from which a person – a speck in the distance, on some distant ridge – is perpetually waving.

In youth we wave back to the figure on the cliff.

I remember us on the bench together drinking warm Coke from the same bottle, two beings about to plunge into their own lives. How soon would we reach the bottom? While at the university in California my class read *The Odyssey*. It interested me because it's not only about the sea but about love and recognition. My father is like Odysseus, but so is my mother. Odysseus is Everyman. All seas lead to one home or another. Every path is the right one. And Magda has disappeared from the earth.

Now, in America, where I have made a home for myself, it is fall, the season of memory. The old car leans to one side. It, too, has strayed from time; it has no designations. It is a car only in name, but in essence it is a sigh.

The sky is beginning to darken. I can imagine my wife napping back at our house. Light spills from a kitchen window on to a patch of flowers.

When my father and I first met Magda at the airport years ago, she was clutching a naked doll with no hair. My father was not expecting a stick-thin girl with one arm, and so he scooped her up and whispered something in her ear. As we twisted our way home along cliffs, Magda looked out at England and then at me, as though I was somehow responsible – as though I had woven everything for her.

Only since becoming an adult have I realized how scared she must have been. She was a child in a place where she could not communicate. Over time her fear became trust and we became a family. When a person is loved, they are granted the strength of all seas.

She never spoke of the violence and abandonment of her early life. It's amazing she even went back. She bore deep scars but through loving turned them into rivers. For some people, life is the process of knocking through walls to get out. For others, it is the building of walls. My father once found Magda crying next to a one-thousand-year-old oak tree not far from the house. She had packed a child's suitcase, though its contents were splayed around her feet. He carried her into the house, and she continued weeping in our room.

That night she admitted her compulsion to escape. She was worried that if my father drowned, or I disappeared, she would be left with nothing. By running away at least she would have the joy of knowing she was missed.

A few days later my father took her on a "father-daughter trip" to London, explaining that he was going to introduce her to our relatives so she might never feel alone. The night they returned after the five-hour drive, we lay in bed together – her hairless doll between us. She explained in broken English how my father had taken her to the monkey cage at London Zoo and introduced her as "Magda the Invincible."

She once told me how she could feel the missing part of her arm – how she sometimes experienced the sensation of a hand – that it is possible to feel something without its physical presence.

Perhaps love is like this and we are all limbs of one giant intangible body. I can see her chopped black hair upon the pillow and remember kissing her shoulder as she slept.

Night can unmoor so many feelings; it is a relief we sleep through it.

Night unravels the day and reinvents it for the first time.

We may mean nothing to time, but to each other we are kings and queens, and the world is a wild benevolent garden filled with chance meetings and unexplained departures.

Magda became so worried that my father would drown in a storm that one morning he woke us up as the world was beginning to crack open. With a special kind of paint Magda and I wrote our names on his surfboard. As we drifted back to sleep – the sound of the Land Rover roaring to life outside in the rain – an umbilical cord of light beneath our bedroom door held the world together.

After leaving for Poland, Magda wrote to my father once a week for two years and stopped when my mother returned from Australia – her skin several shades darker, a cigarette quivering between her lips as she stood before my father in the doorway. I was living in America when my mother appeared and know that my father took her in with no explanation. My mother had been away for eighteen years. She was actually surprised that I was gone, that I had grown up.

She never knew Magda, though I imagine she harbored the same kind of jealousy toward her as my wife does – a strange contempt because it is welcomed by me and probably by my father.

In the gloaming as I open the door of the abandoned car, Magda sings to me through the grinding of iron hinges. I sit inside. The steering wheel is a circle of bone and the chassis rocks with gratitude as I make an indentation in the seat. I am here and inhabit this moment, but I am forever on that wooden seat with Magda, or watching her release steaming eggs from their hot shells.

I never saw her after she left for Poland, but in the letters she wrote in the early years, it sounded as though she was happy. Once she even drew a stork on the envelope.

I know she missed us and that somehow we had given her the ability to live – that my father and I had untied a knot.

And now she is gone. I am not curious as to how it happened; that will come with the telephone call from my breathless father in the early hours of the morning.

I wonder if Magda passed my dreaming wife on her way.

I have encountered thousands of people only once, but they carry a memory of me and everyone else – like sand on a beach, shaping the edge of a living world.

When I arrive home from my walk, it is late and I am drowning in moonlight. I can smell hot coins of rain collecting in the sky, ready to fall. I can see my wife sitting on the porch swing smoking a joint.

The smoke twists upward from her mouth, and, dissipating, it slides over the roof, above the empty forgotten car and the wildflowers, climbing, circling, giving itself to the unknown.

I approach. It begins to rain. My wife looks at me in the same way my mother must have looked at my father. She pats the cushion next to her. The seat takes on the weight of my body, and we both begin to laugh uncontrollably – as if simultaneously realizing that everything is a beautiful trick.

French Artist Killed
in Sunday's Earthquake

T HE FINAL MOMENTS OF her life. Marie-Françoise lay crushed under tons of rubble.

The fish she had been eating was still in her mouth.

Her eyes would not open.

She could sense the darkness that encapsulated her. She could not feel her body, as though during the fall, her soul had slipped out and lay waiting for the exact moment when it would disappear from the world.

Then her life, like a cloud, split open, and she lay motionless in a rain of moments.

The green telephone in her grandparents' kitchen next to the plant.

She could feel the cool plastic of the handle and the sensation of cupping it under her ear. She could hear a voice at the other end of the line that she recognized as her own.

The weight of her mother's shoes as she carried them into the bedroom.

The idea that one day she'd be grown-up and would have to wear such things.

Running into a friend.

That time had passed.

And then the rain of her life stopped, and she was in darkness, her heart pushing slowly against her ribs. Muted noise as though she were underwater.

Then the rain of moments began again until she was drenched by single esoteric details:

Morning light behind the curtain.

The smell of classrooms.

A glass of milk.

The hope for a father and the imagined pressure of his arms against her.

Laying her head upon her new boyfriend's cool back in the morning. She had done it twice. It was as important as being born.

Her grandparents again, but characters in their own stories – walking barefoot in the snowy mud and stepping on a buried hand.

The end of the war.

A bungalow in France.

A daughter.

A granddaughter.

Her mother's elbows as she drove their old brown Renault.

Marie-Françoise could not feel her body and was unable to shout.

There was no sound, nothing stirred but the silent movies projected on the inside of her skull.

She was not so much aware that she was dying as she was that she was still alive. Had she more time, she may have nurtured a hope of being rescued. Instead, memory leaked out around her.

Blowing out candles unsuccessfully – birthday year insignificant, just the aroma of smoke as small fires were extinguished by tiny helping breaths.

Then the sound of footsteps in the hall, and creeping barefoot to find her grandfather dead at the kitchen table with the refrigerator door open.

An egg unbroken on the floor.

Her grandmother's screams.

This memory was not painful to her now. Her life was an open window and she a butterfly.

If not for her intermittent returns to darkness – the body's insistence on life – she could have been on vacation, swimming underwater, each stroke of her arms in the cool water a complete philosophy.

And then she smelled her grandmother's coat, hanging loyally behind the kitchen door with a bag of bags and a broom.

She wondered if she had lived her entire life from under the collapsed building. That her life was imagined by a self she'd never fully known.

And then with the expediency of the dying, she immediately fell in love with the darkness and the eight seconds she had left in it – each second like a mouthful of food to a starving man.

Apples

A s night unraveled through the streets of Brooklyn, the sign outside Serge's shoe repair shop glowed. The red neon burned through evening and into early morning. Anyone pacing the city, anyone lingering in the palm of a streetlight could not ignore the dazzle and low growl of bright gas pumped through tubes like blood in the shape of letters – a promise to all who passed that certain things never need go unmended.

Below the neon sign, Serge's display consisted of several pairs of shoes whose owners had never returned. Serge had painstakingly reconstructed them into sullen models of their former selves.

Under a shelf of dusty Russian magazines was a broken chair for customers to wait while Serge hammered, glued, and stitched. The smell of glue was often overpowering, but it was a thick, fragrant odor that hypnotized customers into waiting quietly in their socks.

The broken chair would not have supported the full weight of a person, but by some miracle had remained intact, beautifully ancient, with one leg suspended an inch above the carpet, as though immersed in a never-ending dream of walking.

Serge was a large Russian with a face like old leather and eyes that over time had been dulled by life. When he was a young man, his hairy arms and beastlike stature were enough to pique the interests of men who enjoyed fistfights. But Serge always backed away from the sly remarks of drunkards, so they assumed him dull-witted or a coward, of which he was neither.

Serge was learning English slowly like an old man entering a sea. He enjoyed it because there were so many secrets entrenched within the meanings and in the pronunciation of each strange word.

Like butterflies, new words flew from Serge's mouth and fluttered about the classroom for everyone to admire.

Serge had taken an English class at a local Russian Orthodox Church, designed after its famous cousin in Saint Petersburg. Serge often overheard neighborhood children discussing the rumor that the church had partly been constructed out of chocolate.

One evening in class, after the teacher had asked everybody's profession, she winked at Serge and explained to the class how the word for the bottom of a shoe and the name for a person's spirit were pronounced without any difference.

That night Serge lay awake beneath a full moon in his bed. His curtains were ivory squares that washed his crumbling apartment white, turning furniture to old wedding cake.

He repeated the word he'd learned in class. He said it out loud from the soft canyon of his pillow. Night had passed, but it was not yet morning.

Serge stopped going to class three weeks later because he couldn't keep his eyes open. He arrived early for his final class and explained to the teacher that it may have been the glue he used in his shop, but he just couldn't stop falling asleep. She was sad to see him leave and advised him to read newspapers in English. Other students drifted in, and within twenty minutes, Serge fell into a deep pool of sleep and then quickly resurfaced in a dream. He was back in Russia. There was a light wind. He entered his family house, and several birds escaped through the open door slapping his head with their wings.

As his classmates practiced the sounds and shapes of their desires, Serge climbed the dark stairs of the house his grandfather had repaired as a teenager. The house had once been the center of village life, where Serge's grandfather held great parties with tall cakes, apple beer, and incense that hung from the fireplace in tight, dry bundles.

A river curled across the property, and Serge's grandfather died one day beside it, while drawing a bird, which he abandoned to a life without flight. Serge had been watching him from the parlor window and, like several village children running through the orchard, had thought the old man to be dozing.

For two blissful years, Serge lived in the old house with his wife, a dark-haired seamstress from a village across the mountain where water froze all year-round.

She died in childbirth almost one year after Serge's grandfather. The birth of his daughter was the saddest-happiest day of his life.

The grand old house soon declined, and within a short time only several of its rooms were comfortably habitable. Their only visitors were a motley group of animals that crept up to the back door at dusk. Serge deposited scraps in several piles to prevent disputes. Serge held his daughter up to the kitchen window so she could see.

While Serge's mostly Russian classmates chained letters to one another, he continued to dream and breathlessly reached the top floor of a house now boarded up and empty. From down the hall, he could hear his daughter crying, but when he tried to move in her direction, an invisible force held him in place. Like all parents, Serge recognized the nuances of his daughter's anguish, and of all the things she could have been crying for; the dream – in a stroke of illusory genius – had merely soiled her diaper.

Serge had often spent whole nights perched over her crib like a gargoyle, afraid for the worst. In Greek myth, Death and Sleep are brothers.

Had it not been for his daughter's crying, Serge would have been afraid and the dream would have been a nightmare – an expression Serge loved because night was like a horse that tore through the forest of memory.

As Serge cupped the doorknob and entered, the crying from down the hall abruptly ceased. In darkness on the broken chair from Serge's shoe repair shop was his grandfather.

As he approached the suited figure, the old man's left foot ascended through a constellation of dust. His eyes glowed like two small moons; his sole had come unstitched.

Under the spell of the dream, Serge knelt down to inspect the damage. His tools appeared.

Only once in his life had Serge repaired a sole that bore the weight of a foot. His grandfather once confessed that such an operation required such skilled stitching and steadiness of hand that it should only be attempted as an act of trust – and reminded Serge of the peasants who tended the feet of Jesus.

Serge's grandfather had not only repaired shoes but also crafted them from pungent sheets of leather and small hunks of oak.

One snowy morning in 1903, a guard from the palace of Prince Romanov rode into the village, his legs numb with frostbite. Across his shoulder in a black satchel threaded with gold were thousands of rubles and a cast of the six-year-old prince's feet.

The guard dismounted wearily and then announced to the growing crowd how the great gilded hall of the royal palace had resounded with the name of *their* local shoemaker. Serge's grandfather was summoned immediately from his smoky cottage on the edge of town.

On his arrival, the guard fell to his knees and begged him to make the shoes his masters had sent him to procure. Serge's grandfather helped him up from the muddy puddle and then listened as the guard explained how, with so much money in his satchel, it was unlikely he'd make it back to the palace alive, and in the event of his disappearance, his wife and child would have to live with eternal shame.

Serge's grandfather was kind, and he assured the guard that he would make the shoes and that for the time it took to craft each piece he would share their home. The palace guard lived in the shoemaker's cottage for two months and, over steaming potatoes, told stories of bravery and last words from the frozen battlefields of Russia's battlefronts.

As Serge stitched his grandfather's phantom shoe, the old man vanished, leaving behind only a few crumbs of soil on the floorboards. The dream, however, remained intact, and he could hear the old man descending the staircase – the chair dragging behind him and clapping each step.

When Serge awoke, class was almost at an end, and the dream slipped from his memory like a pebble sucked back into the sea.

Several months after the dream in that last English class, Serge sat quietly on a B63 bus, watching various workmen settle into their labor for the day. The bus swerved to avoid craterlike potholes. Serge balanced an elaborate lunch on his lap. He had ordered it the night before from a Polish restaurant on the corner of his block. It was a special day, and on the seat next to him was his finest suit wrapped in paper and tied with string.

Although the day's heat was still settling, dark bruises drifted across the sky, stopping above the river to admire themselves. It was a day Serge had been looking forward to all winter, and after opening the shop he unlocked the nightly drop box and set to work on the first pair of shoes – looking up only to greet customers with unusual verve.

It was the day of Brooklyn's only apple festival, and for blocks, in apartments of all shapes and sizes, children were cleaning out buckets and stuffing their pockets with bags in preparation for the evening affair. The ragged homeless had gathered on the corner and were idly watching the stream of commuters disappear into the subway, occasionally asking one of them for a cigarette.

By early afternoon, rain lashed the front window. It was thick and sticky in the shop, especially when the machines were running at full tilt. Moisture in the air prevented the glue from sticking with its usual tenacity. Serge wiped the sweat from his forehead with a corner of his apron. He counted how many pairs of shoes were left to fix and then conducted a triage, placing the most critical repairs at the front of the line.

Each finished pair was wrapped in a white muslin cloth and hung from one of thirty nails hammered unevenly into the back wall with a Russian bootheel.

A small boy from one of the nearby slums often visited Serge at the shop. Omar lived in a damp apartment with his aunt, who had several children of her own. Omar didn't know where his parents were, and his aunt refused to tell him until he was eighteen years old. Omar had once pointed out that Serge's back wall of shoes could easily have been a hiding place for a "spider's future meals."

Serge asked Omar to point out which package looked most suspicious. Omar chose a lumpy white bundle hanging from the farthest, highest nail. Grumbling, Serge took his footstool and plucked it from the nail. He set it in front of Omar and unraveled the cloth. Omar turned up his nose and remarked that it was the biggest fly or the ugliest pair of shoes he had ever seen.

Serge could not remember a time Omar had visited and not pleaded with him to teach him the business of shoes or at the very least let him try his hand on the polishing machine.

"Shoes," Omar once proclaimed, "are the heart's messengers."

Serge chuckled and told him to scram but later wrote the phrase down on some muslin cloth and taped it to the old bathroom mirror.

Omar had not been to the shop since July fourteenth – almost a month. Serge knew this because he marked Omar's visits on the calendar by drawing a pair of round faces: a small head with a smile and a big head with a straight line for a mouth.

Serge's only other friend was a blind tobacconist from Ukraine called Peter, who when not being beaten by his wife played obsolete military songs on an accordion.

Serge sewed the final stitches on a roller skate, as though he were playing a tiny violin. After breaking and tying the thread, Serge held the skate up to the light and inspected each stitch. One of the wheels began to spin. Serge imagined himself on the wheel, spinning through life, moving through time but never actually getting anywhere.

It only seemed like yesterday that small broken wings of snow had silently fallen against the shop window; only yesterday he'd boiled his daughter's diapers on a frozen winter morning in Russia. Without memory, time would be no use to mankind, Serge thought.

Many years ago, his grandfather had bought him a pair of ice skates to use on the river when it froze. In the arms of an afternoon snowfall, his grandfather told him that happiness tears the sky to pieces.

Serge could almost feel his grandfather's hot, smoky breath against his cheek; then a view of the apple orchard; each tree propped on the white tablecloth and the indentations of animals' feet; the hollow bark of an owl through the white falling drops.

On a tattered poster behind the door of Serge's shop was a giant shoe elevated above the heads of several shoe mechanics. They were pointing to the sole and marveling. As a young man, Serge had dreamed of coming to America and purchasing a Cadillac or a Lincoln, like the ones important Mafiosi cherished. About the time he married, Serge daydreamed on dry summer afternoons in the orchard with his back against a tree. The apple trees were always stuffed with birds, and Serge often fell asleep to their evening concert, while his wife dug flower beds barefoot.

He imagined himself cruising down Fifth Avenue, the sparkling dashboard before him, his children reading American magazines in the backseat. Their feet, of course, fitted with the finest Italian leather shoes and their voices light and full of hope.

His wife died a few months later while giving birth to their daughter. Six months and one week after that, doctors from a nearby city explained to Serge that his daughter had a heart full of holes and that she wouldn't last the summer. The doctors agreed that the only two things capable of saving her life were God and money. Serge immediately put the house up for sale, but by the time it sold, it was too late.

Serge removed a small tongue of gum from the roller skate's wheel with a razor. He bit his lip so hard that blood ran down his chin and dripped into a pile of laces. Thirty years later, the shame of how he'd wished away all his money on a car still burned his cheeks.

On a windless day in July, Serge's daughter was lowered into a small hole at the edge of the family apple orchard. A white cross marked the position of her head, upon which gold script told anyone who cared to pass that she was her father's only daughter and that she loved animals. In the box at her feet, Serge placed the family tools, to give his grandfather something to do while they waited for him.

He hung the roller skates from the longest, most crooked nail.

Outside, birds were pulling nets of song through the streets.

Morning's dark clouds had dispersed, leaving a blue shell of sky lightly chalked.

With the skates mounted and the street outside noticeably busier, Serge decided to close up and make his way over to the apple harvest.

He dressed meticulously and combed his white hair in the yellowing toilet mirror. After polishing his own shoes on the machine in his socks, he washed his hands.

Under the sink was a long silver cake knife wrapped closely in white muslin cloth. It was a family heirloom and once guided the weight of two hands across a wedding cake.

Serge slipped the wedding knife into his pocket and flicked off all the lights inside. The outside sign burned all night in dazzling red neon read. It read: ALL SOLES FIXED HERE.

He locked up and stepped onto the street.

Serge hoped he might see Peter the blind tobacconist or Omar – someone to keep him from the company of ghosts. Children rushed past with buckets tied to their backs with rope. Others kept pace with their parents, their faces sour with the embarrassment of a public scolding.

Like a gust of wind, another group of children swept past Serge, gently brushing the edges of his clothing.

The evening was comfortably warm, and for miles around, the piercing freshness of ripe apples poured into people's homes like sunlight.

Serge lived humbly in a basement apartment in the Greenpoint section of Brooklyn. His landlord, who lived upstairs, was a retired university professor who thumped on the floor with a broom when he listened to Beethoven. He was also a widower and the only member of his family to escape the Nazi gas chambers. The weight of their sadness combined would have been too much for either to bear, and so their relationship consisted of a mutual nod whenever they came face-to-face.

On a table next to Serge's bed was a small apple tree, which he tended to every day as responsively as if it had been a dying companion. He purchased the most expensive plant foods to ensure its prosperity. It was almost a foot tall and, with a growing confidence in the world around it, had begun to widen at its base.

In three months, depending on the weather, Serge would have to sneak down to a once-abandoned lot, rip up some cracked tarmac with a crowbar, and plant the tree next to all the others he had planted since arriving in Brooklyn in 1974. After thirty years the wasteland lot had become an orchard and the site of New York City's only apple festival.

Nearing the orchard, Serge could hear the crowd and wondered if there would be anywhere to set up his folding chair.

As he turned the final corner, his perpetually dry eyes were suddenly moist and he felt himself crying. Instead of stopping to forage for a handkerchief, Serge continued his slow rocking walk, for he was sure that no one would look at him long enough to know.

On the eve of his departure from the small Russian village of his birth, Serge had smoked in the family orchard watching workmen board up the windows of his family home with thick planks. The men's wives toiled inside, covering furniture with thick white sheets as though blindfolding them.

Before the men nailed shut the front door, Serge carried his suitcase outside and set it on the grass. It was dusk. The river that flowed across the property was high and thick with the soft black bones of trees.

Like people, all rivers are falling.

With several blankets borrowed from his mother-in-law, Serge made a bed for himself on the grass, six feet above his child.

At dawn, with a film of dew upon his skin and clothes, Serge rose to his knees in order to kiss the gravestone one final time. However, at some moment during the night, an apple had swollen just enough to sit perfectly on the head of the stone. Serge was breathless and picked the apple so the branch – madly and gratefully – could return to the tangle of branches above. He buried the apple deep in his suitcase. On the journey west, six days of hunger and thirst were not enough to tempt him to eat it.

As Serge came within sight of the lot, he was confronted once again with his daughter's legacy and more than a hundred Russian apple trees nodded in recognition.

The curling limbs of the trees were studded with apples, and children grew within the branches, laughing and hanging upside down.

Serge unfolded his chair at the edge of the orchard and listened to the sound of apples punching buckets. Some people had brought barbeques and were baking apples wrapped in aluminium foil.

After several hours, Serge cut his last slice of apple with the silver wedding knife and then wrapped the knife back in muslin cloth. People were beginning to go home. Children dispersed in small groups, their tiny backs bent over with cargoes of fruit. An apple is the size and weight of a human heart; they were carrying the hearts of those not yet born and those lost forever.

It was getting chilly and Serge didn't want to risk his arthritic hands. By morning, his nightly drop box was sure to be full of broken soles and heels worn into smiles.

As he started to rise, Omar pushed through the crowd, his pockets so stuffed with apples that he could only run with his legs straight.

"Shoe-man!" he exclaimed. "I've been looking for you all night."

At the end of the block a firecracker exploded, and Omar grinned.

"Up to your old mischief, uh?" Serge said.

"I bought you a baked apple, but I dropped it and a dog ate it." Omar arranged the apples stuffed into his pants.

"The mayor of New York was here, did you see him?" Omar asked.

Serge said no.

"Someone threw an apple at him," Omar said, laughing.

"Not you, I hope," Serge muttered.

"No, not me – but he said that the city has bought the lot and is giving the orchard to the children of New York." Omar lunged for an apple as it popped free from his pocket and rolled under Serge's chair.

"Who do you think planted these trees, Omar?" Serge asked. "Haven't you ever wondered who started this?"

Omar was on the ground fishing for the lost apple but managed to say, "Nobody knows who did it. The mayor said it's one of the city's great mysteries."

"But have you ever wondered why anyone would do such a thing?" Serge asked.

"Because they love apples," Omar said.

Serge noticed the moon and felt the deep pull of home.

When Omar finally found the apple under the chair, he removed one of his little socks and ripped it in half.

"What are you doing down there?" Serge snapped.

A pair of small hands suddenly began to skate over Serge's shoes. The hands moved vigorously but with controlled strength. Omar spat on the sock and rubbed the heel. Serge tried to get up and shake off the scoundrel, but he had already started the other shoe. Serge sat back and closed his eyes.

Everyday Things

FOR A MOMENT AFTER waking up, Thomas was only vaguely aware that he was alive. Then, like the shock of cold water hitting his body, Thomas remembered that his wife's sister had telephoned during the night, that they had spoken briefly and nothing had been resolved.

He lifted the blanket off his body and waded through a gray light that had seeped through the curtains and into the room. He looked at the telephone with disbelief and then made a pot of tea. While it was brewing, he sat on his bed and fought to remember a dream. He tried piecing it together, but it was as though a feast had taken place during the night in his honor and he had awoken with only a few crumbs. He looked at the telephone again.

He could hear rain spraying the window and decided to write his letter of resignation. He sat at his desk. He swept aside bills and the report he would never finish, then pulled a crisp sheet of paper from the bed of the printer. After finishing a cup of tea, he began to write. He could feel a skin of sugar upon his teeth and after writing his own address, realized he could not steady his hand. It shook like a small, dying animal.

He turned his head toward the telephone but did not look.

Outside, he could hear the increasing traffic. People were going to work, radios were clicking to life in bedrooms, coffee was dripping into glass jugs, bathtubs were filling up. He gripped the handle of the teapot awkwardly and poured himself another cup.

He could imagine his wife in the hospital, her limp body beneath the white sheet like a spread of mountains. In his mind's eye, he pictured the nurse's white shoes and his wife's bare feet parted beneath the hospital sheets.

Her sister had called in the early hours, but he had spoken very little because each time he thought of a word, it had popped like a bubble before he could nudge it past his teeth and into the telephone. Nothing had been resolved, and he thought of the hospital corridor, a long river of plastic with brightly colored lines upon the floor. He could sense the tension in her sister's voice as she imparted everything the doctors had told her. All he could think was how beautiful the word *triage* was.

He dressed. The house was cold and quiet. He poured himself more tea and drank it cold. As he poked his arms through the sleeves of his jacket, his eye caught a pair of her boots. He wanted to slip his hands inside, through the dark leather mouths and into the stomachs that cradled her feet.

He tried calling her sister. Her telephone rang for a long time. He replaced the receiver, feeling that life was disordered in a way he had never imagined.

He looked at his watch and thought of his old self driving to work, listening to the news, sipping coffee. He felt a strange sense of shame and naivety and knew that if he let his mind regress, it would pass a countless number of occasions in which he could have been a stronger and brighter version of himself.

After tying his shoes, he reached into the closet for his raincoat. Instead of yanking it from the hanger, he tugged slightly at the arm and felt his hand begin to wander. It brushed against different fabrics and then stopped at her favorite coat, a long camel-hair one with a thick belt. His fingers crawled into the pocket and swam around between coins, slips of paper, and mints. The secrets of a hand.

He drove to the hospital. The hand that had been in her coat pocket exuded a light aroma of perfume. He thought of her spa and pictured the shelf of tiny bottles above her desk, each one containing a distilled floral essence, each bottle an olfactory fingerprint.

He remembered the faces of her clients as they hung their coats and then peeled a magazine from the stack on the table. He remembered watching their eyes sail slowly through the pages as they anticipated the warm, scented oil upon their faces and the soothing calligraphy of his wife's hands.

The road to the hospital became narrow and straight. It stretched through a forest like a gray bookmark, and dead leaves – like brittle letters – bounced across the highway on their brittle ends.

He tried to hold a portrait of her face in his mind but could not weave each detail simultaneously. He thought again of the small bottles above her desk.

At the hospital he stood above her and listened. Birds muttered on the window ledge, a machine clicked. He sat in a chair and studied her fingers. They were long and evenly spaced. On her wrist was a clear plastic band with her name written by a computer. This made him angry. He leaned in and breathed upon her hand. It was warm, and he shuddered as his breath pushed against her skin.

He felt numb, as though during the night his body had been filled with plaster. He wondered what was happening inside her head. He imagined a garden with the noisy dots of birds.

The day of the operation had been the worst day. Now it was a waiting game, said her sister.

After napping, he awoke to a shadow cast over his wife's body.

"Good morning, Thomas," the nurse said.

He nodded and asked if there was any change in her condition. The nurse consulted her charts and replied that there was no change.

"Would you like to wash her face?" the nurse asked. He turned to his sleeping wife and imagined swishing a wet cloth through the tiny canyons and then across the plains of her cheeks. He felt awkward and his hands turned to wood.

"I'll get you some warm water," the nurse said.

She returned a moment later and placed a bowl and some cotton balls beside his wife's bed. Thomas dipped a ball of cotton into the warm water and then squeezed it. He swished it along her forehead. She did not move. When he had finished, he patted her face with a soft towel, being careful not to cover her mouth or nose.

The operation had lasted six hours and twelve minutes. During this time, Thomas left the hospital and walked to a park where he sat on a bench and wept violently for several minutes. He then smoked a cigarette and watched two boys throw a football to one another. In the December twilight, a dog barked. Then the park was swallowed by darkness. As he had walked back to the hospital, he felt ashamed that he had left even for a moment and wondered if her sister would be angry with him.

He stood before the automatic doors at the hospital for a moment before continuing.

As he had made his way back to her room, he remembered the boys playing football in the park. He thought to himself that one year from this moment, everything would be different – for better or worse.

★   ★   ★

The nurse returned and took away the bowl and cotton balls. Thomas remembered his wife's voice from years ago, expressing a wish to see the lavender fields of France.

Next year for definite, he thought, when all this is behind us, we'll do something like that.

Four days since the operation, and everyone who visited commented on how she had lost weight, as though it were somehow complimentary. It was an uncommonly warm afternoon, and Thomas decided to walk to the park again. It felt good to walk, and he tried to imagine the splintering glass, the spontaneous explosion of the air bag – her face and crumpling body.

He saw the park up ahead and slackened his pace. He tried to see the faces of people driving past him. They eyed him for a split second and were gone.

A sudden loathing filled him.

As he sat down on an empty bench he resisted an urge to sprint back to the hospital and carry her from the bed to their house and then lock all the doors.

At that moment, Thomas realized he had changed, that he was not the same man, but like everyone else, he was the result of an accident that had once taken place between nature and chance.

An old woman with hanging cheeks sat down beside him and sighed.

"The evenings have become so cold," she said. She offered him a stick of violet gum. He slipped it into his mouth and chewed. They sat mostly in silence.

"This time next year," Thomas suddenly remarked to the woman, "my wife and I will be in France."

"Oh, that's nice, dear." The old lady seemed delighted but then looked away. "My husband and I always talked about going to Europe."

"They grow lavender and you can smell it in the air as you amble through the villages," Thomas said.

"Wished we'd gone when we had the chance," she said, "but life just swallows you up, doesn't it? Just swallows you up with its everyday things."

That evening at the hospital, Thomas insisted that he stay with his wife – that he hold her hand and burn some of her favorite distilled essences.

"Most people go home, get a good night's sleep, and come back first thing," the nurse said as she folded a towel.

"I'm not most people," Thomas said and truly meant it. The nurse left the room without a word.

Conception

I AM SITTING AT THE kitchen table with the lights off. There is
broken glass strewn across the red stone floor. The back door is
wide open, and moonlight drips through the trees and pools in the
doorway. I am sitting at the table drinking tea in darkness, while
my wife is somewhere in the fields that stretch endlessly behind our
house. I hold the cup with both hands, as though engaged in holi-
ness. I can imagine her in mud up to her ankles, her glasses spotted
with rain, hair breaking like black sea on her shoulders.

When I arrived home and saw the broken glass and the open
door, I knew she had received news from the doctors. Flapping in
the breeze on the table like a white tongue is the letter, which may
confirm her worst fear. I dare not read it. In the darkness I can see
the cluster of words scattered across the page; like small fallen bodies
they reach out for us.

I wonder if she smashed the glass on purpose or if one of her
walking poles nudged it as she twisted her back and thrashed all
limbs, negotiating her crutches like giant chopsticks as she made for
the empty, moonlit pasture.

Her legs are so deformed you'd think they were rubber. I touched
them for the first time on our wedding night at a bed-and-breakfast
only eight miles up the mountain. On a clear day you can see it from

behind our cottage. I remember the bed and the crisp, yellowing sheets. I wondered how many people had slept in it. I marveled at how the pillow, like a small theater, had staged countless dreams. At dusk, when I smoke in the garden, the lights of the bed-and-breakfast flutter beneath a faint flock of stars and remind me of our first night. We touched with a softness that pushed through the skin into memory, like arms plunged into a river – we could feel the weight of each other's stones.

My wife's legs are so unnaturally twisted that when she was a girl her classmates boasted of frequent nightmares in which their own legs melted into dead white snakes. And they called her names that pierced her like arrows. Every night she fell asleep bleeding and dreaming that one morning she would awake with legs as straight and strong as trees and that on Saturday morning small pink fingers would push the doorbell – a prelude to the breathless voices calling her out to play.

My father was a miner. Her father was a welder who repaired steel-frame supports in the shafts. She dreamed that when her bones woke up and joined hands, her father would light his welding torch and turn her poles into a bicycle with a basket on the front, the sort other girls used to ferry hot parcels of fish-and-chips or crab apples poached from a tree by throwing sticks into the branches.

Once, she threw her poles into the branches of a pear tree that grew at the edge of the schoolyard. They stuck, and when the bell rang summoning children back to their cold desks, she sat shivering outside until a teacher noticed a speck by the fence and sent for the caretaker and his retarded son, who dragged the ladder across the yard pulling faces to the window of every classroom.

My wife is out in the fields, in the shadow of a mountain crowned by mist. Perhaps she is leaning against a stile and watches the drifting cows, their eyes as still and black as well water.

Conception

The village we live in erupted from mud, and mothers wage an impossible war against the perpetually dissolving ground. Above the village, the sky is so stuffed with cloud that water, like some curious animal, finds its way into everything and lives on the backs of the people – slowly drowning them.

On Saturday the unmarried and the widowed kiss and fight at the Castle Pub on the hill. Anyone not at the pub or in the ground is sprawled before blazing fires in cottages, which, like sad ornaments, dangle upon the hillsides on smoky threads. Children watch black-and-white televisions in kitchens as fathers chop heads off fish and smoke cigarettes, peering into back gardens until evening, like a grieving stranger pulls his cloak across the day.

My tea is cold, and the moon, anchored by the hopes and wishes of those abandoned souls churning their way home from the pub, has drifted deeper into the sky.

My wife and I have been back and forth to Wrexham Hospital in the rusting truck. They slide a needle into her spine, which like lightning splits me in two.

And there's the letter that I daren't read, because I have wanted a son since my father was crushed in a collapsed shaft.

I was a boy in this very kitchen, perched at the table in darkness waiting for him to come home and take me to the fair. I had my heart set on the acquisition of small orange fish, which were being dispensed liberally to children in thin plastic bags.

When suppertime passed and my father was still not home, I was so angry that I drew a picture of him and then stabbed it with my pencil. I pictured him at the pub, his face smeared with coal dust, sitting quietly with his workmates rolling cigarettes.

Eventually, a neighbor knocked and entered. She set a plastic Thermos of soup in front of me and explained how my father was stuck in a mine and that it would be on the news. I thought of the drawing and cried.

My mother waited at the entrance to the shaft for three days, and I slept at the neighbor's house beneath a crucifix made from clothes pegs. I imagined myself wandering the grassy mountainside and then digging with the pencil I'd used to stab my father until his hand pushed through the soil holding a bag of fish.

My wife is the neighbor's daughter. Before the night my father died, I'd only seen her on Sunday afternoons tilting around her front garden like a broken toy.

She told me that while my father's body might be crushed under tons of black earth, the body is nothing but camouflage. She whispered that every soul is a river trying to find its way back to the sea.

I have wanted a son since my father's accident. I will continue where he left off. I hoped I was the crucial link. When I can bury every ounce of my disappointment about what I think the letter says, I will slip through the gate into the fields and bring her home. I never want her to know that fatherhood was the ambition of my life. I don't want her to feel as though she has let me down; yet for a moment I consider what would happen if I packed a small bag and escaped, perhaps to London where I could work on a market, or up to Scotland where I'd mine deep lochs for eels. It's tempting to imagine how we could hurt someone close, because it reminds us how fiercely we love them.

In this very kitchen I would listen to my mother tell stories about my dead father. The Sunday afternoon they drove up Sugar Loaf and listened to the crackling radio with a blanket spread over their legs. It had rained, she said, and I imagined the beads of water on the windshield like a thousand eyes, or each drop a small imperfect reflection of a perfect moment. She told me about their first weekend away in Blackpool, fishing for crabs off the pier with cans of beer and hot sausages wrapped in newspaper. She told me that love is when a person introduces you to yourself for the first time.

After he died, I began to imagine the deformed girl from next door as my lover. I imagined driving her up Sugar Loaf Mountain on the back of my bicycle and then touching her legs, and then kissing them with the coyness of snowfall. I imagined defending her in the playground, and with my pillow I practiced punching the rubbery noses of my schoolmates should they dare open their mouths and spill ugliness upon her.

Years ago, I wrote to doctors in America and asked how much it would cost to straighten her legs. Every single one of them wrote back requesting charts, personal information, and, most importantly, photographs. The only photographs I had of her legs I took surreptitiously while she was asleep. I sent them all. There is nothing they can do now, they said, but advances in technology are made every day, and I should keep in touch – which I secretly do. Every Christmas twelve doctors across America each receive a package of tea from Wales.

But if she were whole and her legs were capable of symmetry, I would no longer lift her in and out of the bath, nor drive her to the library where she stamps books and enrolls new members, for these are rituals of marriage in which I lose myself.

I imagine if she were like everyone else: scrambling from the truck on Sugar Loaf Mountain to chase one another. It would take ten years off our lives to run like that. All couples should run away from each other and then collapse in a knot.

Everyone in the village knows me as they knew my father. Once my wife took some coal from the burner and smeared a little dust on my face. She told me I look like him – that our eyes contain the same color water. Death ends a life but not a relationship.

I sweep up the glass on the red stone floor, then find my rubber boots. She won't have eaten. I will carry her home and then lower her into a hot bath. She will cry, and I will say nothing.

It is almost midnight and wind throws light rain against the cottage, whipping the windows and softening cemented stones. The ground beneath the gate has been churned by the split hooves of cows. The mud is thick with puddles as deep as buckets.

As the ground begins to harden I hear the frantic call of some animal. The pasture is free of cows and glistens like wedding cake. As I trudge across it, I notice a white speck in the middle and realize that the noise is the sound of my wife's laughter.

I quicken my step and begin to pant. Drops of rain, silvered momentarily by moonlight, plummet through white plumes of my breath like stars.

My wife is standing without her poles and for an instant I suspect a miracle, but as I approach I see that she is up to her knees in mud and that her poles have been tossed out of reach by the same passion that makes her laugh.

Before I embrace her, I turn around. Mist has swallowed the house. Only the white field and our two shaking bodies inhabit the earth.

As I fall to my knees and reach for her torso, I feel her fingers press against my scalp. Her voice is light and powerful.

"The letter," she says. I try to pull her from the mud, but it holds her as though it were holding its first flower.

"Did you read the letter?" she says again.

"I don't care about that anymore," I say, but a burst of wind carries away the words and she laughs again, lifting her arms to the sky as though channeling some great force through her body.

Save as Many as You Ruin

B Y THE TIME GERARD leaves the office it has stopped snowing. Lights are coming on, but it's not yet dark. At the end of each block the sidewalk disappears under a pool of gray ice water.

Gerard thinks of everyone's footprints in the snow. Manhattan was once a forest. He imagines the footprints of an Indian slipping home, on his shoulders a warm carcass with clumps of snow stuck to its fur.

Gerard thinks of his own footprints and how soon they will disappear. He exhales into the world and his breath disappears. He recalls Rilke, *what is ours floats into the air, like steam from a dish of hot food*. He wonders if his life is an extraordinary one.

Gerard remembers the freezing cross-country races at his English prep school. Bare white legs spotted with mud. Plum-sized hearts thumping.

He remembers Hetherington, the physical education teacher, his strong jaw and sweet blue eyes – the desire to see his boys drink up the glory of victory. Hetherington ran in the 1936 Olympics in Berlin. He won a medal. Hitler watched. Millions were about to be killed as a teenage Hetherington crossed the finish line. A few years later, children walked into gas ovens after a long journey from home. They were scared but trusted their parents.

Gerard feels stabbing love for his daughter. He crosses Fifty-third Street. Her name is Lucy, and she is eight. She has short brown hair with Hello Kitty clips pinned cleanly to her head. Gerard once sat next to a rabbi on the train to Southampton. The rabbi had just returned from England. He was making a documentary about the war.

"But there are so many already," Gerard had said.

Walking up Fifth Avenue he cringes at the insensitivity of his comment. He must have thought I was like everyone else, thinks Gerard. Am I like everyone else, he thinks. The rabbi had merely put his hand on Gerard's cuff for a moment.

It suddenly begins snowing again.

Yellow taxis are nodding through the snowy dusk. The lights from shopwindows are beckoning. Gerard thinks of the mannequins. They are very still, perfectly still. They are talking about something they've never done. They are sitting down to meals they'll never eat; tucked into beds in which they'll never dream.

He pictures Lucy in their warm apartment perched at the table reading a simplified *Black Beauty* in large print. Her legs are swinging under the table in concentration. He has never known such devotion.

Gerard is handsome. He has slept with many women. Most knew he would never love them, so they kept a distance, sparing themselves the grief of an ancient pain. Gerard loved one woman once, but not Lucy's mother.

Lucy is at home with Indira, a heavy-set Barnard student from New Delhi who cooks dinner every weeknight and helps Lucy with her homework. Gerard and Lucy love Indian food. Indira often stays and eats with them – at first she wouldn't. She is becoming part of the family. Her father died.

The snow is covering everything. Gerard remembers *The Invisible Man*. A crackling film from the 1930s. He watched it one night with

Lucy. She'd seen it listed in *TV Guide* and wanted to watch it. It was on late. She fell asleep after five minutes. Gerard could feel her heart thudding like a soft, warm rock. As he carried her to bed, she asked him what happened to the invisible man. Gerard told her that he was caught because it began to snow and he left footprints. That's beautiful, she said, without opening her eyes.

It's a blizzard now.

Flakes like clumps of fur ripped from winter's back.

And then he sees Laurel through the falling snow.

Eight years have passed.

He can't believe it and stops walking.

A woman with bags bumps into him and curses.

Laurel is a few feet away.

He steps over to the glass and taps gently on it.

A line of people inside the shop turn to face him like a sleepy jury.

Her face is still sharp and angular like a Cubist painting, but softened now by her eyes, which have sunk or regressed partly into memory. He thinks she is more beautiful than ever. Her mouth opens in the shape of an almond. Gerard cannot tell if she is smiling.

All this happens within five seconds.

Gerard wonders if he has done the right thing. Perhaps he should have walked on. Later at home in his study, he could re-create the moment he saw her in line at the shop and let the memory spill over like a faucet left running.

She is holding a tray of raw fish and a bottle of iced tea. In that moment of recognition he is not consumed by a rushing sensation of love – quite simply a door opens to a room that has never gone away. The years apart were just years without one another.

They were together only a few months. They met at a dinner party given by one of Gerard's colleagues. There were candles, and wine, and the women wore dresses that left their shoulders bare. The candles made their shoulders glisten. Even unattractive women have beautiful shoulders. He and Laurel talked for hours. He felt as if they were catching up, though they'd never met.

When he finds her in the line she is about to pay, but Gerard quickly hands the cashier a few bills.

Laurel blushes.

"I can't believe it's you," she says.

"I know," he says and tries to maintain eye contact, but people are pushing past.

"So, how are you?" she says.

"Fine," he says. "And you?"

"Good," she says. "How is your daughter?"

"She's wonderful, just wonderful."

"How is her mother?"

Gerard pauses.

"Dead," he says.

"Are you kidding?"

"No."

"Oh, my God." Laurel is genuinely shocked.

"When Lucy was six months old, Issy went back to Los Angeles to fulfill her ambition of becoming an actress," Gerard said.

"What? She left her child?"

"Four years later she died."

It still felt uncomfortable to say her name in front of Laurel.

"That's crazy," Laurel says, "really crazy."

"That she died?" Gerard asks.

"Yeah, that, but for a mother to leave her child."

"It's what she did."

"I know, but it's crazy."

"Yeah."

"Did she ever visit?"

"No."

"Wow. I'm sorry, Gerard."

"It's okay. Lucy has no memory of her."

"But she was still her mother."

"Sure."

"Does she know?"

"No. I'll tell her when she is older, in high school maybe. I cannot bring myself to hurt her with the truth now. Something like that can destroy a child."

"You're still kind," she says.

"I love her, I'm her father. I want what's best for her."

"You were kind to me, too."

"Was I?" Gerard says. "I don't feel as if I was."

"You were," she says, "despite everything."

Gerard went to Issy's funeral in Los Angeles four years ago. She was found floating in a pool. She'd written Gerard's name as her next of kin. Los Angeles was seventy-five degrees and dry. The air-conditioning in his rental car smelled like candy. Issy had played the part of a psychic on a soap opera. People exchanged business cards at the buffet after the cremation. Gerard told Lucy he had to visit Hollywood on business. She wanted to come. Indira offered to sleep over and did. Gerard brought Lucy a present back. He wanted to buy many but stopped himself. He didn't want LA to have a special significance. He brought Indira a gift, too – a tote bag from MoCA with little birds on it and French writing. Lucy had asked about her mother recently. Gerard didn't know what to say. He was planning on going to a child psychologist to ask for advice.

Gerard met Issy a month after he met Laurel. A decade ago, Gerard had never met any of them.

Gerard vaguely remembers the feeling of being in love with Laurel and the desire to have sex with Issy. He knew that other men enjoyed the occasional partner outside of long-term relationships, and he wanted to try it. Issy was an incredible lover. She sprayed perfume on her thighs. She was uninhibited and never took her heels off, even after. Issy wasn't upset when Gerard told her that he was falling in love with Laurel. She laughed and then cried and told him she was pregnant. Gerard thought it was a joke. She was always telling lies. Then he felt something crack inside him because she wouldn't stop crying and he knew it was true. He told Laurel the next night, and she said she understood. A week later, Laurel broke it off in an e-mail.

Gerard agreed to move in with Issy.

Gerard still has Laurel's wristwatch at home in his bedside cabinet. She left it in his apartment eight years ago. Miraculously, the battery still works. Sometimes at night Gerard takes it out and falls asleep as it drips from his fingers.

Laurel is forty-three now. She is a senior editor of business books. She had a cat, but it died. Gerard buys some coffee and asks if they can walk together. Of course, she says, and then looks outside at the blizzard and laughs. She is wearing the same kind of heels Issy used to wear. As they leave the deli, there are people getting out of a taxi.

"Quick," Gerard says and they get in.

In the cab they talk about the president, their parents, and Laurel's brief marriage. She is divorced now, and her ex-husband is living with another man in Brooklyn Heights. She laughs, but Gerard can see she is disappointed.

When they get to her building, Gerard's nose starts bleeding. Night has fallen upon the city, but the snow isn't stopping.

"Oh, my God," Laurel says, and tips Gerard's head back. People watch them.

"Jesus, come inside, okay?" she says to Gerard.

"Okay," he says.

In the elevator they talk about their jobs. He can feel the blood clotting in his nose. Tiny fragments of snow have lodged in Laurel's eyelashes.

Upstairs, Gerard calls Indira to say he'll be back a little later. Then he and Laurel make love first in the kitchen and then in her bed. Her body is not as he remembers it. It is softer and somehow more pliable. Her toes seem perfect.

Her apartment smells of expensive scented candles. She makes coffee after. Her furniture is modern and gray. He feels somehow inside of her – held by her, and he remembers as a boy, swimming to the bottom of a thick pond in summer.

When he arrives home, Lucy jumps down from her chair and runs into his arms.

Gerard kneels and her weight becomes his.

"Why aren't you in bed, pebble?" Gerard says.

Indira appears in the doorway. "School is canceled tomorrow because of the snow, so I didn't think you'd mind if she waited up."

"Of course, Indira, it's perfectly fine."

"Why are you so late, Daddy?" She is kissing him all over his face. Gerard imagines her mother floating in the pool.

"I love you," he says.

"I love you, too, Daddy, but where were you?"

"I met an old friend and we had dinner," he says. Lucy can smell a lie a mile off.

"Is your old friend an old woman?" Lucy asks.

"Yes, how did you know?" Gerard laughs.

"A daughter knows," she says and runs back to the table, laughing and flailing her arms as though they are about to become wings.

Indira won't stay, so Gerard gives her more than enough cab money and thanks her for staying late. She kisses him on the cheek and he holds her. Her hair smells of onions.

After a bedtime story, Lucy asks if she can meet her father's friend.

"I think that would be nice," Gerard says. Lucy looks shocked, as if she'd expected him to say no. Children are difficult to read sometimes.

"Does she like ice cream?" Lucy asks.

"Yes, she eats it every day."

"Are you going to marry her?"

Gerard pauses. "Wait and see."

"Does she have any children my age?"

"I don't think so. Do you want her to?"

"Only if they're not boys."

She asks her father to sit on the edge of her bed until she falls asleep. He says yes, as always, but falls asleep first, as always. Soon they are both asleep.

The snow is blowing against the window.

The room glows with the breath of streetlight.

Around midnight, Gerard wakes up. Lucy stirs.

"Daddy, where's panda?" Gerard finds her stuffed panda and lays it next to her. She goes back to sleep immediately.

In the kitchen, Gerard pours himself half a tumbler of whiskey. He turns out the lights in the apartment, checks the front door, and then walks barefoot into his study.

Instead of taking down a book from the shelf, he looks out the window. He can see all the way up Lexington Avenue. The snow is drifting across the city in waves. Traffic is thin. A few glowing eyes.

He knows that before long Laurel will move in with them. He thinks of Issy. He remembers her laugh, then the roar of snapping flames at her cremation.

All of a sudden he feels a chill like cold water down his back. The tumbler of scotch slips from his fingers and shatters on the floor. Gerard spins around. His heart leaps into his throat. Someone was there, he could have sworn it. But in the space between him and the world he can see only air, only air and the auras of the day past and the day to come.

He thinks how strange life is with its frayed edges and second chances; and though by morning he will have forgotten that he ever thought it, Gerard feels as though he is being followed, that there are voices he can't hear, that the footsteps of snow on the window are just that, and like Lucy's conception – life is a string of guided and subtle explosions.

The Still but Falling World

I LIVE IN ROME WHERE people sit by fountains and kiss. The sound of water is the sound of love rushing between them.

In the morning, the marketplace outside my apartment smells like artichokes. They grow on thick stalks. People forget they are flowers. Some leaves are the color of a blushing cheek. The hard leaves protect a heart.

Tomatoes are more delicate. The vines are laid in rows. Each vine bursts open in several places with a red fist.

The man who sells garlic comes from the south and doesn't sip coffee with the others at dawn. I watch him from my window. I, too, am from the south and know the loneliness of mornings.

Last week it was my cousin's son's birthday, and I sent a gift. I've been thinking a lot about my cousin lately. I'm starting to understand why she lied to us. She and her husband live with their children in the village where I grew up. It is called Morano Calabro, and the small stone houses wrap around the mountain like a cloak of many pockets. At the top of the village are the ruins of a Norman castle where teenagers hide from their parents. It is always windy. They learn how to smoke and drink beer. They watch the drifting lights of cars in the valley. There's talk of moving to Naples, Rome, Venice, but most stay in the village and have beautiful children who grow quickly and want scooters.

Morano Calabro is about 500 kilometers south of Rome. In spring, it is common to see flocks of five or six butterflies. My father told me when I was a child that butterflies are just flowers that have come loose. Childhood was hard for me because I worried about everything. I worried about the end of the world, diabetes, earthquakes, asphyxiation, each of my family members slipping into a coma, one by one (as if going off to look for the others).

At age eight I would set my clock to rise in the early hours and check the regularity of my brother's breathing against my palm.

Life now is sometimes difficult, but at least I know that my condition is a condition and my concerns aren't always serious ones. I may not be normal, but I no longer worry about worrying, I just worry and know it's who I am. If you've never heard of such a thing, I'm surprised, as it's fairly common. You probably know someone who has it. Let me give you a recent example.

I was in a toy shop two weeks ago buying a present for my cousin's child. There was a box of lambs. I picked one up. The wool looked grubby, so I put it back and picked up another. Then the one I put back had this look. So I put the second lamb back to go with the first lamb (because I felt sorry for it), and the second lamb also had a look that said, for God's sake, can't you see I need love, too?

The shopkeeper was looking at me. "Can't decide, eh?" he said stupidly. I began to perspire. I looked around. On every shelf peering down at me were little heads, all pleading to be taken home and rescued from the darkness of a loveless existence. I almost slipped into a panic attack, which, if you've never had one, feels like you're free-falling in darkness (like Alice).

After twenty minutes, the shopkeeper said something else. I couldn't stand his looking and decided to buy them both. It was settled. I scooped them up in a moment of ecstasy and relief.

But two remained in the box. They both had looks. And one had a missing eye. I picked him up. I now had three lambs. There was one very lonely lamb left. He was very lonely. So alone he couldn't even look at me. And so I had all four sent in a box with the store's shiny wrapping paper and a sticker with their address on it. As he addressed the package, the shopkeeper asked me if Morano Calabro had a place to buy toys. "Of course," I said. You could tell he lived only for his shop.

My cousin's husband called during the birthday party a week later. There were children everywhere, he said. They were wearing paper crowns of different colors. I could hear them in the background, a jumble of soft, shallow voices. It's amazing to think they will age together, love one another, deceive one another, weep for each other, and in old age congregate at the public gardens and lock their arms. He put his son on the phone. "I'm three," he said. "Would you cry if I died?" "Yes," I said, and he blew me a kiss. I wonder if he thinks I'm really in the handset, tiny and groping.

The handset is sometimes like my body.

His father came on the phone. He wanted to know why four lambs. "Are they supposed to look the same?" he asked. "They don't look the same," I said. Then I told him they came as a set, which really wasn't a lie. "But why not three in a set like musketeers?" he asked. "Why not four," I said, "like the Ninja Turtles." "I suppose that makes sense," he said, having watched *Teenage Mutant Ninja Turtles* with his eldest boy that very morning. Never admit you have obsessive-compulsive disorder to someone who doesn't have it because they'll think you're crazy.

But the reason I'm telling you all this is because his wife, Isabella, who he thinks is my cousin, is not *really* my cousin. My entire family and her husband and children are living the most beautiful lie.

Her real name is not Isabella Ferrari, but Jocasta Lefferts. She's from Queens in New York City, and her last name is the name of the street she was found on by the local New York police. She came to my village five years ago. It was winter. She showed up and said her name was Isabella. She had a photograph of distant relatives, my grandmother's uncle, Luigi, and his wife, Luciana. Luigi was a metal craftsman. Luciana made clothes. She was partially sighted from birth. In 1917, Luigi's younger brother died in his older brother's arms from shrapnel wounds. Luciana waited for Luigi at the edge of the village to return from the war. When he did they walked to his mother's house in silence. His mother was outside hanging clothes. The sound of drops into dry earth, then footsteps. She turned around. It was the saddest-happiest day of her life.

Luigi and Luciana were soon married in an olive grove high above the village. The spot has not changed but for an old washing machine abandoned on the road halfway up the mountain. In 1920, they departed Morano Calabro for Argentina. No one knows anything about their lives after they left the village.

Isabella's Italian has improved over the past few years since she arrived from North America. From her look, I actually think her ancestors were West Indian, but that doesn't matter. She arrived with an elaborate story of how her grandmother (who was the daughter of Luigi and Luciana) married a Canadian soldier after World War II and moved to Toronto.

Isabella now has two children with a man from the village. She met him soon after arriving. He is handsome and wears Versace glasses. He works the village espresso machine at his newsstand. He dresses so fashionably tourists think he is from Rome or Milan. He is worldly without having gone anywhere, so nobody in the village was surprised when he married a stranger.

I think my grandmother knew Isabella was lying when she first came to the village five years ago. I wonder why she didn't say anything. She is a quiet woman. Her husband was older. When he was alive he worshipped her like a teenager.

My grandmother may know that Isabella is not really part of the family, but only I know her real name and her history (which is bleak). No, I would never say anything because everyone in the family (including her) is in love with one another.

She, her husband, and their two boys take a vacation once a year (nowhere special – Sicily or Bari), and at Christmas Isabella and her husband watch, from a sea of other parents, their children in the Nativity play, dressed in a patchwork of cloth and old carpet. I remember being on that stage dressed as a little bear. I was so nervous. I thought I was going to die out there and was sure that my outfit was teeming with fleas. After the play my father scooped me into his arms and I felt brilliant. For weeks, I felt brilliant. I even asked for a book on real bears.

Now I see it was such an insignificant event to the world. But then every beautiful moment in my life has been an insignificant event to the world.

Even though Isabella doesn't know it, I can relate to her. I know how it feels to be an outcast.

I left the village because I'm gay. And it's hard to be gay in a small place like Morano, even though it's beautiful and the streets smell of wood smoke, and you can go anywhere at anytime and you'll never be turned away by anyone. You must understand, it's a question of practicality, not a question of acceptance. Times have changed. In Morano, if you're loved, everything else falls away. My grandmother knows I fell in love with a man from Rome (the relationship has long since finished), and I pursued him here, which is where I've lived for four years.

Maybe I'll move back to the village in my twilight years. Perhaps I'll have a partner to take long, slow walks with. It's such a beautiful place. The Dutch artist M.C. Escher loved Morano. In 1930, he quietly made a woodcut of the village on Japanese paper. It hangs in the National Gallery of Canada.

We also have a fifteenth-century polyptych by Bartolomeo Vivarini in the main church, the skull of an old castle at the top of the village, a convent, ancient houses built into the mountain rock, and a public garden with a chuckling fountain where teenagers gather and explain the world to one another.

I wonder if Isabella suspects I know the truth about her. I don't have the courage to say anything, even if I could say I love you in the same breath. But then I don't see the point of truth anymore, it causes just as much heartbreak as lying.

Isabella told us five years ago when she arrived that her family was dead and that when she was going through her grandmother's things she found a photo with information written on the back.

She was actually in the village for two days before we met her. She arrived a few days before Christmas. Everyone was excited for the holiday, and it snowed through the night. The scent of trees blew down from the mountains in the morning, but by lunchtime this was replaced by the smells of baking, which spread through the streets like long fingers that pulled on everyone's tongues. Everyone had put up their decorations. You could sense the excitement of every child in the village, and they walked around in the evening with their eyes turned upward.

Isabella had taken a night train to Spezzano Albanese. After coffee and a croissant she hitchhiked to Castrovillari. The man who picked her up called his younger brother and asked him to drive Isabella to Morano Calabro. He had just worked a night shift and had to take his daughter to school. "She's from America and has come to find her family," he had said to his brother, which piqued the interest of their grandmother, who secretly listened in on her grandsons' conversations from an upstairs phone. The silence over dinner would be like cotton wool in the grandmother's mouth.

When Isabella arrived at the village it was the afternoon. She was cold and went to the village's grandest church, the Chiesa di S. Maria Maddalena. She fell asleep on a stiff pew. When she woke up, a man was sitting next to her. He had watery eyes. He asked her why she had come to the village.

She showed him the photograph of Luigi and Luciana. He hugged her. He explained that his own mother had died when he was six. He said it was like God had taken a bite out of him.

Isabella's Italian was very limited then. She didn't understand much that was said to her, but she hugged the man back. His sincerity made a deep impression.

Together, Isabella and the man with watery eyes went to the house of the local police inspector who had access to all the village records. He lived in a stone cottage on via Chiazzile. There was a pink plastic cup on his front step.

The man with watery eyes knocked. A man with white hair poked his head out of an upstairs window. "I'm trying to watch the news and my wife has a headache," he said. The man with watery eyes explained everything passionately. "One moment," the police inspector said, then closed the window.

In a few minutes, it began to snow. Then, the police inspector, dressed in full uniform, complete with medals he'd been awarded for bravery, quietly closed his front door and led them to the building where records were kept. The man with watery eyes pointed to the police inspector's medals and narrated the rescue of two boys from a frozen pond in the 1960s. Isabella asked where the brothers are now. "Costa Rica," the police inspector said. "I just got a Christmas card from them."

At around three in the morning, the police inspector tapped a name in a dusty book. "I have found your family," he said. "I will call them at dawn." And the three of them sipped wine around the space heater until the sky turned white.

Isabella was kissed and hugged more than she had ever been in her life. The building of public records was a scene of great joy. The children of the family wondered what they would give her for Christmas. The man with watery eyes was the last to go home.

The day after Christmas, the police inspector and the man with watery eyes knocked on the family's door. The police inspector had his hat in hand. They had made a mistake, he said. They were not Isabella's real family.

There was anger and confusion. Isabella was summoned from an upstairs bedroom. One of the youngest children cried so hard it became his first memory.

She trudged back to the building that contained the public records. The wrong family followed. When my family arrived from the other side of the village, the wrong family eyed them jealously. Then the wrong family demanded to see the records for themselves. An unmarried uncle of the wrong family pointed out to my father that the police inspector had made one mistake, so was certainly capable of making a second. My father agreed this was a possibility.

Before leaving to come home with my family, Isabella promised the wrong family she would visit them and said kindly that you never know who is who and that she was sure they were her family, too. My mother agreed that God often did things like this for good reason.

I was in Naples visiting my uncle when all this happened and came home the next day to find an American girl sleeping in my bed. My English isn't bad, and I told her I didn't mind and then listened to my mother's story of the mix-up and how the police inspector is really too old to be in such a position of power. But then my father added that it was all the police inspector had and to take his position would destroy the man's spirit.

Isabella presented me with the photograph. Written on the back were the names of my grandmother's uncle and his wife, the name of the village, and the date they left. The photo was taken in an orchard. Nobody knows where. Luciana is smiling in the photograph. "Perhaps she was pregnant," I said. My grandmother looked at me sadly from the kitchen as she dried her hands on a dish towel. Then she looked at Isabella.

I'm going on a second date tonight. Marco is a restorer of Renaissance works, but he is really a sculptor. I met him on via Condotti. We've sipped coffee together. His hands are beautiful.

It is quiet in my apartment as I pick out my clothes. I can hear the future getting into position, like shuffling actors on a stage before the curtain goes up.

Last night in bed, the idea of going out with Marco kept me awake. My pillow must have soaked up a thousand conversations. Then I imagined Marco choking on a piece of penne. Then I saw myself doing the Heimlich maneuver on him. But then I awoke from this half sleep, this shallow river of worry, and realized that I don't even know the Heimlich maneuver, and had to go online at 3:00 a.m. and find out. Then I practiced in front of the mirror with a pillow.

This morning when I woke up I felt like a fool. I drank green tea and thought about Isabella as I watched the men in the market set out their day's vegetables and fruits. I then remembered the four lambs I had bought Isabella's son. One had a missing eye.

After Isabella had been with us a week, I decided to find out more about her because while looking in my room for something, I saw her passport poking out of her suitcase. I looked inside, and it said that it belonged to Jocasta Lefferts.

There was also a business card for a social worker. I wrote to her pretending to be the Italian authorities. I sent Isabella's passport as verification. It wasn't a very kind thing to do, but I was worried. Isabella didn't even realize the passport was missing. She hasn't left Morano since she arrived. The social worker I wrote to was assigned to an orphanage in Queens. She sent me a copy of Isabella's file. She had the file officially translated, but in clumsy guidebook Italian; the social worker had written, "Please take care of her" on the front of the file.

According to the file, an unnamed child was discovered by police in May of 1981 next to a Dumpster on Lefferts Avenue. As a teenager, she ran away several times from the center. She became a prostitute for two months to pay for her boyfriend's drugs. He died. She was beaten several times. There were other things, too. Terrible things.

After reading her file I began to love her. Whoever she is, I thought, she's now a member of the Ferrari family, and in the name of the Virgin Mary, I thought, we're claiming this child as one of ours (and I'm not even religious).

I rode my brother's bicycle up into the mountains and burnt her file along with her passport in the body of an old washing machine abandoned at the side of the road. There were wildflowers everywhere.

My grandmother saw I had received a package from America but said nothing. She and I are very close.

It is a beautiful evening, and I am walking through Rome to meet Marco. I am passing the Coliseum. I can imagine Marco waiting for me at the Piazza Navona beside the fountain of meeting rivers. There are tourists everywhere. They are taking pictures. I wonder what will happen to each photograph in the future. Strange to think photographs outlive us. The Roman Coliseum was once the scene of mass slaughter. People watched people being torn apart and crushed by wild animals from all over the world: lions, elephants, crocodiles, hippopotamuses. The Romans, the Romans. I can't stop thinking that everybody is somebody's child.

I once heard a guide explain to a spellbound crowd of tourists how when the Roman Empire fell, the Coliseum was abandoned and became overgrown with exotic plants and flowers, the seeds for which had been carried in the feces of animals brought from Africa, Asia, and Europe.

I'm now walking through the Roman Forum. If you ever come to this magnificent city, you'll be delighted to learn that it's all free. And bring your children, Italians love children. They'll be treated much better than you and given things to nibble on in every shop.

There are men strolling around dressed as gladiators. They will take a photo with you for a price. They play their parts well. Perhaps they really feel like Roman soldiers. Maybe they tell their wives over supper they were born too late.

I wonder if things can happen too early or too late or if everything happens at exactly the right time. If so, how sad and beautiful.

I'm almost at the Piazza Navona, which is where I'm meeting Marco. The alleys are choked with tourists. I'm tired. I haven't slept, remember. The sky is the color of a peach. It's evening, but it looks like morning. Every moment is a beginning and an end.

Isabella's children will never know their mother's sadness. It would destroy them because she is their mother and you only get one mother in this world. The thing I think about most is why she chose us. It would *seem* obvious to say that she is the lucky one, but I'm not sure it isn't the other way around. Her children's laughter falls through open windows into the village street. The man she married is deeply in love. I wonder if he bit his lip when he first saw her.

I am taking a shortcut. I am threading my way through secret alleys. There are dogs lying perfectly still. There are bags of trash and empty oil canisters. There are waiters smoking with their shirts unbuttoned. *Ciao* they say because I smile at them first. I think most people in the world are decent if they're not suffering.

It was hard for me to leave the house tonight. I couldn't stop checking the gas knobs. They were all off, and there was no hissing sound, but I just couldn't stop looking. And then I checked all the plug sockets and listened to the toilet in case something unseen was overflowing. And then when I did finally leave, I had to try the door handle ten times, just to make sure. The whole door is coming loose, but then if I leave the apartment three times a day, that's 210 times per week the handle gets jiggled. Maybe Marco could tighten it up for me. I can see his hands upon the hinges like two horses.

My neighbor is used to the sound of me jiggling the lock. If I were ever being broken into, she'd never suspect. I buy her a bottle of wine every now and then. I wish she could find someone.

I wonder if Isabella found the photograph of our family in a thrift store in New York City. Perhaps the real Isabella gave it to her on her deathbed.

The mystery is how the photograph traveled from Argentina to New York.

It took only moments for Isabella's husband to fall in love with her. And only a few moments for Isabella's biological mother to set her down on the street and walk away forever. Perhaps, desperately, her mother now has something to hope for. Like a lighthouse, her child missing in the world is a light diffused by the fog of her own despair; a despair beyond sadness.

Isabella's real mother felt her only power was to give up on everything, like Pontius Pilate washing his hands before the hot crowd. But her child went searching, and on a quiet Italian mountainside she found a future waiting for her.

I think we keep these moments of rejection and acceptance very close. I think we carry them always, like cracked shells from which a part of us once hatched.

I see Marco in the distance. He is holding two oranges. I can feel him without touching him. I stop walking. I want this moment never to end. I want to hold on in this still but falling world.

He sees me. We walk toward each other.

Sometimes the man with watery eyes calls on Isabella. She always asks him in. Her children sit on his lap and feed him little pieces of biscotti. They want to hear the story of the church, they want to hear the story of mama. They want to know everything.

The Mute Ventriloquist

I

O SKAR WAS A POLISH ventriloquist who lived in a basement apartment in Brooklyn. People thought he was mad and were afraid of him. Sometimes he went for long walks. He never spoke to anyone he saw, but carried small bits of meat in his pocket for passing dogs. Those who didn't know Oskar was a ventriloquist might have thought him mute, but with a small wooden puppet on his knee, the words and sentences flowed like water out of a tap.

Upstairs from Oskar lived a boy called Drake and his mother. The address was 999 Lorimer Street. Red paint peeled above the front door. The stairs groaned when Drake ran up and down them in his socks. His best friend growing up was called Kristine. She was very tall and flopped her legs when she walked as though stepping over something invisible. Drake liked to mimic the voices and sounds he heard coming from the man in the basement because it made her laugh. Sometimes, when he and Kristine talked in whispers on the steps, Oskar would suddenly appear with two plums.

They put on the years like new coats. But by the time they were teenagers, Drake and Kristine had become strangers to one another. The intimacy of unbroken silence was replaced by the awkwardness of conversation.

★ ★ ★

Twenty-five years later, Drake saw Kristine at a sales convention in Glasgow, Kentucky. At first he didn't recognize her because she was so much bigger. Then he felt suddenly very light. His breath quickened as though he'd been running. There is little joy in those first moments of recognition – for most first glances of love come to nothing. And while the sincerity of that rare moment when your heart is bursting should be the signal to fling yourself on the ground in the path of this stranger – it's the depth of such sincerity that paralyzes you, holds you back from the possibility with phrases like "hello" and "good morning."

Drake approached the woman cautiously. She was seated on a folding chair. When someone passed her table, her arm reached out mechanically with a brochure for testing rings and hydraulic gauze. The lights of the convention center were very high up.

The carpet beneath their feet was a tight brushed red. People had come from all over the world to compare filters and demonstrate new hydraulic methods by lowering small machines into buckets. At some tables people were given rubber aprons and invited to try for themselves.

When Kristine saw Drake, she dropped her stack of booklets.

When he picked them up, he saw very pretty shoes. She was wearing a company T-shirt and a shawl. When she pulled the shawl over her shoulders, Drake noticed marks on her neck, a faint mess of hands. He stood looking at her. She arranged the booklets on her lap.

"You're pregnant," he said.

They shared a quiet, Chinese dinner at the mall. They found a table in the corner near two machines. One was full of tiny rubber balls. The other was a glass case with a mechanical claw that dangled over slumped toys. Small bulbs in the claw machine made Kristine's wedding band sparkle. When they finished supper, Drake stacked their plates on the plastic tray and carried it to the trash. Kristine watched. Earlier, when he picked her up at the hotel, she had changed into a long-sleeved blouse and a skirt with flowers stitched into the hem. Her pocketbook had a gold chain strap. Drake opened the door for her. When he got in to drive, a car bell chimed loudly, as though calling back to the faint thud in his chest.

Drake spent the evening at her Holiday Inn listening to the child in her belly softly juggle its new limbs. They ate peanut M&Ms and watched TV.

Later on, back at his own hotel, Drake stood at the window looking out at the parking lot. The cars below gleamed like unclaimed prizes. Insects swirled the streetlights.

Drake thought about all those years without her. When she looked at him, he felt like a clump of ice breaking under a stream of warm water.

He tried to sleep but lay on his back listening to the muffled shouts from a television in the next room. About three o'clock in the morning, he drove to a Super Walmart he had seen returning from Kristine's hotel. He figured there were a few things she might need for when the baby came.

He was half asleep when he dressed and couldn't find his socks. For three hours, Drake drifted through the aisles like a ghost. Everyone he passed seemed very friendly. A woman called Dorothy wrote him a list of things a baby might like to wear, or play with, or even chew on. Drake also talked for a long time with a man called Kevin about young feet. Kevin was looking at shoes for his girlfriend's kid. He said that you could tell a kid's personality from the shape of their feet.

The two men sat in comfortable chairs they would never buy. Kevin ate crisps from a large bag. Drake wondered if he had paid for them. Then Kevin admitted that he'd been coming to Walmart because he had lost his job as a night-shift packer. His girlfriend still didn't know.

The next morning at breakfast with Kristine, Drake ordered a triple stack of pancakes, extra home fries, three Belgian waffles, sausage, bacon, oatmeal, fruit cups, tea, and a pitcher of orange juice.

The waitress said, "Are you serious?"

Drake pointed at Kristine's stomach.

The sign for the Pancake Cottage was set very high up in the sky on a metal pole. The waitress said it was so that truckers could see it from the highway. She said that at night it was the brightest thing out there and drew people in from the darkness.

After breakfast, Kristine followed Drake into the parking lot to get the stuff he had bought at Walmart. She shook her head and said in a high voice, "Oh Drake, why did you do this?" Then she wiped her eyes with a tissue, forced a smile, and said, "It's really great, Drake. It's all really helpful."

She watched as he demonstrated the smooth action of the wheels on her new suitcase.

"Now you don't have to carry anything ever again," he exclaimed.

A truck growled past slowly on its way to the exit. Its chassis tilted as the front wheels negotiated the uneven ground. The puddles around them were wide and deep. A trainer lay upright – half in the water, like a small animal dipping its head for a drink. A forest lay beyond the restaurant. Slack power lines stretched between the trees like someone learning to write.

Shreds of cloud hung meanly on the far horizon. Then moments before she drove away, Drake rushed back into the restaurant and bought:

1. Five Hostess cherry snack pies
2. A six-pack of sparkling water
3. A box (the red one) of Ritz crackers
4. Bananas
5. A small polar bear holding a giant red heart that said "Kentucky"
6. Flares
7. A gallon of milk

He carefully set the brown bag on the passenger seat of her old sedan. She looked at it and said, "You're going back to Brooklyn?"

Drake nodded.

"When?"

"Tomorrow."

She sighed and looked at the road ahead.

"Let's say good-bye like we said hello," Drake said.

Kristine looked at him without blinking her eyes.

"Just something from a song," he shrugged.

As she drove away, Drake noticed how the paint had worn off the boot of her car. The roof upholstery was the color of a tongue and sagged. There were two uneven holes in the back shelf where speakers had been removed and sold for a few dollars.

Two months after the convention in Kentucky, Kristine appeared at Drake's front door. She was holding a suitcase of clothes and a lamp.

"Hello, Drake," she said.

"That's a nice lamp," he said, shocked by her sudden appearance on the steps.

He took her suitcase.

"It needs rewiring," he said.

The taxi driver waved. Drake waved back, and he drove off. Kristine had run away from her husband. They lived in Franklin, Wisconsin. Kristine said it was famous for frozen custard. Her husband worked at the plant. He was a supervisor. They had bought an extra freezer for all the free custard.

She looked tired. Her wrist was broken and in a sling. Drake didn't ask any questions. Her stomach was so large, it seemed as though she might tip over.

His living room became her bedroom. He changed his whole routine – even working different hours without telling anyone why. To the neighbors, Kristine called herself Drake's housekeeper, but they knew – and the older ones appreciated the veil of modesty. Drake liked to rub her stomach at night. He was amazed how people could grow inside one another. In the evening, Drake put on Bach's Goldberg Variations. One night, the child kicked. Drake danced around the room.

Then they held hands on the couch that they would share that night as a bed.

On Sunday morning a week later, they sat up in their couch bed and ate popcorn. Drake asked Kristine if she remembered the mute Polish puppeteer who lived in the basement.

"I do," she said.

Drake told Kristine everything because she seemed interested. His mother first took him to one of Oskar's performances on his fourth birthday. They took place in out-of-the-way places like smoky gypsy basements with grand tables on which stood steaming bowls of stew with small legs and wings poking through a film of oil and onion skins. At the first performance Drake attended, it was smoky and dim. A single stage light dangled above a straw ladder-back chair like an orange eye.

Oskar hobbled onto the stage led by his puppet. Oskar had dark skin that had come loose with age. The puppet resembled an Indonesian boy-prince, bare from the waist up but with a jeweled turban wrapped about his small head and a crown of hair as black as a bird's wing.

Oskar's performances were unforgettable, though specific details remained a mystery. His audiences included everyone from old homeless men to the sons and daughters of kings. One night, in the basement of the Tomkat factory in Long Island City, Japanese gangsters shared a table with the Hungarian king (then a teenage prince with an insatiable curiosity for the bizarre). When the puppet spoke, it was as though he were talking to each individual person. The wisdom of the puppeteer came only through the puppet.

After Drake's first performance, his mother took his hand and led him through the bewildered crowd to the stage. They climbed up and slipped under a violet curtain into a dark room that smelled like Bruson's Lime Hair Tonic. Drake remembered sitting on Oskar's lap. Oskar brushed Drake's hair with his hand. Drake wondered why his mother had never taken him downstairs to see where Oskar lived.

Drake remembers his mother kneeling to explain that the man upon whose lap he was perched could not speak, whispering to her son that the ventriloquist probably had something wrong with his own voice.

But Drake found nothing so strange about someone unable to find words for life. Children spend the mornings of their lives in a sea of imagination before being hauled out onto rocks by jealous adults who've forgotten how to swim.

Another performance took place in the Norman Avenue subway station at three minutes to six in the morning. Drake wondered how anyone could have known it was going to happen. When the puppet spoke, his wooden body rattling, a Chinese woman holding a bag of oranges let go of the straps. They rolled onto the tracks. People looked and pointed as the oranges settled like balls on a roulette table. Trains pulled into the station, but nobody got on or off because the doors wouldn't open.

Eventually the police came. They listened for a minute to size up the old puppeteer sitting on an upside-down bucket. But after a few moments, the police found themselves mesmerized by what the puppet was saying. And the next day, they woke up and felt great joy at being alive. One of the policemen decided he was going to take piano lessons after all.

On the day Drake turned six, his mother tied several balloons to a parking meter outside their house. He felt too old for balloons but didn't say anything. When his friends arrived, there was a party, a birthday cake, and presents. That evening, watching her pop balloons in the street, Drake said, "Why don't I have a father?"

She sighed and undid the string and torn pieces of rubber from the mailbox. Then Drake fell down the steps and split his chin open. He opened his birthday presents when they got back from the Old Stone Hospital four hours later.

Kristine wanted to know what she had told him about his father.

Drake thought for a minute and sipped his tea.

"She said that he was gone and that was that. I assumed it was her first husband. She talked about him so much. There were pictures everywhere. I even thought we looked alike."

It wasn't until Drake was in college, years after Oskar's last performance at the Greenpoint Working Men's Horse & Pony Raceway, that Drake's mother told him that actually Oskar was probably his father.

"Probably?" he had said. "What do you mean probably?"

Her jaw trembled.

Drake was furious.

"My husband of fifteen years who you didn't know had been dead five years. Oskar sometimes drank tea with me in the evening. I never thought we'd get married or anything. I mean, he was quiet then, but he at least used to speak. We saw each other often, and occasionally he'd stay the night."

"One day he found a puppet in the trash. Then he changed a lot. He became a different person – or more who he already was I guess – not unkind or anything, but not really here, not here in this world."

"I didn't want to interfere – and I was already pregnant with you by then, my little love. What a surprise you were – what a sweet surprise."

Years later Drake's mother got a disease.

Alzheimer's is like having your entire life written out on the beach, and then washed over by the sea at every tide.

A month before the birth of Kristine's baby, Drake began to have dreams. He called them dreams because they happened at night, but they seemed too vivid to have been imagined. It was as though they were imagining him. That he was *their* dream.

In the dreams, the old ventriloquist beckoned Drake to the Greenpoint Racetrack where the old man had given his final performance more than twenty years before.

At first Drake didn't tell Kristine about the dreams, but then he realized that she was his best friend – and so he thought to hell with it, and told her one night as they shopped for toys at the CVS Chemist on Manhattan Avenue. The chemist used to be a movie theatre, then a dance club in the 1970s. A disco ball still hung from the rafters.

Faded posters gripped the walls behind thin metal shelves crammed with toilet paper and boxes of crayons. As she stood in line at the checkout, Kristine told Drake that he should go to the raceway. "But it's only a dream," Drake had said.

"That doesn't matter," she replied. "It still means something."

That night, as they were folding out the couch that had become their bed since the baby kicked, Kristine said to Drake that maybe he was having dreams because Oskar was his father and soon he was going to be a father himself. Drake dropped the cushion he was holding and went into the kitchen. He stared out the window into the quiet street, his eyes blazing. Kristine followed. Her hands appeared on his shoulders like two slow birds. Drake reached for them.

They stood in silence for the first time since childhood.

Two nights later at the racetrack, tired horses limped the oval to the delight of a few gamblers. A short man wore a dark green bird tattoo on his hand. He shuffled inside a long leather jacket. He stood on the concrete floor staring up at televisions suspended by metal braces in flashing squares of nine.

Occasionally something would happen, and everyone would rush over to a different part of the stand. Then something else would happen, and the attention would turn there. People won and lost until the lights were turned off one by one and the stadium was swallowed in gulps.

The horses nodded quietly in their stables at night like old trees. Great fires had once burned in their glassy eyes. Drake peered up – up past the arena into the grey windless sky. Dark clouds were merging in the east. When small drops began to fall and darken the world in penny-shaped circles, no one around him scurried for cover.

The whole scene before Drake would have been exactly like the dreams except that he couldn't feel Oskar hovering at his shoulder guiding him like some fugitive limb. As the rain at the raceway turned cold and pooled on the track, horses drank from puddles and fanned their tails. Drake stepped through the old arches into the covered part of the arena where a uniformed attendant stood outside the toilets selling single cigarettes and plastic flowers. Drake was going to where (in the dream) Oskar had guided him.

A very old woman sat behind a glass window and took bets. Then the sound of shoes echoed through the great hall as one lucky gambler ran toward the window clutching his stub. Everyone stopped what they were doing and looked with reverence and envy upon this lone figure tearing across the stone floor. But they would not look for long because they knew that as soon as the envelope had been slipped under the window, its contents would be counted and then pushed back inside the booth in time for the next race. The raceway had been the site of Oskar's last performance. In the dream, the puppet was in a plastic bag behind a curtain.

After that last performance so many years ago, Oskar simply disappeared, but no one worried because all his things were gone too. The neighbors asked Drake's mother if he had paid all the rent before he left. She said that he had paid several years in advance when he first arrived and moved out at exactly the end of his term without saying good-bye.

In the dreams, behind a curtain in the back bar was a length of wood from a Polish forest near Biskupin that had been carved into the shape of a small person. Drake continued up the stairs to the lounge. The track would soon close. Kristine was waiting anxiously at home. The stairs smelled of Bruson's Lime Hair Tonic.

The bar at the raceway was empty, and the shelves wore heavy coatings of dust. Three dim light-bulbs glowed. Drake crept through the stale air, casting only the faintest of shadows.

At the back of the room was a curtain. As Drake fingered the drape, he hesitated. If he pulled it back and found the puppet, then his dream would have been some kind of omen. It would be his father's final performance, a message from the billowing world of apparitions.

That night, Kristine went into labor.

Drake got home to find her sitting on the couch next to a green suitcase of clothes. "My water broke outside Peter Pan Bakery," she said.

Her baby was born eight hours later on a snowy Christmas Eve at the Old Stone Hospital. When Drake saw the child, he felt as though he had known her all along and they were merely being reunited. He felt they were like two halves of an apple that had never been cut.

Three years later, it snowed again on her birthday, but this time so heavily that people on the first and second floors of Drake's brownstone were completely reliant on their third floor neighbors for news of what was happening. Their windows were almost completely snowed in. Then mysteriously in the afternoon, the first and second floor occupants lost power.

Kristine filled Tupperware with Hamburger Helper. Her young daughter slowly carried the bowls down-stairs. One of the Polish boys who had just arrived from Warsaw lit her way with a candle. His blond hair glowed in the flickering light. Everyone thought it was pretty how the two children made shadows on the wall. Someone said that one day they might get married.

Later on, when it got dark, the neighbors came up to Drake and Kristine's apartment and played birthday and Christmas games. Then they all watched *A Charlie Brown Christmas*. The old woman on the second floor had a tin of chocolate hearts. At first, the lid wouldn't come off, but when it did, the hearts spilled everywhere and people had to grope around on the floor. Then they had birthday cake, even though it was Christmas Eve. Drake wondered if other people outside Greenpoint had such unique lives.

After his daughter went to bed, Drake picked up the phone and called his mother. She lived in a small wallpapered room in an institution for people with Alzheimer's in Plainview, Long Island. The nurses were mostly from Haiti. One of them put his mother on the phone. She said nothing, which meant she was happy. Drake told her about the snow and then the birthday party – chocolate hearts all over the floor.

He recited his favorite line from *A Charlie Brown Christmas*.

She laughed and then said, "Why don't I feel the way I'm supposed to feel?" Which is another line.

It was a cartoon they had always watched together, a sort of living family photograph. After hanging up the phone, Drake imagined the contents of his mother's life spread out before her like wreckage on the sea. Since becoming a father, Drake had begun swimming out to her more often.

He even took Kristine and the baby to meet her. The old woman had reached for the baby almost instinctively. She held her firmly on her lap *oohing* and *aahing*. Then she touched the baby's cheek and said, "My darling beautiful little Drake."

Kristine had wanted to name the baby after Drake's mother.

"We named our daughter after you," Kristine said softly. Drake's mother looked down at the child in her arms as though it had just appeared.

"This is me?" She said in horror.

Kristine took the baby.

The bedroom at the nursing home smelled of milk and bleach. The floor was plastic tile and there was a low sink with a cord attached that could be pulled for help. Drake's mother was wearing slippers that Drake had bought her on Manhattan Avenue in Brooklyn.

Drake wondered how she and Oskar had met. There was quite an age difference between them. Drake wished he'd paid more attention to Oskar. After all, he had lived in the basement only steps away.

As they drove back to Brooklyn from Long Island, Drake looked at the other drivers on the Long Island Expressway and realized that anyone could be anyone's father, that anyone could love anyone under certain circumstances, and that life is a museum of small accidents.

After hanging up on his mother, Drake sat for a long time next to the telephone.

Then he remembered it was Christmas Eve. On the table in the kitchen were the Christmas cookies and the glass of milk left out for Santa Claus. Next to that, an uneven stack of dirty plates from the impromptu birthday party with neighbors. Drake remembered everyone sitting around watching television.

He drained the glass and ate a few of the small cookies. His daughter's mittens were also on the table, two wool sacks for two tiny hands. Drake boiled the kettle and brewed some tea. He drank it very hot. Kristine had fallen asleep in the next room.

Drake remembered his night at the racetrack, standing for so long at the curtain, wondering what lay beyond. If the puppet was there behind that curtain, then to put his hand inside and walk him home across Greenpoint, past the ships lugging their cargo up the East River, past the glistening men in the tugboat café and the Old Stone Hospital – to give life to the puppet and take up the art would have meant total surrender of his *own* life.

The more he thought about it, the more he was glad that he walked away without looking to see if the puppet was there.

Drake looked into his mug. It was empty but still warm, like his mother's life.

Kristine was sleeping on the couch. Drake would have to wake her to pull it out and put the sheets on. He ate a few more of the Christmas cookies. Then he went into the room where his daughter slept. The two people he loved most in the world were asleep where nothing could harm them.

Wisps of hair fell down the child's neck. Her head rested on her hand. Her body rose and sank, as she, a tiny vessel, sailed through a dream toward morning.

And then Drake picked up the fleshy star of her hand. It was probably going to snow all night, and the heavier it got, the quieter everything became – until the city of Brooklyn itself fell asleep and dreamed it was once a wild, deep forest where owls looked out from trees into windy plains.

Acknowledgments

FOR *LOVE BEGINS IN WINTER*

Beverly Allen; Amy Baker; Bryan Le Boeuf; Darren and Raha Booy; Mrs. J. E. Booy; Dr. Stephen Booy; Douglas Borroughs Esq.; Milan Bozic; Ken Browar; David Bruson; Gabriel Byrne; Le Château Frontenac in Quebec City; Justine Clay; Mary Beth Constant; Christine Corday; Donald Crowhurst; Dr. Silvia Curado; Jennifer Dorman; Cathy Erway; Danielle Esposito; Patricio Ferrari; Peggy Flaum; Dr. Giovanni Frazzetto; Pippo and Salvina Frazzeto; Léon and Hélène Garcia; Colin Gee; Joel Gotler; Lauren Gott; Dr. Greg Gulbransen; Audrey Harris; Dr. Maryhelen Hendricks; Nancy Horner; Mr. Howard; Lucas Hunt; Tim Kail; Carrie Kania; Alan Kleinberg; Hilary Knight; Claude Lelouch; Eva Lontscharitsch; Little M; Alain Malraux; Lisa Mamo; Michael Matkin; McNally Jackson Booksellers; Dr. Bob Milgrom; Dr. Edmund Miller; Carolina Moraes; Cal Morgan; Jennifer Morris; Samuel Morris III; Bill Murray; Dr. William Neal; Ermanno Olmi; Lukas Ortiz; Jonathan Rabinowitz; Nonno Nina and Nonna Lucia Ragaglia; Alberto Rojas; Russo Family of Morano Calabro, Italy; Leah Schachar; Stephanie Selah; Ivan Shaw; Michael Signorelli; Philip Spitzer; Jessamyn Tonry; F.C.V., Eve K. Tremblay; Wim Wenders; Dr. Barbara Wersba.

Simon Van Booy

FOR *THE SECRET LIVES OF PEOPLE IN LOVE*

I wish to directly acknowledge these people:

Darren Booy (for knocking on the wall), Joan Booy, Dr. Stephen Booy, Ken Browar, Sandra Buratti, Justine Clay, Christine Corday, Lindsay Edgecombe, Danielle Esposito, Patricio Ferrari, Peggy Flaum, León García, Francis Howard, Lucas Hunt, P.K., Dr. Mickey Kempner, Hilary Knight, Bénédicte Le Lay, Laura Lyons, Michael Matkin, Mary McBride, Anne Michaels, Dr. Edmund Miller of Long Island University, Samuel Morris III, Dr. William Neal of Campbellsville University, Jonathan D. Rabinowitz, Sheridan Sansegundo, Paula Sinnott, Jessamyn Tonry, Keith Usher, F.C.V., Lorilee Van Booy, Wim Wenders, Peter Handke, and Jurgen Knieper for *Wings of Desire*, Dr. Barbara Wersba, and the Russo family of Morano Calabro, Italy.

I also wish to acknowledge:

Greenpoint Café

Humanities Department at the School of Visual Arts, New York

Musée de la Résistance Nationale, Paris

Shakespeare and Company, Paris

Wellspring House, Massachusetts

About the Author

Simon Van Booy is the author of two novels and two collections of short stories, including *The Secret Lives of People in Love* and the Frank O'Connor Award-winning *Love Begins in Winter*, now published for the first time as one volume by Oneworld Publications. He is the editor of three philosophy books and has written for the *New York Times*, *Guardian*, NPR and BBC. His work has been translated into fifteen languages. He lives in New York with his wife and daughter.

www.SimonVanBooy.com

Also by Simon Van Booy

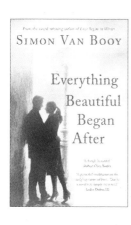

Everything Beautiful Began After

ISBN: 9781780743783 eBook ISBN: 9781780743790

Simon Van Booy, winner of the prestigious Frank O'Connor International Short Story Award, brings his gift for poetic dialogue and sumptuous imagery to this debut novel of longing and discovery amidst the ruins of Ancient Greece.

'A powerful meditation on the undying nature of love and the often cruel beauty of one's own fate. This is a novel you simply must read!' **Andre Dubus III**

'Haunting.' *Daily Mail*

'Vivid and meticulous.' *Metro*

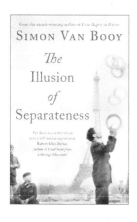

The Illusion *of* Separateness

ISBN: 9781780743943 eBook ISBN: 9781780743257

A luminous story of how one man's act of mercy during WW2 changed the lives of a group of strangers, and how they each eventually discover the astonishing truth of their connection.

'A delicate, complex, moving novel, one to withstand – demand even – an instant second reading.' *Daily Telegraph*

'The elegance of Van Booy's evocative prose has led to comparisons with F. Scott Fitzgerald; it's some claim but one this little gem of a book completely justifies.' *Daily Mail*

'There is a sustaining pleasure in wondering how the strands of the story will tie together.' *Guardian*